True Companion

To: Keeley

I hope this story warms your heart!

M Janes

A novel by Margie Janes

True Companion

All Rights Reserved

COPYRIGHT © 2022 Margie Janes

This book may not be reproduced, transmitted, or stored in whole or in part by any means, including graphic, electronic, or mechanical, without the express written consent of the publisher except in the case of brief questions embodied in critical articles and reviews.

ISBN: 978-0-578-94044-1

Cover design by Sooraj Mathew

Edited by Hilary Jastram

Bookmark
PUBLISHING HOUSE

Dedication

For Billy

My hilarious, fiery, and supportive husband

Table of Contents

Introduction 1
Present 3
   Chapter 1 – Invisible 4
   Chapter 2 – Eastern 8
   Chapter 3 – New Course 20
Then and Now 23
   Chapter 4 – Running Back 25
   Chapter 5 – Reunion 30
   Chapter 6 – Sanctuary 34
   Chapter 7 – First Dance 40
   Chapter 8 – Auntie Helen 44
   Chapter 9 – Reconnect 48
   Chapter 10 – Playing Dead 56
   Chapter 11 – Speedbump 63
   Chapter 12 – Everybody's Happy 68
   Chapter 13 – Snowball Fight 72
   Chapter 14 – Roasting Marshmallows 77
   Chapter 15 – Jason 87
   Chapter 16 – Playdate 94
   Chapter 17 – Breaking a Sweat 99
   Chapter 18 – Something's Wrong 104
   Chapter 19 – Valentine 107
   Chapter 20 – Storm 112
   Chapter 21 – Field Day 116
   Chapter 22 – Crushed 123
   Chapter 23 – One of the Girls 126
   Chapter 24 – Torn Apart 131

Chapter 25 – Birthday Bash 134
Chapter 26 – Escape 139
Chapter 27 – Apology... 146
Chapter 28 – Broken 151
Chapter 29 – Comfort 161
Chapter 30 – Sidelined 169
Chapter 31 – One on One... 172
Chapter 32 – Sunset 177
Chapter 33 – Boiling Point... 179
Chapter 34 – Sinking.. 187
Chapter 35 – Fallout... 189
Chapter 36 – Nightmare... 192
Chapter 37 – Ditching.. 195
Chapter 38 – Gone 197

Future **201**

Chapter 39 – Spring Break 202
Chapter 40 – Camping 210
Chapter 41 – Breathing In.. 221
Chapter 42 – Visitor 227
Chapter 43 – Carlyle 234
Chapter 44 – Second Kiss.. 240
Chapter 45 – Vows... 251
Chapter 46 – Revelation 264
Chapter 47 – Truth 268
Epilogue 273
Acknowledgments 275
About the Author 277

Introduction

When you struggle to find yourself, you start becoming someone else.

That is unless you have a true friend to hold up a mirror and remind you who you are.

Rebecca, the main character in this story, has been lost for most of her life. She is the fill-in daughter for a sister's shoes she will never fully fit into. Walking the line of breaking free and upholding expectations is exhausting for Rebecca. During the second semester of her junior year in college, she is given a gift from her past in the form of a now grown-up TJ, the only person on Earth who ever understood and accepted her. His reappearance, like a ghost from her childhood, may finally give her the courage to move forward out of the shadow of her sister and into the light of her own self-acceptance.

As the youngest of four in my family, I tried to find my individuality. One of my greatest hurdles was that I was painfully unathletic. But it did allow for more time to simply *play*.

Growing up in the south suburbs of Chicago, I spent my childhood days outside with my brother, Mark, and our neighborhood friends. We rode bikes constantly, played at the park at the end of our block, swam in friends' pools, and played football and Running Bases. We ran. We collected toads, lit fireworks in the street, played HORSE, drank Kool-Aid, and picked raspberries off our neighbor's bushes. What a free and open space for me to develop. To be a kid. Free to explore and be unencumbered.

When I wasn't outside, I created imaginary worlds for my dolls and Barbies, dreaming up plots and characters. I organized drama and cliffhangers, first loves, and last fights. These dolls were my actors, and I was the director.

INTRODUCTION

Thirteen was a transitioning year for me. Too old to play Barbies in my crawlspace, too young to hop in the car and drive my friends to the mall, I traded my Barbies for pencils and notebooks to create stories. These stories told of longing for acceptance and friendship, and true love.

At that same time, in April of 1990, the very impressive Phil Collins released a music video called "Do You Remember?" I watched this video time and time again, cross-legged on my front room carpet when it would pop on MTV or VH1. (When those stations used to actually show music videos). The video features a young boy and girl who meet, develop a friendship and then become separated by an event. I was so infatuated with this video (that I watched repeatedly), my imagination lit up in a profound way. The idea for *True Companion* was born.

It is a story about finding that one person who gets you. Who will always be true to you. The one who doesn't get offended when you lose your cool. The one who speaks up for you. The one who knows your heart without you explaining. Your most loyal partner.

I am thankful now, for having that summer, for the opportunity at 13-years-old, to write my heart out and be a creator.

This story, very much like me, has grown and changed from where I wrote it in cursive writing in the original Datamark spiral notebook to the penning of it in a college-ruled spiral after I earned my bachelor's degree to the continued development of it on a desktop using the Times New Roman font my sister, Sue, typed for me to my laptop. I made hundreds of edits in between teaching and raising my two babies. Having worked on this story on and off for thirty years, living through the eyes of my characters as children and adults, I am so proud that it is *finally* out in the world. The same world that beheld my anxieties and awkwardness as an adolescent and teen. The same world that offered me a new space in college to branch out and find my people and my path. The same world that guided me toward love and family and teaching.

Sometimes your dreams can become a reality. Just put your pencil to the paper. And find yourself.

PRESENT

CHAPTER 1

Invisible

My sister died today.

Sixteen years ago, but it might as well have been today. I don't remember Rachel; I was barely four years old when it happened. I have tried to picture in my mind what she would've been like now, her adult face, her body, her mannerisms, the sound of her voice, but my imagination gets off track, and I just fill in the gaps with what little information I can decipher from my dad and even rarer detail from my aunt. My mother won't talk about her. Even now.

Over the years, I have discovered the cause of Rachel's death. Influenza B wreaked havoc on her nine-year-old system with fever, vomiting, shortness of breath, and one complication after the next. Then pneumonia set in. She died in the hospital. My mother died in her own way from unimaginable grief at home.

I paced the kitchen floor near the table where a bouquet of pink roses and baby's breath was clustered in a clean, white vase. The card on top of the gorgeous blossoms read, "Suzanne, always with you. All my love, Robert."

It was a waste of the last day of break.

I should've been more considerate of my mother's grief about my dead sister and cried from the loss of her. But, instead, I felt tense. I took in a long breath, trying not to be annoyed. It didn't work.

I was leaving to go back to college for the second semester of my junior year. My best friend Lindsay and I should've been on our way to my boyfriend Jason's by now.

He was going to drive us from his house to school. My older brother, Ryan, had moved out two years ago, and my dad was on another business trip. I still did not have a car of my own, so my mother was supposed to take Lindsay and me. Instead, she was lying on her bed in pieces. She'd shut herself in there all day.

I'd made a few attempts to check on her and comfort her, but she'd dismissed me with a wave of her hand. It might as well have been a slap. It stung the same.

Then the buzz of an incoming text from Jason: "Rebecca, where are you?"

I clenched my jaw and took another long breath before texting back: "Sorry, change of plans. Can you just pick us up at Lindsay's? Give me a few minutes. Thx."

Then I sent Lindsay a message to prepare her for the alternate agenda.

The two overnight bags were already packed, thanks to my mother. My clothes were freshly washed and folded. The amount of care and attention she put into those bags of fresh laundry was laughable. Although now, staring down at them, I felt the rise of stinging tears and burning in the back of my throat.

I shoved my arms roughly into the sleeves of my coat, threw my bags over my shoulders, and charged out of my house.

Then I ran.

The January wind cut into my hair and whipped my face and eyes. I grasped the handles of my bags tighter and sprinted, my feet lunging off the sidewalk and down the street, headed toward Lindsay, and ultimately Eastern, far away from my mother.

In an instant, that old summer memory came rushing back.

***

My mother was sobbing alone at the dining room table. My four-year-old self stood near the table watching her. She hadn't looked at me the whole day, almost as if I was invisible. She hadn't looked at me since Rachel hadn't come back from the hospital five months earlier.

Dad had finally gone back to a steady workweek, and Ryan had been sent to a day camp. My mother and I spent our days in silence.

Sliding my fingers back and forth along the length of our dining room table, I watched her nervously. I saw my mother's back jerking up and down, her arms folded beneath her head. The strangest deep moaning muffled through her sleeve and howled through the empty house. That noise scared me so badly it made my lip quiver. In one exhalation of breath, I ran from the dining room and out our front door. She didn't move from the table.

My soft bare feet slapped the paved sidewalk. Thwack, thwack, thwack, they echoed on the deserted block. The sun felt warm on my tear-stained cheeks. I ran further down the block and turned the corner. My heartache deepened with a new worry: *Would I find my way back home?*

I slowed down when I saw a woman approaching with a stroller. She had wavy strawberry blonde hair and a bright smile. I stopped and locked my feet in place as she drew nearer.

"Well, hello there." The woman's voice coated the air like honey.

I stood frozen, looking up at her.

All at once, a flash of golden hair burst into view beside her. It was a boy a few inches taller than me. He had scabbed knees and dirty fingers. His hair was a mop of sweat and golden tangles. His eyebrows were crunched together in surprise, calling my attention to the most striking blue eyes I had ever seen. I stared at him, mesmerized.

"Who are you?" he asked.

"Rebecca," I mumbled.

"Beck?" the boy asked.

I just wrinkled my forehead at him.

"Is it Becky?" the woman asked.

Again, I could only stare up at her.

"Mom, this is Beck," the boy said determinedly. "I'm TJ."

The woman laughed loudly at this, which startled me.

"Oh, really?"

"Yeah, Dad said it's short for Thomas John." He nodded at her.

"Funny, I thought I knew your name to be Tommy." She leaned in and tickled the boy on his side.

He giggled for a moment, and then a high-pitched whine came from the stroller.

"Uh-oh, we're waking up Katie, shhh," the woman hushed us and moved the stroller back and forth as she stayed in place. "So, Becky, I'm Mrs. Lawson. Is this your house?" She turned, smiling, and indicated the white stone house beside us.

I followed her gaze and shook my head.

Then a different emotion overtook her face; it was a mask of concern. Her eyes flew to my bare feet, then scanned the street.

"Where's your mom?" the boy asked, drilling his blue eyes into mine.

"I lost my mom."

He grabbed my hand. "Don't worry, Beck. I'm good at finding things."

**

The memory made me gasp. Stumbling, I rushed to catch my feet up to my body. I threw my bags down with a clunk on the salted sidewalk and covered my face with my freezing hands. Then I peeked through my fingers and looked for TJ. But of course, he wouldn't be here. Not the right time or place. Not even close. God, I hadn't looked for him in so long. I couldn't stay in that memory. It hurt too badly to see him. I had to keep running. Lindsay's house was only a few more blocks.

I gritted my teeth and sniffed the cold air. "Keep going," I told myself, throwing the bags over my shoulders and charging forward. Then I pushed off the concrete with more determination and, within a few minutes, rounded onto Lindsay's street.

"Are you nuts?" Lindsay yelled at me from her front door. "I think it's time to chill on the running obsession, Rebecca. For real."

"It's what I do." I panted, lugging my bags up and through her doorway. I couldn't let Lindsay have any of my grief, so I buried it again.

CHAPTER 2

Eastern

Although it was almost too dark to see, I recognized the faint image of rushing fields outside the passenger window. Every few seconds, I would brush away the fog on my window to see the edges of the highway speeding past. The moon was a mere slice of gold in a pit of black sky. It followed us, yet everything was passing.

Most of my friends, Lindsay included, were anxious about returning to school. Unlike them, however, I enjoyed the monotonous three-hour drive south on I-57. It gave me time to breathe and clear my head. I needed that, especially today, on the anniversary of Rachel's death.

I was glad to get away and start a new semester with fresh possibilities and freedom from my mother. Even though we'd had a good break together up until this weekend, it was never really easy with her. She still maintained control over most everything. That iron grip lessened in my mind with every passing field between us. The haunting memory of Rachel unwound with each mile, too.

It was ironic that a party campus, loud neighbors, and course criteria deadlines could make me feel at ease. But it was time away from the fake smiles of my mother and her tribe of social media friends. Time away from my mother was time away to mess up outside Suzanne's line of sight.

Being home for two weeks on Christmas break made me feel like a captive out on parole. I had to check in with her for permission to go anywhere. But I could see Jason, of course. *Anything for Jason.* By the last day of my break, my repressed anxiety levels had peaked. I just needed to escape.

Jason's hand cupped the curve of my knee, bringing me back to reality. His jaw was set, and his eyes focused. I hoped he'd have the will to fight off impending sleep to make it back forty-five minutes to U of I after dropping us off. I covered his hand with mine and gave him a squeeze. Then I lifted his hand and kissed the back of it.

My heart clenched uneasily for a moment. We had spent nearly every waking moment together over break. Now, we would be put through the test again: two separate campuses, miles between us, our paths diverging. Jason wouldn't give up on me; I knew that. He had fought hard to win me over early on, and he didn't like to lose.

"Okay, I really don't think I'll make it," Lindsay urged from the backseat.

"You've got to be kidding me." Jason peered at Lindsay in the rearview mirror.

"Sorry, but, you know…." Lindsay said.

"Linds, we just stopped at the rest station like forty-five minutes ago," I said gently, sensing Jason ready to erupt.

"I know, but I have to go."

"No. Not stopping. You'll just have to hold it. We're almost there anyway," Jason protested.

"Uhh! You're the worst," Lindsay moaned.

"Try walking to Eastern next time."

I rolled my eyes and exhaled, used to the two of them bickering by now. Lindsay was an easy mark. She was very sensitive and naïve and a true sweetheart. But she was a bit clueless.

I was used to Jason's antics. I should've despised him for his lack of tact at times, but I was attracted to him all the same. His defined, angular face, sturdy jawline, and determined eyes below his perfectly placed, dark hair drew me in.

I also reveled in the fact that our relationship was never too serious.

"Why did I agree to pick her up?" Jason complained, glancing at me.

"Because you like me a lot," I said wistfully. He softened his eyes and smiled.

"I do like you a lot." He leaned over and kissed me.

It was our inside joke. Jason had fumbled to find the right words to tell me how he felt after dating me for a few weeks. He'd tried to confess his feelings once but ended up sounding like a twelve-year-old boy with a crush instead of the confident, cocky adult he could be.

"We're still driving. Eyes on the road, people," Lindsay said. "You can continue in a few minutes, ya know?"

Jason grimaced and pulled away from me. We exited the highway, skirted off the ramp, and headed into the heart of Charleston. I grinned at the almost rural feel the town had. We lived in the northwest suburbs of Chicago, surrounded by high-end, gated neighborhoods. Trendy stores at every corner. Elite golf courses and fine dining. Outlandish community gardens and high-tech fitness centers. In Charleston, other than Wal-Mart and Kroger, there wasn't much to look at but fields and flatlands.

I felt welcomed at Eastern, though. Their motto was "Big enough to matter, small enough to care." That was one of my selling points with my mother as she'd tried her hardest to get me to attend a big name, big bill, and big bragging rights university. My dad had helped me convince her that EIU was a better fit for me. Small-town life just suited me better. The introvert in me could shine a little brighter at a place like Eastern than at an intimidatingly large campus where I would get lost in the crowd.

We passed the Castle at Old Main. The lights strung across its edges, covered with a dusting of snow, glittered beautifully. A soft smile perched on my tired face as the sight of the university's iconic student hall lit up my spirits. I was happy to be back. Snow-trodden footprints led from Old Main to Marty's. A rite of passage hangout bar. Even amid frigid temperatures and snowstorms, students had their priorities.

"Rebecca, I need your phone since mine is trash. I have to let my mom know we made it." Lindsay popped up from the backseat.

I rummaged through my purse and found my cell. When I tapped on the screen, I saw a torrent of missed calls and texts from my parents. My stomach dropped. "Hang on, Linds," I said, swiping on the phone screen to erase the alerts. "I thought you asked for a new phone," I said, distracting myself from the reality of my unread messages.

"So, when does asking ever mean I'll get it? Erin didn't even get the laptop she asked for, and she's the good kid." Lindsay sighed. "Oh my GOD, I have to pee!"

"So, what did you get then?" Jason asked Lindsay, shooting her a glance in the mirror.

"Get what?"

I eyed Jason, knowing he would let out another disappointed sigh toward Linds. We hadn't even been dating a year, yet I knew his responses before he did. He was about to begin another tear on Lindsay for being a little lost in conversation.

"Context clues, Linds." Jason was getting irritated. I looked out the window waiting for the conversation to be finished.

"What is that? Context clues?"

"You just explained five seconds ago that you didn't get a phone for Christmas, and your sister didn't get the laptop. I asked you what you got..."

"Yeah, I get it."

"And you can't follow that line of thought?" He cut her off, louder than necessary. "Are you not in Elementary Ed?"

"Jason, come on," I breathed, annoyed by his relentless digging on Lindsay.

"You really should use your context clues to figure things out. I mean Christ, you'll be teaching soon."

"Well, thank you, Mr. All Knowing and Most Powerful. Let's see, for Christmas, I got a copy of *Jason's Guide to Context Clues*, and I'll make sure I set it out in my classroom for my students one day. How's that?"

I let out a giggle, and surprisingly, he did too. Lindsay was always good for a laugh at her own expense.

We pulled up to our apartment complex on the backside of the campus. Its location made getting to classes on time challenging, but it was a great apartment. It had three spacious bedrooms, two bathrooms, plus our outrageous roommate Amy's favorite perk: friendly neighbors with connections to lots of parties.

Jason pulled up to the nearest parking spot to allow us a quick route to the entrance. We got out of the car, and he popped the trunk.

"You're gonna call your mom, right?" Jason asked.

I looked up at him, stunned. He couldn't have known about all the times she'd tried to contact me on the ride. *Right?* "Yeah," I said casually, not meeting his eyes.

"You better call her, or you know she'll just call me."

"She won't call you today. She's ... busy." I flinched from the cold. "I'll just text her that I'm here."

Lindsay grabbed her bags from the trunk. "Well, thank you, Jason," she called and bolted up the steps.

Jason grabbed my bags from the trunk and handed them to me.

"Thanks." I kissed him quickly on the lips. I feigned normalcy, pretending this was a typical goodbye kiss instead of a long goodbye, wanting to keep moving, wanting this day to end.

"Rebecca," Jason said, pulling me around to face him. "You're going to miss me."

He gave me his almost-smile. I was never an open book with Jason, yet he knew full well I couldn't resist that face. So, I softened my resolve, set my bags down, and wrapped my arms around his neck.

"Miss you? Hmm." Jason's determined hands captured my waist. "What exactly am I going to miss?" I teased while he tried not to smile. "You mean, I'll miss your constant phone calls and texts and dropping by unannounced every day to see me? Is that what I'll miss?" I pulled away, looking at his lips, knowing his kiss would interrupt me any second.

Jason pressed his chilled, firm lips to mine for a few moments and pulled away. "You like it when I bother you," he said, kissing me again.

Loud cheers and jeers of college boys and girls from nearby windows suddenly echoed in the still parking lot, dissolving our intimate moment.

"Text me later," he said, ducking into the driver's seat.

"We might be out later."

"You can't send me a text from wherever you're going to be?" he asked like a scolding parent.

"I'll just talk to you tomorrow. Thanks for the ride. Be safe," I called.

He raised his eyebrows at me. "Call your mom," he ordered again and drove off.

I grabbed my gear, stepped inside the main hallway, and trudged up to our door. Amy's calico cat, Scooter, greeted me immediately, meowing while stalking my every move. Her eyes accused me of being gone too long.

"Hi, Scoot!"

She purred, brushing her side into my leg. "Whatcha doin', huh?" I stepped over Scooter, shut the door, and moved to my room down the hall. Lindsay was just emerging from the bathroom.

"Phew! That was a close one. Really nice of your boyfriend to cause my bladder to rupture. And Amy's not here," she said.

"Figures."

Scooter followed me into my room. She was beautiful but illegal. We weren't allowed to have pets in the apartment but had managed to keep her a secret. Amy had found her at two in the morning outside a Denny's on her birthday, so she took it as a sign that we should keep the cat. Scooter jumped up on my bookcase while I emptied my luggage and put away my clean clothes.

Lindsay whined from across the hall, "God, my room is such a disaster! Why did I leave it like this? That was really dumb! Can you clean it for me?"

"Not a chance. I clean too much as it is," I replied.

Lindsay came into my room, her eyes searching my tidy space. "Yeah, you really do. I've gotta learn some organizational skills."

"Feel free to stay a week or so with my mother," I offered.

My mother had a rule: "There's a place for everything, and everything has its place." If you didn't pick up your toys, you wouldn't have them anymore. Fold your clothes corner to corner and stack them neatly away in your drawers with T-shirts on one side and shorts on the other. There was no need for exploding drawers of fresh laundry. Your closet should have wooden hangers, and clothing should be arranged by color and style.

When I closed my eyes, I could still visualize my orderly and perfect closet in my old, yellow bedroom. My clothes mixed in with Rachel's relics and her dresses all arranged together, untouched. Even now, I kept things orderly. There were some habits from my mother that I just couldn't shake. Two hundred miles between us didn't matter one bit.

The door slammed, and Scooter hopped off to investigate.

"Where da hoes at?" Amy called. Her keys hit the table with a clatter. Lindsay and I shared a grin.

"Speak for yourself, skank," Lindsay answered.

"Where were you?" I asked.

Amy walked into the room and held up her now five-pack of beer. "I stopped somewhere," she said as she plopped belly-first on my bed. She looked up at us with her brown hair flopping over her wild, green eyes. "What's up, bitches?"

I laughed.

"Jeez, you look like shit," Amy stared at me.

"Thanks, Aim." I laughed dryly.

Amy was a one-of-a-kind, playing the ultimate double life. She had a brilliant mind, although you wouldn't know it from her GPA. She consistently skipped classes, argued with professors for a condensed workload, and the assignments she did complete were usually late. Lindsay and I, however, saw enough of Amy's calculating mind and sheer determination to know her real potential. She was a total fireball.

"So," Lindsay said, "How was it? Or should I say, *who* was it?"

Amy raised her eyebrows and took a sip.

"Yeah, Aim. You've been gone over two weeks. See any of your *old friends*?" I inquired, glad for the distraction of my rowdy girlfriends.

"Of course."

"Tony?" Lindsay asked.

"Naturally," Amy replied.

"Ew! He's like your best friend, though." Lindsay squinted at her.

"Ladies, we've been through this. What ARE friends for?" Lindsay and I rolled our eyes and laughed. "I'm totally going to hell, though!" Amy snorted.

"Why this time?" Lindsay asked.

"Jon came over while my parents were at church last Sunday...." She covered her mouth. Lindsay's jaw dropped.

"You're so bad," I said.

"Jon, too? You know, one of these days, I'm gonna tell your parents who you really are," Lindsay threatened.

"They know who I am. I'm Daddy's angel," Amy said, pulling up the back of her shirt and exposing a pair of wings and a halo tattoo on the small of her back. Of course, Amy's dad didn't know about that. All part of the double life.

"Sure. You keep telling yourself that, and it might just come true," Lindsay said.

Amy lived in a small town and apparently had a lot of "friends." Lindsay and I didn't quite understand her friends-with-benefits situation. Even more mysterious, she somehow kept her parents in the dark about her many infractions. She was a church-going, sweet, innocent gal back at home, but we knew the truth. She could be hell on wheels at any given time.

"Are we ready to go? You ladies need to work on your dance moves for this week, right?" Amy asked.

"Yeah, I am so freaking excited! Dance is going to be the greatest class ever!" Lindsay proclaimed. "I can't wait to meet some hot guys finally! Elementary Education is totally lacking."

"Yeah, but you might just have a bunch of theater majors and fatties instead," Amy added, stroking Scooter.

"Shut up."

"What did Jason say when you told him you'd be dancing with other men, Miss Rebecca?" I shrugged and continued to put away my clean laundry.

"You didn't tell him, did you?" Amy asked. She was clearly reveling in her infamous people-reading skills.

"He doesn't know?" Lindsay questioned.

"It's no big deal."

"Yeah, that's true. Besides, it was your mom's idea," Lindsay argued.

"Uh, it was her mom's idea to do aqua exercise, not ballroom dance," Amy said.

Lindsay's eyes popped. "Wait, your mom thinks we're in aqua exercise?"

Amy's grin stretched across her face.

I hadn't intentionally gone behind my mother's back. She had suggested that an aqua exercise class as an elective would be a great way for me to continue to build tone since gymnastics, swimming, and soccer had gone by the wayside when I started college. She thought it would do me some good to be involved in a class like that.

So I took her suggestion about a course providing physical activity and tweaked it ... just a little. I actually didn't mind the idea of an exercise class but was eager to finally have a course with Lindsay, so it was decided. Something fun to keep us fit, and as a bonus, Lindsay had the opportunity to meet the hot guys that she so desperately wanted. Lindsay was all too excited to take Ballroom Dance with me.

I shrugged again, hoping to end the conversation. It was annoying but true that my mother was completely in charge of my course list each semester. As usual, I gave up the fight like my dad normally did and allowed her to reach maximum power. She chose what she thought I should do and be, and I obliged, shushing the resentment in my subconscious. It was easier to let her take control. All part of the "Rachel life" that I couldn't quite lead yet couldn't avoid attempting.

"Are we going out or what?" Amy barked, standing up.

"Are you driving? I'm too tired to walk," I admitted.

"I'm sort of out of gas."

"What do you mean sort of?" Linds asked.

She pointed to the beer. "It was either that or beer. Give me a break."

"Priorities, right, Aim?" I muffled a laugh.

"I'm not walking. It's too far and too cold," Lindsay protested.

"Then stay home, loser," Amy teased.

"So, *sort of* out of gas…." I said.

"Good point. I may have enough to get us there."

"Fine, I'll walk home, but only if I'm drunk enough," Linds agreed.

"Done," Amy said.

***

We dragged ourselves back to the apartment around one a.m., battling the loud ringing in our ears. As I was getting ready to lie down finally, I checked my phone. Then I wished I hadn't. Two missed calls from my dad and ten missed calls and texts from my mother. My mind was a little fuzzy, but words like "irresponsible," "inconsiderate," "didn't even know where you were," "so upset," "at least acknowledge your safety," and "disappointed" stood out in the messages. Jason was right; I should have called her.

I tried to shake off the uneasy feeling that I had let my mother down but knew I would be cursed that night with the Rachel nightmare. It was my punishment for blowing off my mother. By this time, I could almost cause them.

The nightmare started just before dawn.

As always, she walked ahead of me on a secluded, winding trail that seemed to go on forever. The sun had almost set. I rushed to catch up to Rachel, but I couldn't reach her. She didn't turn around, despite my calling and pleading with her. I fell and scraped my knees, got up, fell again, and scratched up my palms. Panting from exhaustion, I lost my voice but kept mouthing her name. She finally stopped walking and turned her head. Where her face should have been, my own face looked back at me, blank, hollow, vacant.

I jolted up in my bed, breathing heavily. Once again, the dream unsettled me. It was six a.m., too early for Lindsay's rants or Amy's protests. So, I did what I usually did when I needed to escape from a Rachel nightmare and took a morning run to help settle myself, saying another silent prayer that she would stop haunting me.

After my run, I tucked my tail between my legs and sent my parents the apology they were waiting for, including a separate one just for my mother.

"Mom, I'm sorry. Had to get going though, I ran over to Lindsay's. Jason had a lot of driving to do. Hope you are ok."

"Very irresponsible to leave so hastily without even telling me, Rebecca."

"Sorry."

"You need to be more responsible. Tell Jason thank you for driving."

I stared at her texts. Of course, they were only surface deep. She wouldn't acknowledge actually being hurt by me or by the anniversary of Rachel's death. I took another minute to look over her words, then set my phone aside and tried to prepare myself for a long day of new professors and information.

I could hardly keep my eyes open during my morning sessions and repeatedly yawned, unable to control my sleep deprivation. After the nightmare and text exchange, I was grateful when the day brightened. A gorgeous afternoon beckoned crowds of spring-hungry students to the east quad. It was still chilly, but there was no breeze. Lindsay and I met up with Amy and her friend Megan between classes on the benches alongside the quad.

"What's with you?" Amy asked.

"I didn't sleep well," I admitted, trying to stay awake. I left out the part about the Rachel nightmare. I never told anyone about them. Instead, I asked Lindsay to fill us in on her morning and endured five minutes of her complaining about her professor for Children's Literature.

"You would not believe the amount of papers I have to write for his stupid class."

"I'm sorry," I said.

"Yeah, mine's no picnic either," Amy chimed in. "Want to join Molecular Spectroscopy with me?"

"Huh?" Lindsay's eyes popped.

"Seriously, Linds, try Finite Math," I suggested.

"Ugh." She shivered.

We casually watched a group of guys throwing a football around across the quad. A tall guy with a bright blue beanie and a large build launched the ball as hard as he could. His dark-haired teammate had to scramble toward us to make the catch.

"Sorry," he said before hurrying away.

"Check out sizzling." Megan puckered her lips.

"Which one? They're all hot." Lindsay smiled.

"The blond over there," Megan said. "Gray shirt. The tight end. In more ways than one." She smirked.

We all fixed our eyes on the blond, racing his teammates and winning every pass. His animated energy seemed unmatched.

Megan practically burned a hole through his clothing the way she eyed him.

"Too tall for you," Amy teased.

Megan was petite and gave off the first impression that she was a sweetheart. In reality, she was a pistol, and she did have a way with the boys.

The football players who had finished their game began talking to a few girls.

"We'll see about that," she smiled and trotted off toward the blond. They were flirting within seconds. I stared for a while, intrigued.

"How come I can't do that?" Lindsay complained. Megan was already touching the blonde's shoulder and laughing.

"Don't worry, Linds," I soothed. "Keep thinking about Ballroom Dance."

"Yay! Tomorrow!" Lindsay cheered.

CHAPTER 3

New Course

Tuesday was a different day altogether. When I got back from Managerial Accounting and Business Statistics, Lindsay was waiting with a letter in her hand.

"We totally screwed up! Dance starts at noon, not twelve-thirty!"

"Uh-uh." I scanned the course letter anxiously.

"We're never gonna make it."

"Yeah, we will," I said. "We just have to sprint. Come on!" I pulled her through the door, and we booked it double time.

"Oh, great. I'm gonna be all sweaty and exhausted right before I have to dance with a hot guy," Lindsay panted between breaths. I tried not to laugh so I could maintain our pace. We cut across the south quad and dodged oncoming traffic on Fourth Street. Our sneakers splattered the slush with every step.

"Well, at least Coach Teague would be happy," I breathed, then laughed to myself at the memory of our high school soccer coach hounding Lindsay for being a running wimp.

"Slow down! You know I can't keep up with you."

"You can do it! We're almost there."

We sprang up the ten steps to the gymnasium and hurled the doors aside, then ran down two corridors and through one more set of doors. It was 12:04 as we charged into Mrs. MacFarlane's Ballroom Dance class.

"Here," a voice said.

"Brendan Michaels?" the instructor called out.

A small crowd of bodies stood in a wide circle in the dimly lit gym. We tried to be as unobtrusive as possible, yet we were clearly out of breath and panting loudly.

"Here."

"Oh, God," Lindsay gasped, hands on her knees, doubled over.

"Taylor Nelson?"

"Here."

"Next class, we'll leave earlier," I whispered.

"Ya think?" she asked.

"Trevor Pomeroy?"

"Here," said a husky voice.

"Hey, that's the guy with the football from yesterday," Lindsay nodded toward the guy with the deep voice. "And isn't that the hot blond Megan was talking to?" she asked, trying to flatten her static-stricken jet-black hair.

"Keep working on the hair, Linds," I said, chuckling.

"Natalia Santana?"

"Here."

"He is *really* cute," Lindsay said.

"Casey Sherman?"

"Here."

I looked over to where she was staring, dabbing sweat from my neck. The blond raised his hand and gave a friendly nod. He stood next to some of the other football-throwing guys from Monday.

"Gabriel Valdez?"

"Here."

"Look at all these beautiful men!" Lindsay whispered ecstatically, tugging on the sleeve of my shirt. I smiled at her immature nature but found myself peeking again and again at the blond, not knowing why. Each time I looked up, he focused on me intently then looked down.

"Rebecca Winslow?"

NEW COURSE

"Here," I called out shyly. I was glad Lindsay was there as a comfort. She would provide comic relief, too, no doubt. I still hadn't completely kicked my shyness in new situations. Junior high had been brutal and high school had been awkward at best, but college was becoming manageable.

"If I haven't called your name, please come see me," Mrs. MacFarlane announced. Just then, the doors swung open, and a group of students sheepishly entered.

"Oh, thank God, more late people," Lindsay said, walking away to check in with the instructor.

I looked up and accidentally locked eyes with the blond football player from the other day. He stared at me in utter amazement.

"No way," he mouthed.

I furrowed my brow and looked side to side to be sure he was referring to me. His mouth widened into the most adorable smile and his eyes danced. "There. Is. No. Way!" he yelled.

A few guys around him followed his gaze across the circle and stared at me.

My face blazed with embarrassment. I looked again at his golden hair and perfect grin, and in that second, I knew.

"Oh my God," I whispered.

The realization that it was him made me feel like I was falling backward without touching the ground. Falling into memories from our last summer together so long ago. In a frenzy of images, I saw bits of him, of us. His golden hair, his wide grin, his crystal blue eyes, his bicycle, his arms reaching out and grabbing the football just like he did yesterday. Then back in time. Eleven years ago.

He took a purposeful step toward me.

"Beck?" he asked, grinning from ear to ear.

"TJ."

THEN AND NOW

CHAPTER 4

Running Back

Ten-year-old TJ leaped across the field and captured the football easily as if his hands were magnets pulling the ball seamlessly into his grasp. I was amazed that at his age, TJ had the athletic skills to shade anyone in his path.

Upon hearing a barrage of complaints about a redo, TJ tossed the football back to Bobby, who was, as always, whining about some cause for his less-than-stellar performance. That awful pass Bobby threw out of bounds was supposedly Garcia's fault. As a defensive lineman, Garcia was supposed to wait five seconds to give Bobby a chance to get a pass off before plowing into him.

"Come on! Garcia keeps moving in too fast!" Bobby shouted, spiking the ball in frustration.

Bobby was always quarterback because he liked being in charge. He was super competitive and was a pretty good quarterback, but not as good as TJ. Bobby knew that deep down and tried his best to mask his lack of ability by blaming anyone else on the team for his shortcomings. Garcia wasn't moving in too fast; he was just too much kid to get around before our agreed-upon play clock time was up.

"No way, man, I counted to five before I moved in on you, and you know it!" argued Garcia.

"Ar-right, let's just start over, come on." TJ was always the mediator.

"Okay, ready, hike," Bobby called as Garcia started his countdown.

"One."

Bobby jabbed his neck into the side of Garcia's beefy head, who was waiting to pounce at five seconds. TJ was all over Pete, even though Pete was a good three inches taller than him.

"Two," Garcia called.

I was guarding Mikey. Being kind of scrawny, he could move quickly, but he wasn't much of a receiver. He was the second-fastest in our neighborhood, second only to me.

As the ball left Bobby's hands, I leaped toward it, but it was far over our heads. Mikey ran for it and caught it in a near-fumble, tripping over his feet. He gained control and darted for the goal line, which was an area of shaded, fresh, green grass amidst the sunburned field. He was getting close, but I was a half-step behind his every move and charged into his back, knocking him down. I landed on top of him with a thunk. My shoulder smashed into the earth.

"Yeah, Beck!" TJ cheered.

I jumped to my feet and held my hand out to help Mikey. I didn't celebrate the tackle; it wasn't the first time, and it wouldn't be the last. I was more reserved than most other nine-year-old girls, and hooting and hollering just wasn't me.

The boys regarded me as *almost* equal. TJ always made the effort to prove I was as good a teammate as any boy.

We huddled back with our teams and got into position again.

"Nice tackle," Garcia said, wiping his sweaty forehead with a huge, dirty palm.

"Jeez, Mikey! Can't you even run it in?" Bobby spat.

"Give me the ball, Bobby. I'll get it in," Pete pleaded.

"Then you better get open and dodge him. Tommy's all over you," Bobby scolded, collecting the ball, brushing his right hand on his shorts, and setting up for another play.

I heard the familiar honk of my dad's Honda pulling up opposite the field and glimpsed him entering the T-intersection that curled around our corner house and into the driveway. I waved at his car, but I was still focused on keeping in front of Mikey.

"Okay, get open now. Hut, hut, hike," Bobby called, shooting sideways out of Garcia's block.

He launched the ball immediately to the left of the field near TJ and Pete. Pete, who had been charging backward at the break, veered left until TJ stretched his right hand up, tipped, and then captured the ball. He sped off in the other direction, Pete trailing behind him. Bobby wove left and right, trying to grab TJ. He scraped through Bobby's extended reach and passed over the goal line.

"Yeah! Oh, yeah! Go, Tommy! Go, Tommy!" cried Garcia, doing a little dance.

I ran up to TJ and gave him a high five. He bent low to catch his breath, smiling his adorable smile at me as sweat dripped off his head.

"I can't believe you couldn't get that one, Pete. God!" Bobby sulked.

"Bobby, he was totally blocked! What's he supposed to do?" Mikey snapped.

"I can't believe *you* couldn't sack Tommy!" Pete got in Bobby's face.

I heard my mother's voice ringing out over the field. "Rebecca, let's go! We're eating dinner!" Her head poked out the front door.

"Wait, Beck, do you have a second to kick it in?" TJ asked.

"Sure," I said matter-of-factly. I was the designated kicker on our team. My record that summer was 10-1 mainly, in my opinion, because of a bad hold by Garcia. I took the ball from TJ and walked to the center divot in the field. It was our marking spot for all extra points. The ball needed to get through the two evergreens on one end of the field.

We set up the play. TJ snapped the ball, and Garcia lined it up. I rushed forward with a crushing blow to the ball, sending it soaring through the air, passing it directly between the two evergreen goal posts. 11-1. Not bad.

"Ar-right! Good kick, Beck!" TJ skipped over to me and patted me on the back.

"Rebecca! It's dinnertime. Now!" My mother yelled, leaning halfway out the door.

"Uh-oh Rebecca, watch out! Mommy's upset with you," Pete joked.

"What about our game? We're not done. It's not over yet," Bobby whined.

"I gotta go. You lost anyway." I smiled at my bold statement.

"If you wouldn't ditch out, we'd beat you guys," Bobby argued.

"Good game, Beck," TJ called. I headed toward my front door feeling sticky, dirty, and satisfied.

My sweaty arms tingled at the chill of our air-conditioned foyer. My eyes adjusted to the dim indoor lighting as Buddy, our retriever, strutted toward me, his tail dashing back and forth.

"Hey, boy!" I bent down and kissed his snout as he licked my grimy nose.

"It smells delicious, Suzanne." My dad cooed at my mother, sneaking behind her in the kitchen, clasping the back of her shoulders, and kissing her cheek. She grinned and patted the back of his head. I kicked my shoes off into the front closet, came up to the dining room table, and opened the lid on the serving dish to spy on the meal. I was immediately bewildered.

"But Ryan hates chicken fettuccini," I said.

"Ryan won't be home for dinner. He's staying at Scott's overnight," my mother replied from the kitchen, her back to me.

"Yes!" I threw my fists up in celebration. A whole evening without my brother. Just Dad and me.

My dad brought drinks over to the table. "Looks like you and I got a date with ESPN, kiddo. Sox are home tonight." He smiled softly and kissed the top of my sweaty head.

"Rebecca, don't be rude about your brother. I really wish—" My mother stopped mid-sentence, her mouth gaping. She pursed her lips together while staring me up and down. "Look at you," she said, setting the cucumber salad on the table. "Have you at least *washed* your hands?"

"No, not yet."

"Well, what are you waiting for?"

I headed down the hall to the powder room and scrubbed my filthy hands.

"And you'd better grab a rag from the closet to sit on," my mother yelled from around the corner. "You're not sitting on my good chairs with a bottom full of grime."

I splashed water over the edges of the sink to rinse off the newly added dirt droplets, grabbed the hand towel on the counter, and dried my hands. Then I took an old towel from the linen closet and skipped back down the hall until I passed by the china cabinet. My steps slowed to purposely avoid looking at Rachel's picture. I knew she was watching me anyway. She always did.

As my mother filled my plate with chicken fettuccini, I slid into my seat. "What time is the game?" I asked my dad.

"Seven."

"No, no, no. After dinner, you are taking a shower, and then you can watch the Sox," my mother interjected.

"Right. After your shower," Dad agreed.

"I should've had you come in earlier to shower before dinner."

"I would've missed the football game."

"That was a great interception by Tommy." My dad grinned, then stuffed a forkful of pasta into his mouth.

"You saw it?" My eyes lit up. "Yeah, it was pretty good, huh? Mom, you should've seen it. Bobby was so mad."

"I didn't see you all day today. Out running here and there and off to Tommy's again." She gave me a scornful look.

"TJ needed me."

Being with TJ all day, every day, was the only thing I ever wanted to do. My mother didn't understand, no matter how many ways I'd said it before. My dad found our friendship adorable. My mother? Not so much.

CHAPTER 5

Reunion

"Oh my God," I said in a stunned, quiet voice, still staring dumbfounded at this figure of a man standing a few feet in front of me. A small group of people near TJ turned around to see what was going on.

"Holy Christ!" he exclaimed. The next thing I knew, he had picked me up and swung me around. "Beck!"

"Oh my God," I said again, starting to process what was happening. TJ let me go and backed away to look at me.

"Rebecca Winslow," TJ declared, shaking his head.

"What are you doing here?" I finally said.

"Pickin' up chicks," he laughed, holding his arms out as if the answer were obvious. "Your ankle's all better, I see."

"What?" I furrowed my brow, awestruck by his smile and glittering blue eyes.

"Aren't you going to introduce me … Rebecca?" Lindsay questioned.

Without taking my eyes off TJ, I sputtered, "Lindsay, this is TJ." Then I smiled, shaking my head. He looked at her, then back at me smiling, too.

"Unreal. I can't believe you're here," he said, almost to himself.

"TJ?" asked the dark-haired boy, laughing at TJ's apparently unknown nickname.

I glanced at both of his friends, who looked amused, then back at TJ, who was grinning broadly. "Tom, Tommy," I explained to Lindsay, who obviously didn't get it.

"Focus everyone," Mrs. MacFarlane directed.

"Nice to meet you, Lindsay." He shook her hand heartily. "This is Trevor and Freddie."

"Tommy Lawson? Something the matter?" Mrs. MacFarlane called when we didn't turn toward the group. All eyes darted in our direction. I couldn't believe I'd heard "Tommy Lawson" announced.

"No, we're all good, Mrs. Mac. Just havin' a little reunion back here." He winked at me.

"Can I be so bold as to ask that you halt your reunion so we may begin?"

"Absolutely! You know I've been looking forward to this one. I got my dancin' shoes on," he called.

"Uh-huh," Mrs. Mac said, rolling her eyes, a smirk on her face. Some girls nearby eyed TJ up, too. It was perfectly clear he had kept his classic charm. I was amazed that he was there, standing beside me, eleven years later and still the same TJ.

Mrs. Mac went over guidelines and intros, then handed out packets of information, which I was certain no one would glance at. She told us to get ready for the ultimate entertainment workout. I could hardly process what Mrs. Mac said. It felt like I was in a trance, mesmerized by TJ; I was unsure if I'd ever come out of it. Each time I looked at him, I put back another piece of the puzzle from my younger years. It was almost as if I had locked TJ away with the earliest parts of my childhood. As if I had forgotten who I was back then with him. I was awed to see him yet anxious that my life was about to unravel.

As class wrapped up, Mrs. Mac said, "See you all Thursday—on time."

Lindsay and I picked up our belongings and pulled on our coats. TJ looked as if he was making a polite getaway from a girl yapping at him. We were casually strolling toward the door when he stopped us.

"Hey!"

"See ya, Tom!" Trevor passed by us on his way out the door.

"Hey, later, Trev." TJ high-fived Trevor and focused on me. "Where you goin' now?" he asked.

"Um, Coleman Hall."

"You have another class?"

"No, it's… I'm an office assistant for Dr. Miller. He's one of the business directors."

"Oh, cool. Well, hey, walk me to work. It's on your way," he insisted.

"Where's your work?"

"The Rec Center."

"Sure."

"What about you? Where are you going?" he asked Lindsay.

Lindsay blushed, "I have class at Old Main. So, I gotta run, but it was really nice meeting you, Tom, Tommy, TJ," she said, eyeing me.

"Yeah, same here," he said.

TJ and I headed down the steps, both of us buttoning up our coats against the blast of cold air we were about to plunge into. The sky had turned overcast and gray.

I couldn't help but feel awkward with TJ. I had no idea what to say. *How do you pick back up after half a lifetime apart?*

"So how the hell are ya, Beck?"

I smiled, still dumbfounded by the now grown-up TJ.

"You look a lot different." He tilted his head, squinting a little. "But you still look like you."

I glanced at him with a grin, at a complete loss for words. That was always his department anyway.

"You ar-right?" He laughed.

"I'm sorry. I'm just shocked to see you."

"It's pretty crazy, huh?" he asked, smiling. "How long have you been here? Freshman? Sophomore?"

"Since freshman year. I'm a junior now."

"I've only been here a year. I started at a community college at home, and then I came here with Mason, my cousin. He's my next-door neighbor too. We have a house here a few blocks down on Fourth Street." TJ stopped speaking for a second and shook his head lightly. "Man, I can't believe I haven't seen you around until now. Where've you been hiding out? You go to the Rec, right?"

"Yeah." I nodded.

"Amazing." He shook his head as if trying to remember something important. "I can't believe I haven't bumped into you before now."

"Maybe you have and just didn't make the connection."

"Oh, I doubt that. You and I always had a connection, ya know?" His eyes were endearing and honest.

He was so comfortable talking that it made me feel guilty for keeping quiet. He always did wear his heart on his sleeve, though. TJ never left any room for second-guessing.

"Well, here I am. Thanks for walking me to work, Beck."

"You're welcome."

"I'll see ya on Thursday. Save me a dance."

I nodded.

"Rebecca Winslow," he said, shaking his head as he walked through the Rec Center doors.

I watched him walk further into the building, sensing that somehow this carefully plotted path my mother had laid out for me had just taken a detour.

CHAPTER 6

Sanctuary

I awoke the next morning from a brilliant stream of sunshine dancing across my clamped eyelids. I peeled my eyes open, looked at the clock, saw that it was already 9:30 a.m., and jumped out of bed. Rubbing the sleep out of my eyes, I almost fell over Buddy on the way to the bathroom that I shared with Ryan.

I washed my face and brushed my teeth, threw on a dirty pair of jean shorts and tank top, and headed downstairs.

"I cleaned it out yesterday, Mom," Ryan told my mother from in the kitchen. His tone indicated he was obviously lying about something.

"No, you didn't. You were at Scott's all day. You'll have to skim the pool and pick up after yourself if you want him to come over."

"Why are *you* back from Scott's so soon?" I inquired, opening the refrigerator to select a carton of orange juice.

"Good morning to you, too, dearest sister," he said, in his typical sarcastic tone.

"Rebecca, Ryan, be civil, please."

"Like the Civil War?" he asked. "Can we use cannons?"

My mother sighed loud enough for me to hear.

I ignored Ryan and walked over to the patio door, scooting on my sneakers.

"Excuse me, where do you think you're going?" My mother had an empty cereal bowl and spoon in her grasp, gestured toward me.

"I'm not hungry," I protested, my hand clenched on the handle of our sliding glass door. I just wanted to escape to my outdoor haven.

"Nonsense," she said.

It was useless to argue with her. I took the spoon and bowl, poured some cereal, and joined my brother at the table.

"God, can't you close your mouth when you eat? It's disgusting." Ryan sneered. I opened my mouth as wide as possible, just to spite him. A chunk of cereal slipped out and fell on the table.

Ryan slowly shook his head as his upper lip curled in disgust, a hint of laughter behind it. I chuckled.

My mother must've missed my cereal dribbling. Otherwise, she would've pointed out my unladylike behavior like always. She was busy straightening up her new shipment of summer catalogs from the jewelry company she worked for.

She came over to the table and set a stack of catalogs down. I felt her staring at the top of my head.

"Hmm," she moaned weakly. "It should grow out a little before school," she said more to herself than either of us. Ryan narrowed his eyes at me.

What my mother was sighing about was my latest mistake in the Winslow house. My formerly long, bouncy, chestnut brown hair was now chin-length and choppy.

One particularly hot day two weeks ago, I'd had enough. So logically, I cut it off. I thought I'd done a tremendous job, but my mother's appalled shriek when she saw the cut led me to believe she was not thrilled with my new look. I don't know why I was so surprised. I knew messing with my hair was forbidden. The little voice inside my head had yelled at me to put the scissors down before I'd hacked at it, but I did it anyway.

My mother had tearfully hauled me off to the beauty salon. After a week of constantly explaining that the long hair was too hot and kept getting tangled, I found it was in my best interest to keep quiet.

"So, Mom, can I call Scott over?" Ryan asked, bringing her back to reality from my botched head.

"After you clean up outside."

"Fine." He dropped his empty cereal bowl in the sink and went out the sliding door to our backyard. He was having his only friend over to swim, which meant I didn't want to be around the house. Ryan was bad enough, but Scott was in a whole other league.

Then the phone rang, and my mother answered it and started jabbering. I guessed she was talking to my Aunt Colleen. I quickly washed out my bowl and set it on the drying rack. Then I slipped out the patio doors and past Buddy. He was heartbroken, shattered that he wasn't invited where I was going.

"Sorry, Buddy," I whispered.

I hopped on my bike and headed three blocks to the Lawson's. The short trip to TJ's always seemed to transport me to a different place and time.

With each pump of my pedals, older sets of houses came into view. The new, suburban brick homes with three-car garages from my block made way for the aged, detached-garage houses nearer to TJ. Thick trees towered over the parkways. Sidewalks cracked, and veins of weeds snaked through. The houses got steadily closer to each other, separated by sagging chain-link fencing. These were tired streets, but it all felt more like a neighborhood to me.

TJ's house was a lot different from mine in ways that my mother didn't approve of. The appliances were run-down. The bathroom tiles were a little dingy and broken here and there. Even the wrought iron front porch railing was paint-chipped and loose. His house was much smaller, with a tiny damp basement and an even tinier attic on the top level. Mrs. Lawson had turned the hideaway into a bedroom for TJ. He called it the penthouse. He loved it even though he often hit his head on the slanted ceiling if he didn't walk straight down the center of his room. It was sweltering in the summertime and freezing in the winter, but he never complained.

TJ's six-year-old sister Katie had the room on the main level next to Mrs. Lawson's room. But she rarely slept there. Most nights, she just curled up beside her mom in her big bed. Their house didn't have four bedrooms, three bathrooms, or a three-car garage hiding a Honda and BMW. No swimming pool or golden retriever running around a large wooden deck out back. Yet it was my safe haven, my home away from home, and for most of my years up to that summer, I would've sacrificed all I had in a heartbeat to live there.

I rode up the front walkway. Katie was playing with her Barbies on a blanket. Like all of the Lawsons, Katie knew me well enough to know that I didn't play Barbies. Since I was there for TJ, she didn't ask me to join her.

"Hi Becky," she said in her sweet way. "Tommy's been waiting for you."

"Thanks, Katie. Is your mom still home?" I asked, confused to see the Lawson's brown Caravan parked along the curb.

"Yeah. She forgot a file, so she had to come back for it."

"Why, hello, Beck," came the voice of Thomas John Lawson from the side of the house.

"Hello, TJ."

"Sleep well, did you?" he asked in his goofy tone. "The sun's been up for hours, you know. I've been waiting all morning to show you something."

"Did you take the garbage out, sunshine?" TJ's mom called as she hurried out the front door.

"Yeah, I put it in the bin."

"Oh, my goodness. Thanks, baby." She let the door fall shut behind her. TJ's mom looked entirely out of place in a suit coat and skirt. Her typical outfit was outdoor-casual. Her wavy strawberry blond hair was loosely piled up in a big, black clip at the back of her head. She looked frantic yet happy at the same time.

"Hello, my sweet Becky," she said, a broad smile softening her freckled face. She kissed the top of my choppy, brown hair.

"Goodbye, sweet pea. Muah!" She gave Katie a big kiss on the lips.

"See you, sunshine," she said, moving over to TJ and kissing him on the lips, too. He didn't wince or say anything at all. It's what separated him from most every other ten-year-old boy. He understood how important his family was. That was TJ's serious side, and it was a huge reason that I admired and envied him.

"Now mind Auntie Helen, won't you? See you guys," she said as she closed the driver's side door and drove off.

TJ retrieved his bike from the weathered one-car garage. He crossed the yard to tell his next-door neighbor, Auntie Helen, that he would be riding around for a while, that Katie was in the front, and he'd be back by lunch. Then he gestured for me to follow him toward the backwoods on the west side of town.

"So, what is it?"

"I found something yesterday after you left the game."

We headed through the woods on the bumpy path. Big tree roots stretched over the path, which twisted and turned the further we rode in. TJ usually led the way to the trail because he was better at navigating and knew when the drop-off was coming up. The drop-off was a dangerous section of the woods that jutted down three feet from the narrowing trail. You had to be sure to stick to the right of the flattened path, or you could crash down into it. Just slightly past the last sharp turn, the trees scattered out, and the outline of the pond appeared.

TJ and I enjoyed playing around at the pond. It was secluded from the rest of the world and filled with tons of slimy creatures that we liked to study. My mother thought it was filthy. "Snakes live there!" she always said. Although the two species of snakes I ever saw there were completely harmless, I didn't usually mention my visits.

We parked our bikes near the murky water and walked along the edge. "There," TJ said in a hushed voice. He pointed to a newly dug, deep hole with fresh grasses thrown on top of it. It barely looked any different from the surrounding area. He squatted low to it, took a quick look around, and slowly pulled back a section of the mud. Then he whispered, "Can you see them?" He'd uncovered a nest of turtle eggs.

"Oh yeah, they're awesome."

We had a large population of painted turtles in the pond. They basked on the rocks midmorning until late afternoon. But that summer, there was a mild drought, and the number of turtles we saw was limited.

"How many?"

"I see seven."

"Okay. We gotta check on them every day and maybe make a trap for any snakes, huh?"

I paused, considering the nest. "No, we shouldn't bother them. I hope they'll be alright, though."

"Yeah, you're right. Their mom's gotta be looking out for them."

We stayed there for a while, looking around for garter snakes, frogs, and minnows. I was fascinated with animals. My bookshelf was crammed with books on all different species. I remembered most of what I read and what I couldn't find out in my books; I learned from Animal Planet.

I could've stayed there all day, hands on my knees peering into the muddy water watching for signs of life. But when TJ told me he was starving, we hopped back on our bikes. He entertained me by horribly singing his favorite tune, "Walking on Sunshine," all the way back home.

CHAPTER 7

First Dance

Little by little, scenes from the past flashed across my mind. I found it hard to concentrate on much of anything besides memories of TJ. It was as if I was awakening from a deep sleep.

I felt so grown up at the thought of how much time had passed. I wasn't the same sulking tomboy I used to be. That girl was left behind, but now I wished I could go back to her strong will and independence.

I didn't tell my parents or Jason about TJ. Whether that was intentional or not, I didn't know.

Lindsay was another story. She gave me the third degree about Thomas John Lawson. Why hadn't I said anything about him before? Was he always gorgeous? When did I see him last? Where did he live? She was, as she stated, "very interested." It was good to see Lindsay looking forward to something; this something happened to be Tuesdays and Thursdays at noon.

On Thursday, Lindsay and I charged through blistering cold and whipping winds to reach Lantz Gym on time for dance class. She was acting strangely paranoid. I assumed it had something to do with TJ. My face was cold and tight, and my eyes were watery from the icy breeze.

"I'm down to my last tissue," Lindsay said, blowing her nose for the fourth time and sniffling.

"Use your sleeve."

"There he is!" she exclaimed quietly, shoving her tissue into her pocket.

TJ stood with a crowd of guys and girls from our class. When he saw us come in, he gave us his big, adorable smile. We walked over to join him.

"Hi Tommy," Lindsay said excitedly.

"Hey," he said, "Lindsay, right?"

"Yeah." She blushed.

"Lindsay, this is Taylor, Natalia, Freddie, and Trevor. You met Trevor before, right?"

"On Tuesday. Hi."

"Hey Beck," TJ said. I smiled in return. "Guys, this is Rebecca Winslow." He smiled warmly.

"It's nice to meet you," I said.

"Hi, I'm Taylor," said the tall girl beside me. She had short, coiled black hair with burnt-orange tips.

"Aren't you on the soccer team?" Lindsay asked her.

"Yeah."

"I thought I recognized you," Lindsay continued. "You scored in the divisional game against Terre Haute, right?"

"Good memory," Taylor said.

"You're such a star, Taylor," Natalia said.

"Bite me."

"Are you a soccer fan, Lindsay?" TJ asked.

"Yeah, Rebecca and I played in high school."

"Soccer player, huh?" TJ asked me. I nodded. "No football?"

"I wasn't exactly allowed." I shrugged.

"That never stopped you before. What about intramural?" he asked.

"She could probably take Trevor's spot," Freddie said, laughing.

"You still on the team, Freddie? I haven't seen you make any plays recently," Trevor sniped.

"Ouch," Taylor said.

"We could use her. She's a great athlete. Fast. At least she was. Right, Beck?" TJ asked.

"Alright now, let's gather around," Mrs. Mac called out. "Today, we're going to start with a basic dance. The foxtrot."

There were a few groans and jokes.

"My grandpa does the foxtrot," a boy yelled.

FIRST DANCE

"Now, the foxtrot has a lot of basic fundamentals for dance," Mrs. Mac instructed. "It keeps to a 4/4 time for rhythm and is characterized by long, flowing moves across the floor. The man leads, as is the case with all the dances. We'll start in two groups, the boys' group and the girls' group."

Mrs. Mac's dad came out then to show the men their steps while she showed us ladies how to move. We all thought it was so charming that a little eighty-year-old grandpa was teaching.

"Gentlemen, left foot forward. Slow, slow then quick, quick to the side," Mr. Mac croaked in his raspy voice.

The dance was incredibly easy for most of us, yet several boys had difficulty. Outbursts and cackles punctuated the air every now and then. Soon enough, Mrs. Mac said to find a partner to try it for real. One second after her instructions, TJ had my hand and pulled me away from the rest of the group. Poor Lindsay looked destroyed until Mrs. Mac announced that the gentlemen would rotate clockwise to experience an array of partners. She started the music, and we started dancing.

TJ was obviously a novice. He was very choppy with his moves and started off on the wrong foot most of the time, yet didn't seem to care. He still had a million questions for me.

"So, how ya doing, Beck? You don't mind me calling you that, do you?" he asked.

"No. Do you mind me calling you TJ?"

"Not at all. It takes me back." He smiled. "So, where are you living now? In the dorms? On campus? Do you live with Lindsay, or is she just a friend from home?"

I had to stifle a laugh.

"What?"

"I forgot how much you could talk. A million ideas at once."

He grinned, "Am I moving the right way?"

"Not really. It's just four steps, though."

"I'm a little slow at this," he admitted.

"Okay!" Mrs. Mac clapped her hands together to get the attention of the class.

"Are you working, or do you have class after this?" he said in a rush, knowing that a partner change was about to ensue.

"No."

"Let's have the gentlemen rotate clockwise and introduce yourself to your next partner," Mrs. Mac directed.

"You're coming over then," he stated. I raised my eyebrows in surprise. "That's that."

He moved over, rotating to Natalia. It was amazing to me that he could just pick up exactly where we had left off. I felt hesitant to take his invitation. But, seeing him glide to Natalia, greet her warmly, and talk with her effortlessly, I knew he was still the same TJ. And I knew full well that TJ was one to be trusted completely.

CHAPTER 8

Auntie Helen

"Here you are, dears," Auntie Helen said, handing TJ, Katie, and me each a sandwich. "What a lovely idea, Tommy, to come sit in the screened-in porch this afternoon."

"I really like it in here," TJ said, throwing on the charm and shooting me a knowing, mischievous grin. It was all I could do to bite my lip and keep a straight face. He was famous for his charisma, especially with adults. His grandma said it was a Lawson trait.

The only reason TJ had suggested sitting in the screened-in porch was that it was hardly ever breathable inside. The house was small, stuffy, and exceedingly hot three hundred sixty-five days a year. The most noticeable aspect of it was that it smelled of air freshener and bird droppings.

Auntie Helen was known to the neighborhood as the Bird Lady. She had eight birds: six parakeets and two lovebirds in three birdcages in her living room. Since she was unable to get around much because of arthritis, she didn't clean all three birdcages as often as she should have. Most of the time, she just piled on the newspapers and sprayed air freshener to cover the scent.

Auntie Helen had lived alone in that house for twenty years since her husband had died. She had one daughter, April, who we never saw. The last Mrs. Lawson had heard about April was that she had moved to Miami with her lady friend to open a tattoo shop. Auntie Helen never mentioned April, so I never asked about her.

I was surprised to find out that "Auntie" Helen wasn't related to TJ at all. She was a lonely but polite elderly woman who always wanted company. The Lawsons had simply adopted Auntie Helen as theirs. Mrs. Lawson helped her with groceries, and TJ mowed the lawn in exchange for babysitting five days a week. She always told Mrs. Lawson that it was too sweet of a deal to look after such dear children.

"Thank you, Auntie Helen," Katie said, taking a bite of her sandwich.

"Yeah, thank you," TJ and I chimed in together.

"You are welcome. Eat up, eat up," she said as she crept back into the kitchen for some lemonade. I took a bite of my sandwich and slowly chewed the odd texture. It was a chunky, cool mush with a bitter taste. I didn't know whether to keep chewing or spit it out, so I moved the bite around in my mouth until finally forcing it down.

TJ must've seen the gross expression on my face and wrinkled his nose. "You don't like tuna fish?"

"Oh." I didn't know what to say. I looked down at the sandwich as someone might look at a glass of curdled milk. My stomach churned. I felt queasy and hot. I had to eat it but had no idea how to do it without it coming right back up. I couldn't break this poor old woman's heart and deny what she had given me.

Just then, TJ asked Katie to get another napkin from Auntie Helen and some cookies, too. I looked up; he was eyeing me with a mixture of concern and humor. Katie, the doting little sister, got up and stalled Auntie Helen.

I was certain I would be sick. As I opened my mouth to consider another bite, TJ said hurriedly, "Here, give it to me." He grabbed the sandwich and gobbled it down.

I was shocked, disgusted, amazed, and grateful all at the same time as I stared at him. Katie skipped back onto the porch with a plate of cookies and napkins. Just as Auntie Helen's footsteps neared, TJ put the crust of my sandwich back onto my plate. I covered my mouth and giggled. He then swallowed hard, stood up, and politely grabbed two glasses from the tray Auntie Helen struggled to walk with. He handed me one, then, sitting down again, chugged his own.

AUNTIE HELEN

"Here, Katie dear, is this enough lemonade for you?" Auntie Helen asked.

"Uh-huh."

I finally stopped gaping at TJ and took a sip of my lemonade. Auntie Helen sat down, grinning at us. TJ began eating his own sandwich, although much more slowly.

"Oh, would you like another sandwich, Rebecca?" Auntie Helen asked, reaching for my plate.

"No," I said, quickly throwing my hand over hers. Catching her look of surprise, I said, "Thank you. I had enough." I shyly smiled at TJ, whose eyes smiled back at me through a mouthful of sandwich.

"Well, how about an oatmeal cookie?" She asked, eyeing me suspiciously.

"Sure."

Katie and Auntie Helen stayed in the screened-in porch after lunch. I decided to help TJ clean the birdcages.

"You okay?" TJ asked as we left the room and headed into the house to toss our trash.

"Yeah."

"I thought you were gonna puke all over everything. You turned green, Beck," he laughed.

"I felt like I was gonna. Thanks, TJ," I giggled.

"No problem. I didn't want you to throw up on me."

"I can't believe you ate all that," I remarked while pulling up the newspaper from the corner of a parakeet's cage.

"Yeah, I feel kind of sick right now." TJ held the garbage bag close and made a puking sound. I turned around suddenly with a look of horror. He smiled, clearly faking. "I don't know how you can stand cleaning up all that bird poop." He made a face.

"Well, it's no big deal. They can't do it themselves, and I'm sure they don't like all those air fresheners." We both giggled silently.

Although everyone else in the neighborhood thought Auntie Helen was crazy for having all those birds, I really enjoyed them. I wouldn't sing to them like she or Katie would, but I petted them and fed them from my hand all the time.

Auntie Helen would sometimes get TJ to help her sing to them. He sang a lot, usually out of tune. Whether he intended to or not, I'm not sure. But it was funnier that way.

The three of us played basketball all afternoon in TJ's driveway, which was next door to Auntie Helen. The Lawsons had a big, mobile basketball stand. They bought it at a garage sale years before. We played HORSE, but since Katie was so little, we lowered the hoop for her, or TJ picked her up to shoot. He was a great brother to her—unlike Ryan. She adored TJ just like everyone else did, except my mother.

I had just made a difficult shot when my dad pulled up alongside TJ's driveway. I pouted openly about having to leave.

"I thought I'd find you here." He grinned at me, stepped out of the running car, and motioned to TJ for the ball.

"Hi, Mr. Winslow."

"How are you, Tommy? Katie?"

Dad dribbled the ball and ran in for a layup. TJ's face lit up. He admired my dad so much. Anytime he was around, TJ kept his eyes locked on him. It broke my heart to see TJ with my dad. It was the one missing piece from his perfect family.

"Nice, Daddy."

"Thanks, kiddo." He dribbled again, then bounced it to TJ, who followed his layup. "Great shot, Tommy!"

"Thanks."

"Well, let's get going," Dad said to me. "Mom's got dinner for us." He held up my bike, so I could hop on.

"Good, I'm starving."

"Didn't you have lunch today?"

"Sort of." I looked back at TJ and stuck my tongue out.

CHAPTER 9

Reconnect

When dance class was over, TJ said goodbye to all his new girlfriends. The giggles and open flirting were just the beginning of what was sure to become routine. I found myself thinking that many of the girls in this class must've signed up for the same reason as Lindsay.

TJ politely asked Lindsay if she'd care to join us for a visit to his house on Fourth Street, just a few blocks up from Lantz Gym. She deflated the moment he asked. She had class after dance on both Tuesdays and Thursdays, and she was not at all the kind of student to ditch out. Ever. Sure, she might flirt with the idea, but she would ultimately chicken out. Lindsay was a desperate rule follower.

"Sorry, I can't. See you at home, Rebecca!" Lindsay called.

"Yes, ma'am."

TJ and I headed out toward his house. We chatted about class and how TJ knew Mrs. Mac.

"I had her for PED 1500. It's all part of my Kinesiology and Sports Studies requirements. That's the technical term for PE."

"That's your major? PE?" I smiled.

"Heck, yeah. Can't beat it."

"What are you going to do with that?" I bit my lip upon uttering that question, hearing the voice of my mother behind it.

"Be a PE teacher and coach at my high school back home."

"Really?"

"Yeah, next year the PE teacher's retiring. I'm hoping to take over. That is if I take intersession classes to finish on time. Come on! We can make this light."

We dashed across the slushy intersection while thousands of tiny flakes fluttered down on us. Once on the curb, we settled back into a rhythm of walking and catching up.

"How do you know you're gonna get that position?" I asked.

"I don't. But I know the whole staff. We live in a small town. It's almost like an extended family. I planted a seed in the superintendent's mind about it last fall. So that's the plan."

"Wow." I couldn't believe he had his entire career mapped out already. I, on the other hand, didn't have the faintest idea of what I wanted to do with my future. True, I'd joked initially about TJ being a PE teacher, but it was an ideal job for him. In every sport he played, he was a gifted athlete. He was also an incredibly patient leader, so imagining him coaching a class of students made perfect sense.

"When did you know that you wanted to do that?"

"Um, probably after high school. When I got my head in check."

I looked up at him, unsure what he meant.

"So, this is my house."

It was an old red and brown brick house with a large, elevated porch capped off with four thick posts. I gingerly made my way up the snow-packed porch steps. Apparently, none of his roommates had invested in a shovel. Newspaper covered some of the front windows. My guess was that it was a replacement for window treatments.

Inside, the wall-to-wall brown shag carpeting no doubt hid beer stains. A very used, comfy-looking sofa with a pillow and blanket rolled into a ball was accented by a few mismatched chairs, a decent size TV, and a dartboard on the wall. The house was long but not that spacious. The front room led to the dining room, which led to an open kitchen. Three small bedrooms and a bathroom lined the hallway. A nicely crafted, four-person bar sat in the corner of the dining room, opposite what looked like a sound system.

The decor was universally beer signs and posters covering areas of fresh plaster. The kitchen held a large folding table, chairs, and two fridges.

"One's for a keg." TJ clarified. Off the kitchen was a back patio. Plastic covered the door but didn't keep the cold out.

I smiled to myself, imagining my mother's reaction to the house and to TJ's reappearance. TJ didn't explain or apologize for anything. He seemed proud of his house. I thought that was darling. In truth, it was like any other house of college boys: just a place to sleep and party.

"You hungry, Beck?" TJ said, checking his fridge.

"Not really."

"I'm gonna make you a sandwich. Ham or turkey? Both? What'll it be?"

"That's okay."

"Beck, I'm gonna have a sandwich. It's good lunch meat, I swear. Trevor works at Kroger. He keeps us stocked. Which one do you want?"

My phone buzzed with an incoming text. I paused for a moment, "Whatever you're having. It doesn't matter."

"Ar-right." After washing his hands, he started preparing the sandwiches.

I checked the text. It was from Jason inquiring where I was. I didn't reply.

"Hey, I could make you a tuna fish sandwich. Remember that? With Auntie Helen?"

"Oh, my gosh, yeah."

"She's still kickin'," he said. "Mayo, mustard, both?"

"Neither." I wrinkled my nose.

"You're missing out. Condiments are the key to a good sandwich. Eventually, I'll get you to come around."

He handed me the sandwich.

"Thank you." I took my plate then stifled a chuckle.

"So, Auntie Helen's still alive?" I offered for conversation.

"Yeah, how about that? We send her a Christmas card every year. She's in the nursing home now. When was the last time you saw her?"

"A long time ago."

"What about Pete, Mikey, or Garcia?"

"No idea. We moved to Naperville eight years ago."

"Oh yeah?" He mumbled around a mouthful of sandwich, reaching for a paper towel on the counter. "Why's that?"

I shrugged. "I don't know. My dad got promoted, so my mom wanted a bigger house, better area, I guess." Of course, I knew the answer: keeping up with the Joneses.

My mother never liked our home on Foxgrove. She complained about the layout and the small, separated rooms. She had been trying to get my dad to move since Rachel had died. I understood the feeling of her ghost hanging around in our old house and could concede to my mother's need to move, but Rachel was still there no matter what. The move didn't seem to make my mother any happier. She still had the same dark circles under her eyes and the same prescriptions collected in her bathroom cabinet that I wasn't supposed to know about.

The front door slammed as TJ nodded and gave me a knowing smile. I looked away as two of TJ's roommates came into the kitchen arguing with each other.

"You spineless coward," the big one with curly brown hair and a thick, brown beard said, shoving the smaller one in the back.

"Brandon, Mason, this is Beck," TJ said, tossing his napkin and plate in the trash bin.

"How's it goin'?" Brandon, the big one, said, his voice a low growl.

"Nice to meet you," Mason said politely. He flicked snowflakes from his baseball cap and ruffled his sandy, brown wisps. "Wait a minute." He pointed at me, scrutinizing TJ's face. "This is Beck? As in 'Beck from back home?'"

"The same."

"Huh." He looked me over.

My cheeks flushed.

"I'll give you the tour," TJ said, standing up.

"You look a lot different from your picture," Mason said as I moved past him to throw out my plate and half sandwich. I widened my eyes, not knowing what he was talking about.

"Hey, are you gonna finish that?" Brandon asked, eying my lunch longingly.

"Um." I squinted and shook my head.

"Cool," he said, taking my unfinished sandwich and shoving it whole into his mouth. "Thank you," he mumbled as TJ and I walked upstairs, snickering.

"This is my cousin Mason's room," TJ said, stopping just outside the door at the top of the landing.

"Mason." I looked down, trying to recall what I knew about him. I had heard TJ mention him in the past. Then it hit me. The car accident.

"Yeah," TJ said, gesturing for me to walk into the room. "He's lived with my great aunt and uncle, his grandparents, since my dad and his parents died in that crash. They live right next door to us back home, and …well, it's a little complicated." TJ turned toward the corner of Mason's open closet, where I noticed a pack-n-play, stuffed animals, and a package of diapers.

"His girlfriend and daughter live with him, too. At home mostly, but sometimes they come here to visit. This is Tana." He picked up a picture of a sweet little brunette girl from the dresser. She wore a Christmas outfit and sat in a sea of gifts.

"She's cute."

"Yeah, she's adorable."

I couldn't even imagine trying to juggle a child and college. Worse, I was reminded of that terrible accident that robbed TJ of his dad and Mason of both of his parents.

"So, Mason and Brandon live with you?" I asked for a change in direction.

"Mason, Brandon, and Trevor."

"Who's the lucky one that sleeps on the couch?"

"That's Big Al." TJ smiled. "He's a townie. His old lady kicks him out a lot, so he stays here from time to time. His place is right behind us. There are people here all the time, actually," he laughed.

"Wow, you guys are generous with your space."

My phone rang then, and my heart pounded. "Sorry," I said, reaching into my coat pocket. He shook his head.

I accidentally answered it instead of silencing it, "Hello?"

"Hi." It was Jason.

"Hey," I replied, moving over to the side of the room. I was suddenly uncomfortable being at TJ's, especially when Jason didn't know he existed.

"Didn't you get my text?"

"Yeah."

"Why haven't you called yet?"

"I will. I'm not home right now."

"Where are you?"

"Let me call you back." I glanced at TJ, who grinned and picked up Mason's sponge ball and began jumping around, shooting hoops off his mini basketball net over his door.

"Why? Where are you?"

"I'm at a friend's house. I'll call you back."

"I'm running out soon. Just call me later then." Jason sighed, sounding disappointed.

"'Kay." I hit the end button. "Sorry," I said, shyly putting my phone back in my pocket and staring at the floor.

"What's his name?"

I picked my head up, opened my mouth, and closed it, "Jason."

"Does he go here?"

"No, U of I."

"So, is he one of those academic types?" TJ winked.

I laughed. "Yeah, he's pretty smart."

He had what seemed like a forced grin on his face. We shared a moment of awkward silence before I blurted out, "I've gotta go."

"Yeah, me too. I have to work at 2:30. Let me drive you back."

"No, that's okay."

"I'm driving anyway. It's snowing like mad out there."

"I don't want you to go out of your way."

"Beck." He looked at me seriously, "You will never be out of the way for me. Ar-right?"

I nodded and resigned myself to a ride home. It was sweet of him to take care of me.

TJ's white pickup truck was definitely a hand-me-down. The right front fender was dented, but the interior was very cozy. It suited him well. It was sturdy and comfortable, the kind of vehicle that could handle any road or weather. TJ jammed to the EIU country station, belting out lyrics about heartache and summer nights, and before you knew it, we'd pulled up to my apartment. The snow was dissipating, and the sun covered by dull gray skies.

"This one?" he asked, peering up through his driver's side window.

"Yeah," I said.

"Which floor?"

"Second."

"Cool. So, it's you, Lindsay, and…?"

"Amy."

He smiled and looked at me for a second, "You gotta call your boyfriend back."

"I know. I will. So, thanks." I reached for the door handle.

"Hey, Beck, look," he said, blocking my way out with his arm. "I hope I'm not making you uncomfortable. I'm just glad to be hanging out with you again, you know? It's been a long time, but I still remember almost everything about you. You were a huge part of my life."

His spectacular eyes were so honest and vulnerable that I warmed to him all at once. I saw instantly in my mind the image of my ten-year-old pal.

In that second, he wasn't a college hottie (as Lindsay would say). He was just my TJ.

I ended that internal battle with myself to stay guarded. After I'd spent so much time building my invisible wall, TJ deserved at least a window of entry. I relaxed my shoulders and really inhaled for the first time in forever.

"I don't think I'll be able to stay away from you now that you've resurfaced." He grinned. "I think you're okay with that, but..." He stretched his neck to one side as if examining me. "I'm just making sure I'm not bugging you. You're being timid like always, right?" I smiled. "You don't have to hold back anything with me."

I surprised myself by blinking some tears away, realizing how much I had missed him. I'd just been remembering him when I was on the way back from break, and then he'd popped back into my life from nowhere.

"I hadn't thought of you in so long. But then I did a few days ago," I said cautiously, fidgeting with my coat buttons, not meeting his eyes. He hung on my every syllable. "And now, here you are." I looked up at him. "I feel like I called out to you. Like I summoned you somehow."

TJ stared at me for a second. "I know what you mean."

CHAPTER 10

Playing Dead

"Good morning Buddy, mmmwha." I kissed my dog hello as he lay near the foot of the stairs in the living room. I walked up to my mother in the kitchen. "Morning, Mom."

She looked sideways at me. "Morning. Flip those for me." Her eyes darted to a griddle of pancakes on the stovetop.

"Pancakes! Yes!" I grabbed the spatula and cautiously flipped the six pancakes one at a time, hearing the sizzle of the pan scorch each one.

"That's it. Keep flipping them quickly," My mother called out while grabbing a small stack of plates from the cabinet.

"How long do I wait, Mom?" I asked, patting each as I'd seen her do before.

"Wow! Are you teaching her how to be a girl?"

I snapped my head around to catch the smug look on Ryan's face.

"Ryan, not another word," my mother scolded.

He stared at us both for a second, likely to see if he should risk a retort that would give him satisfaction or if it would push my mother over the edge.

"Take Buddy outside," she demanded. Ryan walked to the sliding door and clapped to get Buddy's attention from where he lay, then guided him out. My mother crossed the room, took the spatula, and removed the pancakes from the griddle.

"Do you want me to pour some milk?" I offered.

"That's fine."

I looked up at her expression. My mother was visibly shaken by Ryan's comment. She wouldn't even look at me. She just spread butter on the pancakes and brought them to the table. I could see her eyes glaze over with despondency. I guessed she was processing the loss of her true daughter again. I felt myself shrinking down once more.

The three of us ate quietly. My mother kept standing up and getting more milk and syrup to escape the tension of our breakfast table. She was an easy target for Ryan's comments. Anything to cause a stir. He barely had anything but snide remarks for anyone.

Ryan hurried through his pancakes, shoving forkfuls at a time into his chubby face, all the while lobbing dirty looks at me. Soon he was out the door, grabbing his skateboard and heading down the sidewalk. I helped my mother clear the table and clean the dishes.

Our doorbell rang, announcing TJ's visit. When I opened the door, a wave of heat wafted through our perfectly air-conditioned house. The sun blazed through a cloudless sky. Humid mist was in the air already, and beads of sweat stood out on TJ's forehead. He squinted at me.

"Jeez, it's hot," I shielded my eyes at him.

"Yeah. I checked on the turtle eggs. They're all still there."

"That's good. Do you want to swim? It's too hot for football."

"Sure, I'll ride back home and get my suit."

"Cool." I darted back inside. "Mom, TJ's gonna come swim, okay?" I yelled, slamming the door, then ran upstairs to get my suit.

"Uh, alright," she replied. "Is his sister coming with him?"

"No, she's probably with Auntie Helen," I hollered down, tossing my shirt and shorts on the ground and climbing into my purple two-piece. I grabbed a beach towel from our linen closet and headed downstairs and out the sliding door.

Just as TJ showed up, my mother appeared, holding a spray bottle of sunblock.

"Rebecca, did you put on sunscreen?"

"Yeah," I lied.

"Hi, Mrs. Winslow," TJ said. He dropped his bike to the ground and petted Buddy, who nearly knocked him over.

"Hello, Tommy. Come here, young lady."

I looked at TJ, who smiled at me while I rolled my eyes.

She sprayed my back and shoulders, then sprayed a bit in her hands and rubbed my cheeks and forehead. "Now, you may swim."

TJ kicked off his shoes. My mother eyed TJ, inspecting him and his worn-down sneakers and cheddar fries-stained shorts. He grabbed his Packers beach towel and wiped his face and head. I climbed up the ladder and dove in so I wouldn't have to see any more disapproval in her eyes. A tingle of icy water swept over my body as I cooled instantly. The water was so refreshing; it took my breath away. I touched the bottom, crawled along it, then popped up, smoothing my hair out of my eyes.

TJ tugged at the back of his shirt, pulled it off over his head, and climbed up the ladder to the deck. He was tall with a lean build. His golden hair glistened with sweat in the light of the sun. His eyes reflected the sparkling crystal blue water perfectly. He reached the top step and somersaulted into the water.

We swam around for a couple of minutes, then timed each other holding our breath. I averaged around forty seconds, but TJ was unbelievable! He could hold his breath for over a minute and a half. Of course, he was blue when he finally came up, but that didn't seem to bother him.

"How do you do that for so long?"

TJ smiled while doing a light backstroke, "I don't know. Maybe I just don't panic."

He made everything look so easy. I liked swimming and had taken lessons at the local high school. That was one of my mother's requirements. I was pretty good and moved up quickly through several levels. On the other hand, TJ was naturally great at virtually anything and everything. He was always good competition for me. I could run just a little faster than he could and was probably a better student, especially in art. And I knew more about animals, but TJ reigned over everything else, even swimming, which was baffling, seeing that I was the one with the pool.

We took turns diving for rings. I had no trouble grabbing them when I could see, but TJ wanted to try a game where we had to keep our eyes closed. He loved a good challenge. No matter where I dropped the rings, he glided along the bottom, running his hands from side to side and finding every ring, every time.

"I can't hold my breath that long," I whined after being unsuccessful a third time.

"Sure, you can. Listen, all you have to do is start at a corner and work your way around. Don't think about breathing. You have plenty of air right above you, so don't worry. Just run your hands over the bottom and move around from that corner. Try it again. Okay?" He dove to place the last two rings, then popped up. "Now, close your eyes."

I shut them and took long, slow breaths trying to calm down.

"They're in place. You can do it, Beck."

I nodded, then backed up to the side by the ladder and dove down with one huge gulp of air. Everything got quiet and still. I felt for the bottom. It was smooth but gritty from tiny particles of dirt and rock. I reached my arms out and swept the bottom while squeezing my eyes tight.

Left, right, left, right. I moved forward. Left, right, left—my hand touched something raised and smooth. *I had one.* Right, left, right, left, right—*the second one!* I started thinking about how many more seconds I could last but then shook the thought from my mind. Instead, I thought, *slow, calm down, left, right.* I had to be close. Then my fingers closed around the ring. I got it! I darted up to the surface, splashed out, and held all three rings up in the air, wiping off my eyes with my free hand.

"See! I told you!" TJ beamed at me.

We floated around for a bit, and then he let me surf on him. TJ bragged about how I had such great balance. I could stand up on him for several seconds without wobbling too much.

"Hey," his eyes grew wide again. "Let's make a whirlpool!"

"Okay!"

We charged through the water counterclockwise, swimming and walking and jogging around. It seemed like a long while that we circled the same direction when we finally noticed a bit of current moving in a circle. At last, we began to cheer excitedly while floating along with our newly created current, and then…

"Cow-a-bunga!!!" A huge figure cannonballed into the center of the pool. Then another. Startled, TJ and I could barely find our balance among the pounding of the water.

A body I recognized as my annoying brother came hurtling toward me. "AAAHH! I'm drowning! Help me, Rebecca, please!"

He wrapped himself around me, nearly pulling me under, pretending to panic and splash like crazy. Ryan's big, dumb friend Scott laughed loudly.

"Get off me!" I snapped, pushing him away. The water finally gave up its current and slowed.

"Hey look, Ry! Your little brother brought his girlfriend, PJ," Scott snorted.

I looked at TJ, and we both knew our fun time in the pool was over. *How long would we have to stay in before we could escape and not be thought of as cowards?* I thought of yelling for my mom, but that would be of no help. She would say, "Share" or "Well, you've been in there all day, let Ryan have a turn."

My brother and his friend looked delighted with each other.

"I know Ry, splash contest!" Scott belted out.

Immediately waves slapped us hard in the face. We tried to splash back, but it was useless. They were so much bigger. Our feeble attempts only made it worse. It was hard trying to find a second to breathe. My eyes stung from the relentless pelting. I choked for breath and turned my head away from a wall of water thrashing toward me.

TJ turned me around and yelled, "Go under and climb out on the ladder! I'll keep them busy!"

I took a huge breath and dove as TJ shoved water at them with all his might. Under the surface, I heard rushing water and loud taunting. I made it to a wall and felt the ladder. There was still so much noise. I knew they didn't see me sneak by. I climbed up quietly and backed onto the far end of the deck behind them. Then one splasher gave up. Ryan and Scott had their eyes shut and continued to bombard TJ, still splashing and breathing hard while hooting.

Then TJ was floating on his chest. I knew him too well to freak out. I smiled sneakily like he must've been doing underwater.

Ryan stopped splashing, wiped his face, and peered closer at TJ. He looked at me, confused to see me safely out of the pool. I instantly made a dramatic, troubled face at TJ but said nothing.

Seconds passed while TJ remained still. Ryan furrowed his brow at TJ. Scott stopped splashing and noticed my brother staring at TJ in disbelief. I quickly stole a glance at the sliding glass doors, hoping my mother wasn't watching. If she found out TJ was playing at this prank, she would be livid. I could almost hear her voice, "Pretending to drown is nowhere near close to humor!"

I pretended to panic and paced the deck. "Ryan, what did you do?" I cried, smiling to myself despite the terrible scene. I knew TJ had to be loving the silence under the still water. They stood there dumbfounded, open-mouthed.

"Rebecca, go get Mom!" Ryan's body shook. Scott was silent; his eyes fixed on TJ's lifeless body. "Get Mom!" Ryan ordered again.

"Hoo-hah!" TJ jumped up, slightly blue, but smiling at their puzzled expressions as he wiped off his face. Ryan's shock turned to anger. Scott still looked baffled.

TJ slid to the ladder. "Thanks for taking care of me, guys. Really," he said, between breaths. "It's nice to know if I'm ever drowning, you'll just call your mom to flip me over." He climbed out.

I smiled proudly at him.

Ryan, seeing I was in on the joke, sloshed a huge wave of water up onto the deck.

We scurried down the steps, grabbed our towels, and rushed toward the screen door. I almost knocked my mother over in my haste.

"Rebecca, what is going on out here? I heard a lot of shouting. You know I don't want you and Ryan messing around in the pool. It's dangerous." She looked annoyed.

"Oh, Ryan and Scott got the deck all wet from splashing."

We covered ourselves and opened the sliding door. My mother set her mouth in an irritated manner, then went toward the boys. I could hear her lecturing them on pool conduct, and TJ, and I laughed as we went upstairs to change.

"You knew I was faking, right?"

"Duh."

"They were really worried?"

"Yeah! Worried that they made you die."

"Did you see Ryan's face?"

We couldn't stop giggling.

CHAPTER 11

Speedbump

I spent the next two nights after my visit with TJ hanging out with my girls. On Thursday night, Amy and I had to talk Lindsay down from the ledge. She'd found out she had sixth-grade practicum. Practicum was a field experience that Lindsay had to complete before she could do any student teaching. Many of her classmates were scheduled to observe and assist in classrooms of sweet little kindergarteners or second-grade cuties. Lindsay was stuck with sixth graders.

"God, this sucks. I don't want old kids. I wanted little ones. These kids are probably going to cuss me out or something," she vented, wiping her red eyes.

"Come on, Linds, look at it this way. Now you get to teach Sex Ed." Amy winked at her. It was probably the worst comment she could've mustered.

"Oh, GOD!" Lindsay cried again.

"Wait a sec, shouldn't it be a requirement to have sex before teaching Sex Ed?" Amy asked herself.

"Shut up, Amy!" Lindsay cried.

"Aim," I began.

"Speaking of Sex Ed," Amy interrupted, "I heard you were at a boy's house the other day, Miss Rebecca."

I had to convince Amy that there was nothing going on with TJ and me. Amy eyed me suspiciously like she was looking for a crack in my armor. Lindsay was interested as well. I had nothing to hide and explained without a hint of a stutter that TJ was just a good buddy from my childhood.

"Well, I don't care. I just wanted to make sure you knew that Megan said she saw him making out with some tramp at Stix last night," Amy said.

"Seriously?" Lindsay asked.

"I'm not surprised at all. You should see the girls swooning over him in class. Even our instructor has a thing for him," I said.

"This sucks. Everything sucks right now. Let's get drunk," Lindsay announced.

"Sounds good to me," Amy agreed.

I designated myself as the sober driver, and Amy and I treated sorrow-filled Lindsay with pick-me-up shots at Marty's, the closest bar. It didn't take long for Lindsay to forget her frustration and hang on the both of us, telling us she loved us and that we were the best. Of course, Amy agreed.

The next afternoon, I finally sat down long enough to have a real conversation with Jason. And I knew that texting promoted bad communication habits, although conversations with Jason were mostly one-sided anyway. He typically ran down his agenda for the day, highlighting problems and how he'd solved them. Or he complained about a professor or moron of a classmate. And he usually went into great detail about how much he missed me. How he missed my eyes, my lips, my legs. I flushed a light pink listening to that as Lindsay interrupted my privacy to borrow something from my closet.

"Sorry," she cringed, wrapping a fleece blanket around her crumpled PJs and messy bun, trying to tiptoe and make a quick escape.

Not wanting to continue our current topic of conversation with Lindsay clearly in the way, I built up my nerve to tell Jason about TJ. I felt guilty about seeing TJ and spending time with him with Jason, so completely unaware. *But then again, why should that matter if nothing was going on?* I didn't tell Jason about new friends in class ever. TJ was *just* my friend. But Jason should know what was going on with me and my weekly experience. He was so willing to share his.

"Want to know something incredible?" I blurted out.

"Sure."

"I ran into my best friend from my old neighborhood. He's in one of my classes. I haven't seen him in forever. Isn't that cool?"

"Cool, that you saw a guy?" Jason asked, already on the attack.

"No, just neat that one of my oldest friends is here at Eastern," I muttered.

"So why are you telling me this?" he asked, a note of irritation in his voice.

"Uh…" I paused. "I don't know. You always say I don't tell you anything."

"So, now you're telling me about some guy friend? What are you trying to do? Prepare me or something?"

"No, Jason, you're reading way too much into this. It's just crazy that he's here when we haven't seen each other...."

"Yeah, okay," he cut me off.

"Come on."

"I gotta go," he said, hanging up.

Figures, I thought.

Unease crept into my belly. Being with Jason was like a tight rope act. It was emotionally draining at times. I could be up so high with him when things were good, but one slip, and I would come crashing down. What had I expected, though, talking to him about TJ? Of course, he would take it wrong. He didn't get it. I stretched my neck out, trying to unwind from our conversation. I knew this stress would cause the nightmare to happen again. And it did.

That night I raced to catch Rachel, but as always, I never got close enough. I just followed her long, brown hair swaying off her shoulders as she walked methodically in a straight path along the trail. I managed to wake myself up before I saw my own face. Then I sat up in bed for a while, unable to return to sleep.

Before long, I became aware of a repetitive bumping noise on the other side of the wall and shook my head laughing. It sounded as though

Amy had a "friend" over. After a few drinks of water, I finally nestled back down and drifted off to sleep.

Later that morning, I made my way over to the Rec Center, where I knew Lindsay would be. I assumed she'd decided to skedaddle after seeing one of Amy's "friends" stumble by in his underwear bright and early, heading for the bathroom. I thought she'd be used to that by now.

As I entered the Rec Center, I passed the registration booth and spotted TJ making conversation with a girl I'd seen before. She was giggling and tossing her head back as he leaned over the counter, babbling, no doubt. I had to chuckle. It was unbelievable how often he flirted with the ladies. He handed the girl a piece of paper. Then she walked away, and he turned to file something. I approached the booth.

"Hey," I said.

He turned around. "Hey, Beck. How ya doing?"

"I'm okay."

"You working out?"

"Going to."

"You want a tour?"

"I've been here before," I answered, smiling.

He laughed. "I could give you the inside tour."

"That's really okay. Is Lindsay here?"

"Yeah. She seems a little out of sorts."

"Right." I glanced downward, fighting my grin.

"What's with Lindsay?"

"Nothing. She just needed to escape from one of Amy's male friends hanging out in our apartment."

"Uh oh. Hey, I told my mom I saw you."

"Did you? She probably doesn't even remember me."

"Are you kidding? She couldn't believe it. Then she started crying. She said I'd be in huge trouble if I didn't bring you home with me soon."

"Uh," I choked in disbelief, then stepped aside for a student approaching the desk.

"Is this the intramural schedule?" The kid asked, pointing to a piece of paper.

"Yeah, here ya go, man." TJ handed it to him.

"How is your mom? She was always so sweet."

"She's great. Working in the park's office. She's getting married." He smiled.

"She's getting married?"

"Yep, in April, to this amazing guy, Howard. He owns a fishing shop right by Carlyle Lake."

"Wow."

"It's so awesome. Howard is a huge fisherman. We go out on the lake constantly. He used to go fishing with my grandpa a lot, but he passed away a handful of years ago, so I've kind of taken it up with Howard. Sometimes Howard asks Katie to tag along, but she isn't into it."

He looked so happy and at ease talking about his family. It was so far off from the comments I made about my family. I envied his pride and passion for those he was closest to.

"Katie's a junior on the cheer squad. She just broke up with her boyfriend, so I'm happy about that."

"Oh my God. What, you didn't like him?"

"Of course not. He was dating my little sister." He stood up to give approaching customers attention.

"Hey, are there any slots left available for racquetball right now?" one of the guys asked.

"Let me check."

"TJ, I'm gonna...." I pointed up to the workout area.

He teasingly looked mad and threw his arms up, "Ar-right, see ya."

CHAPTER 12

Everybody's Happy

TJ's grandma Lawson was coming up the next day. She was so warm and fun. Because she lived in Southern Illinois, she couldn't get up to see his family much, but she and TJ's grandpa would visit from time to time. TJ made an effort to include me whenever his grandparents visited. Like I belonged to them, too. We were planning to camp out the next day when she was over. It was just a matter of breaking this news to my family now.

My mother, dad, brother, and I sat around the dinner table playing happy family, except for the fact that Ryan and I gave each other grimacing looks behind my mother's back.

My dad was usually unaware of what was going on. At least he pretended to be, maybe to avoid confrontation. I guessed he picked his battles and let some issues slide. He was thoughtful, passive, quiet, and caring. My mother often made comparisons between my father and me. She always pointed out that I had his eyes and his face. And he said we were two peas in a pod.

Ryan babbled on and on about some new skateboard Scott had just bought and how he wanted one so badly.

I interrupted him, "So, TJ's grandma is coming in tomorrow." I looked around and waited for any reaction.

"That's nice. You like his grandma." My dad gave a simple smile and continued to delve into his potatoes.

"And?" My mother eyed me, clearly waiting for something more.

"Well, Mrs. Lawson said I could stay overnight and camp out again."

TJ's family owned a campground a few miles from our neighborhood. TJ's mom and dad had started it together several years ago, and Mrs. Lawson had single-handedly run the campground since TJ's dad had died. They didn't have a whole lot of nice, new things, but they had tons of camping gear at their house. Their family did just about everything outside. TJ liked to set up the backyard with all their equipment. I would often camp out at his house with him and Katie. It was a little escape from reality for all of us.

My mother sighed out loud.

"Why don't you just go live with PJ? You're over there enough," Ryan said. "That way, I can turn your bedroom into a game room."

"You know, I ran into Mrs. Abrams last night at work," My mother said loftily, ignoring Ryan's comment and my proposition about the campout. "We both talked about how nice it would be for you and her daughter, Melanie, to get together."

I stared blankly at her, but she was too busy cutting her lamb chop to notice.

"You know, Melanie may be in your class this year."

I tried to picture who my mother meant. When I finally placed her, I realized she and I were nothing alike. She was this little, blond porcelain doll who never spoke to me at school and was usually decked out in some pink, sparkly outfit with a giant bow on top of her head. "So what?"

"Well, Mrs. Abrams mentioned that she and Melanie were free for the next two days. I'm not sure you'll be able to camp out with Tommy's family. I made a playdate for you with Melanie tomorrow."

Ryan's face broke into a huge grin. My mother finally looked me in the eyes.

I couldn't believe what I was hearing. *Melanie Abrams?* I couldn't imagine attempting to play with her. My face grew hot with fury as I stared my mother down, sending her quiet, defiant thoughts until she looked away.

"What for?" I said, trying to conceal how heartbroken I felt.

EVERYBODY'S HAPPY

"I think it would be nice to have some other friends of yours around."

Ryan openly loved this, "That's awesome. Mom made a playdate for you to be friends with a girl."

"Ryan." My mother scolded him.

"Watch it, Ryan," my dad shot him a warning look. Ryan wiped the smirk off his face.

"I don't even know her," I protested.

"Well, you'll get to know her," my mother countered.

"I can't camp out at TJ's?"

"You spend too much time with him as it is. I think it's best if—"

"But Grandma Lawson is coming up, and we were gonna have a whole campout, and…."

"Maybe we could move the playdate to Friday?" my dad gently suggested to my mother. She immediately looked affronted. My dad hardly ever disagreed with her ideas. "That way, Rebecca can stay at Tommy's tomorrow to see Grandma and then be here with Melanie on Friday. You said Mrs. Abrams had the next two days free, so then everybody's happy."

"Everybody's happy? Everybody's happy, Robert?" She was looking to win her fight and have her way.

"Yes, you just said Mrs. Abrams was free for two days, right?"

"Robert, don't you think a little distance from them would be for the better?"

"So, is this about accommodating Mrs. Abrams or canceling plans for Rebecca to be with Tommy and his grandma?"

At this, my mother gaped at him.

"I just don't see why we can't reschedule with Mrs. Abrams?" Dad pressed.

With that, my mother stormed out of the dining room, leaving her half-finished meal. My dad took a deep breath and leveled with me, "You can stay with Tommy tomorrow, but Melanie will be here Friday." I couldn't believe he'd actually refused to back down. I nodded in disbelief that my dad had called one of the plays in my mother's handbook.

That was it. Discussion over. Now they wouldn't talk until my dad apologized.

My mother came back fifteen minutes later, wearing a flattering dress adorned with accessories for her jewelry duties with Aunt Colleen. They both worked part-time as consultants for a trending jewelry company. She grabbed her purse and keys. I knew that she was leaving an hour early for her meeting. Then she was out the door, without a word to any of us.

My dad acted almost as though nothing had happened. He finished his potatoes and lamb chops and then did the dishes. Ryan got up and scraped his plate into the garbage, then disappeared to play his Xbox for the rest of the night. I should've been used to their occasional arguments. They would fight, and then she'd storm off. Now, they wouldn't speak for a day or two until he'd apologize, even if it was her fault. Or he'd let her win her argument to keep the peace. There was no communication in between, and it never got any better.

I sat at the table for a long time trying to figure out what had happened and what upset me more—my mother making friends for me behind my back, her constant attempts to shape me into what Rachel would've been had she not passed at nine years old, my brother and his unyielding taunts, or my parents fighting over matters brought on by me.

Later, I lay on the couch with Buddy watching the Sox at Milwaukee. Buddy licked my chin every now and then as I scratched behind his warm, silky ears. My dad quietly watched from his chair, a bottle of beer in his grip.

I stared blankly as the Sox scored on a two-run home run in the fourth inning. Shortly after that, I dozed off. I felt my dad pick me up off the couch and carry me upstairs. I was suddenly awake, but I didn't open my eyes. I'm sure he knew I was faking being asleep, but I didn't want to wake up just then when I was safe in my daddy's arms.

CHAPTER 13

Snowball Fight

Snow covered all of Charleston for the next few weeks. The landscape was like a scene from a snow globe with little characters and evergreens covered in soft powder. The weather certainly made getting to and from classes arduous. Plus, the honeymoon phase of classes was over as our professors piled on the work.

Lindsay, Amy, and I were trapped in the apartment for two weekends. But Lindsay lived for these moments. She planned major roommate bonding time.

First, she staged a real-life *Dancing with the Stars.* We performed all the dances we had learned while Amy judged us. She must've called Lindsay a dork about a million times before really getting into it. Amy made us change our outfits several times to show more skin so that it could at least be something to look at. When Lindsay tried to dip me, we both fell over. Lindsay literally peed her pants from laughing so hard.

After the dancing, Lindsay made us play charades, Hedbanz, and drinking Jenga. Then we watched her favorite romantic comedy for the hundredth time.

Amy did her best to remind us how bored she was, but she did accommodate Lindsay on the games and the flick. Linds was so easily pleased at times that something as simple as agreeing to watch her favorite movie went a long way with her.

Both of our lockdown weekends solidified how much we counted on each other and how much I loved these girls.

***

I knew TJ itched to go play in the snow. Every day after leaving Lantz Gym, he grabbed a handful of snow and launched it at Trevor to see if it was solid enough for a snowball fight. One Thursday, he convinced Mrs. Mac that snowball conditions were finally ideal, and she needed to let us out ten minutes early for the festivities.

TJ rounded up takers at the early dismissal.

"You're not serious," Lindsay said.

"Yeah, he is," I said, laughing.

"Oh, hell yeah. Come on, everybody outside!" TJ called. Some of the girls rolled their eyes and left, but a bunch of people stayed behind.

"So, is it every man for himself or what?" Freddie asked once we were outside.

"Let's do two teams. We'll split up," TJ said, pulling on his gloves and adjusting his hat.

I joined Trevor, Taylor, and a few others while TJ, Lindsay, Freddie, and Natalia made the other team. We stood several feet apart in the snowy courtyard outside Lantz.

"Ar-right, we're starting in sixty seconds!" TJ shouted, then he immediately started making snowballs and talking strategy with his team. My team got the hint to do the same. Taylor took over as captain.

"I say we all go after Tommy first."

"I like it," a short guy named Casey agreed.

"Ten, nine," TJ counted down.

Some passersby glanced our way as TJ counted down; they turned and walked backward to see what we were up to as they moved away.

"One, fire!" TJ shouted.

His team charged out shooting, but my team stood still a few seconds longer, blocking each other until Taylor yelled, "Now!" Then we pelted TJ so much that he howled with laughter and ducked into a bush. It was a massive free-for-all. Snowballs flew in every direction. TJ got Taylor square in the face, and we were rolling. Clumps of wet snow matted in her lashes and slid down her ebony skin. Taylor swore revenge. She charged at TJ and tackled him. Freddie ambushed Taylor as she tried to get up from the ground.

Lindsay and I were at each other for most of the battle. She had terrible aim but still smacked me a few times. I went easy on her until she lost her glove, then I really let her have it. But once I apparently threw an ice ball at her side, it started her incessant whining. That just made me laugh harder and continue to attack her until we were both out of breath and slaphappy.

TJ was as accurate as ever, and he hit almost every mark, including me. After about eight minutes, the fight was over. Natalia collapsed and made snow angels. TJ and Taylor joined her. It was so much fun to play for a change.

Lindsay finally dragged herself away to try and wipe off the frost from her pants so she could head to class. Everyone else but TJ and I prepared for their classes or ran off toward their dormitories to get warm. I had a grin plastered on my face and just wanted to hang for a while longer. So, I rolled around a ball of snow, attempting to build a snowman. I felt TJ eyeing me and saw him begin to roll a snowball as well.

"So, tell me one thing," TJ said, hovering over the ball as he rolled it left and right near me.

"About what?"

"About you. Like high school or junior high. Anything. I missed out on a lot."

I set my first snowball off to the side and started on the next one, glancing at TJ and half expecting him to let me off the hook for a story.

"Come on.... You can tell me one thing. I know you can." He gave me an encouraging smile. I continued rolling the ball this way and that, gathering more and more snow on it.

What could I tell him? That I fell apart in middle school? I lost myself without him? That I learned to keep my mouth shut to survive my teenage years with my mother? I could tell him about Rachel and that her ghost is the only part of her I know. I shook off these self-indulgent complaints. It was too perfect a day to wallow in past emotions, so I opened my mouth and told him the first interesting idea that entered my mind.

"During my senior year in high school, I dated this nonconformist for a few weeks to irritate my mother." After my confession was out, I grinned at him sheepishly. I don't know what he was expecting to hear, but that certainly wasn't it. His eyes popped, and his mouth curled into a wide smile.

"Really?" he asked. I flushed, thinking I'd said the wrong thing. "And how did your mom react to this delightful suitor?"

"As expected. I guess that's what I was aiming for." He nodded, his grin still hanging on, but he didn't push me for any more details.

"Your turn," I said hastily, trying to interrupt my embarrassment.

"Ar-right, what do you want to hear?"

"Something about high school."

He rolled the base of the snowman closer to me. "Hmm, TJ high school. Ar-right. Late in my high school years, I became a fisherman!" He threw up his arms as if he was making an announcement.

I couldn't hold the giggle bursting out of me. "A fisherman, metaphorically?"

"No, for real. It's sort of my church."

We heaved the pieces of our snowman up and, largest to smallest, set them in place.

"It helps me find peace, get centered," he continued. "What?"

I must've had a look of confusion. "Nothing, it's just...you've *always* been centered." I smoothed the sides to brush off excess snow from the middle snowball and curve the body.

"Not always." He regarded me pointedly as if he wanted to elaborate but thought better of it. TJ then took off to dig around in the bushes for our snowman's features. When he found them, he came back and handed me a few rocks and scraps of mulch so I could create a face. I set the eyes and mouth.

"Not bad," TJ admitted. He had just returned with branches he'd torn off a nearby tree for the arms. I turned and searched under the boughs of an evergreen and found a pinecone that would have to do for the nose. "Aww, nice," TJ said.

I put the last piece in place, and we both stood there admiring our snowman with stupid grins.

"He's awesome," TJ admitted, and I nodded. "What are we gonna name him?" He searched my eyes.

"I have no idea."

"How about Alex?"

"Alex?" I asked, busting with laughter. TJ chuckled right along with me. "Yeah, why not? It's a good name."

"Snowmen aren't named Alex." I removed my glove and wiped my eyes with the back of my freezing hand, still bobbing with laughter.

"Why not?"

"You are so crazy. I have to go."

"Uh, don't forget to say goodbye to Alex." He gestured at our snowman with his snow-encrusted mittened hands.

I turned back around to say goodbye and saw that TJ had removed one of Alex's branch arms. He waved it at me. "Bye, Alex! Bye, TJ!" I said, shaking my head and grinning.

CHAPTER 14

Roasting Marshmallows

TJ and I played catch on his front lawn as we all waited for Grandma Lawson. His mom was off work to welcome her, and although I knew she was excited about seeing Grandma, she looked worn out and distracted and mostly stayed in the house.

At half-past one, a large red pickup truck pulled into the driveway. Mrs. Noreen Lawson glanced up casually from behind her wide sunglasses toward the area where TJ, Katie, and I were standing. She was a thick, leathery woman with scattered white-blond curls on her windblown head. Grandma was a Southern gal who was wise and tough on the outside.

"Gram-ma!" Katie cheered.

Grandma pulled herself out of the driver's seat. "Well, don't you just stand there. You get over here and give me a great big hug!" She bent low as Katie jogged to her. Grandma scooped her up and smothered her with noisy kisses. She moved over to TJ, still squeezing Katie in her arms.

"Hi, Grandma," TJ said.

Grandma lowered Katie down. "Hi, sugar." She opened her arms and bent over slightly to embrace TJ in her hearty fashion. When she let go, she grabbed his chin, surveying him. "Lord, love a duck! You're getting so tall!"

Then she moved to me. "Hi," I said shyly, although I had met Grandma numerous times.

"Becky, darlin', how are you? It's so nice to see you." She gave me a grandma hug, too.

TJ's front door opened, and his trembling mother emerged, eyes reddened. She stood inside the house but held the door open.

Grandma's broad smile slowly faded. She headed toward the open door. Katie and TJ followed her, but Grandma turned around and stopped them.

"Give me a chance to have your momma all to myself for a few, alright? We've got some grown-up talking to do. We'll catch up all evening. Sound fair?"

"But I want to be with you now!" Katie tugged on Grandma's shirt and pouted in protest.

"Sure, Grandma," TJ said, gently pulling Katie back by her shoulders.

Grandma climbed the stoop and embraced her daughter-in-law.

"Hi, darlin'," she rocked TJ's crying mother side to side in her strong, comforting arms. I nervously looked at TJ. He was staring at his mom, cautious concern masking his face.

"Momma, why are you crying?" Katie asked.

TJ's mom took a minute to answer. "I'm just happy to see your grandma, sweetie."

"Now, it ain't the end of forever," Grandma said. She led Mrs. Lawson into the house.

TJ stood there for a minute longer. On the surface, he was unmoved, but I saw the worry in his eyes. I took Katie's hand and left TJ with his thoughts for a few more seconds.

***

Later that day, we all sat around a crowded picnic table playing cards. We played Go Fish for Katie, then Gin Rummy for the rest of us. TJ was as entertaining as usual. During our game of Go Fish, he'd start off with a serious tone, talking to Katie, "Do you have any ... tomatoes?"

She'd laugh, "Nope! No tomatoes."

"I'm sorry, I meant chopsticks. Do you have any chopsticks?"

Katie roared with her catchy laughter until we were all in a fit of giggles.

Grandma was so spirited. She talked for hours about Grandpa and their farm, TJ's cousin Mason, and the rest of the Lawson gang. She, like Mrs. Lawson, TJ, and Katie, treated me like family.

TJ's mom grilled out hamburgers and hotdogs while we helped Grandma whip up her famous bread pudding. Mrs. Lawson seemed relaxed then and in control of her emotions.

"Becky, darlin', I just love your cute little hairdo," Grandma said, patting me on my head. TJ and Mrs. Lawson knew the story and grinned at me.

"My mom doesn't."

"Well, I do. It suits you," Grandma said decidedly.

I thought about her comment and agreed with Grandma. It did suit me just right.

The greatest thing by far about TJ's house was the backyard. It was massive. A collection of evergreens and oaks lined the back of it. They had a vegetable garden on one side of the tall wooden fence, and on the opposite side was the camping area. TJ's father had built a fire pit years ago. There were even big tree stumps all around the outer rim to sit on. This rustic backyard was perfect for a campout.

The five of us sat around the fire, roasting marshmallows on twigs. The crackling fire heated my cheeks and made me drowsy. It smelled of warm ash and sticky, sweet marshmallows. We couldn't see beyond our tight circle. Countless stars sparkled above us in the moonless night. I shivered from a slight breeze in the air, and goosebumps rose on the back of my uncovered shoulders.

"Tommy, go get Becky a sweatshirt." Mrs. Lawson called out.

"Okay." TJ hopped up and ran into the house.

"Katie, darlin', you better turn that marshmallow around. You're gonna drop it in the fire," Grandma advised.

"I like 'em toasty," Katie insisted, keeping the marshmallow burnt-side in. It was scorched on one side and drooping lower with each second. Grandma grinned at Katie as the marshmallow lit on fire. Katie let out a yelp, and Mrs. Lawson leaped up to blow out the flame.

TJ rushed back out the door and over to our spot. "Here," he handed me his favorite Packers sweatshirt. I looked up in surprise that he would offer it. He eyed me quickly, grinned, and looked away as he plunked himself down next to me.

"So, what have you been doing all summer, sugar?" Grandma asked him.

"Oh, the usual: football, swimming, riding around. Beck and I found a nest of turtle eggs," TJ replied excitedly. I proudly pulled his sweatshirt over my head.

"Really?"

"Becky is our animal expert, Noreen," Mrs. Lawson announced. I flushed hot in embarrassment.

"Is that so?"

"She knows so many things about animals. She's got our athlete learning more and more about being quite an environmentalist." Mrs. Lawson winked at me. Now I buried my face in my hands. TJ giggled at me.

"Becky, honey? Is she upset?" Grandma asked.

"No," TJ laughed, "She just doesn't *crave* the attention."

"Unlike other kids we know," his mom teased.

"Boy, I tell ya, you two have something special. You are such tremendous friends." Grandma said.

I peeked at her through my lashes.

"I know. It's amazing, isn't it? They're always together. I believe they're soulmates." Mrs. Lawson got choked up again, looking back and forth from TJ to me.

It was pretty common for her to get emotional easily, but this time pain lurked in her eyes beyond the tears.

"Hey, Grandma, want to see what I can do?" Katie asked, licking her sticky fingers, then rubbing them on her shorts.

"Well, I sure do, sweet pea."

Katie got up from her tree stump, walked back from the circle, and sprinted into a haphazard cartwheel. We all applauded as if it was a perfect ten. Katie grinned widely, then sat on Mrs. Lawson's knee.

"Good job, baby," she said, kissing her cheek.

"That was fantastic, Katie, darlin'. I certainly can't do a cartwheel. How about you, Becky? Can you do a cartwheel?"

"Grandma, Beck can do all kinds of stuff. Backbends, cartwheels, round-offs. She can even walk on her hands!" TJ blurted out. My eyebrows raised in surprise as everyone smiled encouragingly at me.

"Well, butter my backside and call me a biscuit! Can you really walk on your hands?" Grandma hooted.

"Sort of."

"Sort of? Come on, Beck! Show 'em! Come on!" TJ persisted.

"Tommy, Becky doesn't have to show us anything. Let her be," Mrs. Lawson replied.

"Well, okay," I said

I rose from my stump and moved to an open spot in the yard. Kicking up my right leg, then balancing it, I threw myself forward into a handstand. My stomach muscles tightened, and my legs wobbled for a second as I forced them to straighten while blood rushed to my head. I pushed off with my right hand shifting my weight to my left and then repositioned my right hand on the ground in front of me. I strained, keeping my legs level. Shifting my weight again, I moved my left hand and right hand again until I had scooted about two feet. Then I dropped my right and left leg in front of me and touched the ground. When I was done, I flashed a smile at everyone, brushed my hands on my shorts, and quickly sat back down.

"My goodness! That was remarkable," Mrs. Lawson said with a look of awe as everyone applauded.

"Sure was. I wouldn't have believed it was possible unless you showed me," Grandma declared.

"See, you're awesome at that." TJ nudged me.

"Now, what about you, Tommy? What are you gonna entertain us with?" Grandma asked.

"Well, what would you like?" He stooped forward and eyed Grandma with a twinkle in his eye.

"Would you listen to that?" Grandma smiled, shaking her head from side to side. "He's a Lawson, alright. How about something different? Surprise me, sugar."

"I know!" TJ exclaimed. "But it'll take a minute to get ready."

"I ain't going nowhere. You go right ahead and set up."

"Beck, give me a hand."

I followed him into the garage, where he tossed me a baseball. Then he reached into a garbage bag of empty pop cans, pulled out a few, and handed some off to me. Next, TJ turned on the outside lights, which threw a glow on the part of the backyard near the picnic table.

"Ar-right, we're gonna set these up, spaced out on the picnic table," he told me.

We put the five cans on the front end of the table. Then TJ took the ball from me and walked back over to the fire. "Now, Grandma, I'm gonna knock down those cans with this baseball from over by the garage."

"Let's see it!" She slapped her knee and turned around to face the table.

TJ wore a goofy grin as he trotted back to the garage. He lined himself up, took a few pacing breaths, and started his concentrated windup. TJ pulled his arms to his chest with the ball and stared down the target. He waited another second, then exhaling slowly, swung his right arm around, and threw the ball. It sped like a bullet and crashed into a can knocking it down.

"Hot dog!" Grandma proclaimed. "That's one."

I tossed the ball back to him and dashed out of the line of fire. On his second throw, we heard the crunch of crushing aluminum, and it was the same with the third. We all cheered.

"Tommy! That was incredible." His mom was wowed.

He smiled, caught the ball from me, and wound up for his fourth shot.

His shoulders powered the ball forward. It made a dull thud on the edge of the table right beneath the can.

"Dang," he said but smiled just the same.

"Oh," Katie sighed.

"That's alright, sugar, you got one more shot."

I tossed him the ball for his final shot. His eyes narrowed in deep concentration. He raised his arm around past his shoulder blade. The ball rocketed out of his fist and clobbered the final can in a devastating blow. Grandma whistled, and Mrs. Lawson drummed on her tree stump, cheering. Katie let out a whoop and attempted another sloppy cartwheel.

TJ grinned, then recovered the cans and tossed them back into the garbage bag.

Soon after our mini talent show, Grandma said she was ready to hit the hay. Katie pleaded with Mrs. Lawson to let her stay in the tent with us for the night. Mrs. Lawson was concerned about Katie pestering us, but she promised to be good. I didn't mind. Katie wasn't so bad. I knew she would just talk herself to sleep. After a few more pleases, Mrs. Lawson agreed. Katie tossed her Barbie sleeping bag into our tent, too.

The tent was roomy and cool despite our three bodies side by side by side. I breathed in the familiar citronella and firewood scent as TJ zipped us up for the night. The zip was Katie's favorite part. She and I chuckled again and again as TJ played with the zipper, working it up and down at different speeds, matching his silly expressions to the sounds.

After we all settled into our sleeping bags, TJ told knock-knock jokes until Katie fell asleep. Then he started telling me his corny ghost stories. It was a tradition, or so he claimed. Although I couldn't imagine Mrs. Lawson being a ghost storyteller. Regardless, the ghost stories were TJ's favorite part of camping.

"It was a creepy, rainy night on Halloween," he said in a low, rumbling tone. "The ghosts and goblins all ran into an empty house on Elm Street." TJ paused dramatically and widened his eyes in the dim light. I rolled my eyes at him in disapproving delightedness. "As the little children rang the spider web-covered doorbell, a scream inside made their hair stick straight up into the air." At this, TJ shot his arms up, and I jumped in surprise. He widened his eyes and continued with the tale.

"Then the door opened." Another dramatic pause. I was wrapped up in his silly enthusiasm. "But it wasn't a person or a ghost or goblin. It was a giant bloody hand!" TJ threw his hand out toward my neck. I screamed! His hand was somehow covered with a tight red glove. I tried to scream again as he covered my mouth with his hand, and then I couldn't stop laughing. "The hand started choking everyone, reaching in for the candy and—"

Katie sprung up from her sleeping bag, looked around, startled with sleepy eyes, and fell back down asleep without a word.

"Stop!" I giggled, "You're gonna wake up Katie."

"You screamed."

"You're dumb."

We laughed at each other.

"Whose glove is that?"

"Katie's. You were scared."

I smirked and lay on my stomach. TJ removed the glove and tossed it aside as the quiet evening fell back on us.

"I think we're gonna have a rematch tomorrow with Bobby."

"Okay." I yawned. Then I stopped and remembered my dad's deal about Melanie. My stomach dropped, and suddenly, I dreaded the sunrise. "Ugh, no, I can't." I pouted.

"Why not?" TJ laid on his sleeping bag next to me, his elbows supporting his chin.

I looked at him and stalled.

"What's up?"

I sighed deeply to convince him that this was not what I wanted to talk about. "I have to play with Melanie Abrams." I sank my chin onto the backs of my hands. TJ looked confused. "She's coming over to play with me all day."

"What are you gonna play?" he asked, mildly amused.

"Probably stupid dolls."

TJ let out a bubble of muffled laughter.

"Shut up."

He bit his lip in an apologetic manner. "Sorry."

"It's not fair. I wish I could just stay here forever."

We grew quiet. TJ stopped smiling but looked at me affectionately. "Yeah, but you're really lucky, Beck. You have a great house, and Buddy and your dad's so cool." He rolled onto his back, gazing at the night sky through the clear plastic dome in the center of the tent.

My heart sank. I opened and closed my mouth. I didn't know what to say. I wanted to reel back in my spoiled brat comments, but I couldn't.

A few moments went by in silence. Katie turned over. I tried to remember his dad, but only a couple of still images came to mind. TJ's dad chasing him in the yard. Him sitting on the picnic table in the backyard as Mrs. Lawson sat on his lap laughing.

I remembered more than anything, though, the sudden grief that had struck Mrs. Lawson after the car accident that killed TJ's dad and his cousin Mason's parents. My dad dropped by TJ's house again and again, helping TJ's mom with house or yard maintenance until she got back on her feet. As I stared at TJ's profile, I tried to imagine life without my dad. It was an impossible agony.

"Do you ever think about your sister being up there?" TJ asked.

Taken aback, I shrugged my shoulders. I thought about Rachel often. But I mostly thought of an invented version of her. I had no connection to her. Other than articles of her clothing mixed in my closet or her photo in the living room. She was just a ghost. TJ had been around long enough to see her photo. And he also knew that no one spoke about Rachel.

"Cuz I think about my dad a lot." TJ continued.

"Beck, what do you think my dad's doing right now?" TJ asked thoughtfully, peering into the heavens.

The mellowing fire in the pit crackled. We rarely talked about his dad. This time I knew I had to say something—something teetering between comfort and hope. I thought for a moment, and the smoldering fire in the background gave me the answer.

"He's roasting marshmallows in a cloud."

TJ turned to me, a dreamy expression on his face.

"Because you're camping, and he is, too. And he's keeping an eye on the tent. You know, for your mom."

He smiled at me in bewilderment, and so I found the courage to continue.

"And when he pulls marshmallows out of the cloud, it burns the sky and makes the stars," I smiled awkwardly.

TJ was enthralled. His eyes were glassy. He took a deep breath and turned over on his back to look out of the dome, a trace of a smile on his face. A single tear rolled down his temple.

We lay there for a long while, quietly watching the night sky. The infinite space. The blinking stars. The impossible magic—understanding each other's silence.

After a few minutes, he turned to me, his eyes soft and sincere. "Thanks, Beck."

CHAPTER 15

Jason

Jason was the kind of guy who could win over anybody's parents. His confidence and quick wit impressed every adult he met. My mother was one of his biggest fans.

His mom and mine had struck up a friendship on the Facebook page for her jewelry line. Last June, they'd suckered Jason into attending one of my mother's open house events for the jewelry company under the pretense of driving his mom. It just so happened that Jason's mom had teamed up with my mother to play matchmaker.

"My mother directed me to you, saying I had to introduce myself. I'm assuming you're Rebecca," Jason said, staring at me intensely.

I looked over to where he had walked in and saw my mother talking animatedly to one of her acquaintance friends.

Preparing myself to be annoyed, I noticed his determined expression. He told me how he'd begun a debate with his mom over her matchmaking attempt only to confess that his mom had severely underestimated how beautiful I was. We planned our first date for the following evening.

Jason had a lot of conviction. He was pre-law, could hold a debate with just about any taker, and end up winning because he'd argued his side so well. He even avoided a speeding ticket on our second date by citing a flaw in the angle at which the speed limit sign was visible. Jason advised the officer that his record was impeccable, so it would be fair for him to issue a warning rather than an actual ticket. I was fascinated by his candor with the cop. He'd looked him dead in the eye the whole time while explaining valid arguments without showing a bit of embarrassment.

JASON

There was something about Jason. He had this intensity about him in everything that he did. When he was with me, he was almost hypnotic, causing me to block out everyone but him. His deep, penetrating eyes and set jaw reeled me in again and again. Time away from Jason turned out to be easy, though. He was out of sight, out of mind, until he visited and enraptured me all over again.

***

On a Friday evening, Jason showed up at my doorstep looking amazing and carrying a large pizza. That earned him some points from the girls—even Amy, who I knew didn't like him much. It was very difficult for her to be polite instead of honest. Jason and I were typically on our own during visits, but this time he sat at the table with the girls and me for a long while talking. Everyone complained about their classes in a collective bitch-session, which allowed for stress relief. Jason talked a lot about how tough his classes were supposed to be but that they'd ended up being a breeze for him.

Later that night in my room, I listened to him catching me up on his family over rum and Coke, his favorite drink. Jason started to relax more and more, which got me thinking of our previous summer together. He scooted me on top of his lap while his eyes searched me over.

"God, I've missed you," he breathed.

I exhaled and leaned my head closer to his, kissing him. His kisses grew more intense, and he flipped me over onto my bed, promising to show me how much he missed me.

I tried not to look too deeply into our relationship. Yes, I felt strongly for him, but we weren't that lovey-dovey, baby-talk couple that some were. We didn't say "I love you" to each other. He was just stable with me. He didn't seek out too much information about me; instead, he mostly talked about himself. Some people might've seen him as arrogant. I guess he was, in a way. I mostly saw it as a relief that I didn't have to say too much or worry about myself. He definitely helped keep my mother off my back, which was a huge plus for me.

The next afternoon, we hung out watching boring TV shows on the History Channel. Then we went shopping at Wal-Mart and grabbed some beer at the always-crowded liquor store.

For dinner, Lindsay made delicious chicken, rice, and kimchi—a spicy, Korean, pickled vegetable dish that her mom often served back at their house in Naperville.

"Thank you, Lindsay," Jason said as she set a plate in front of him.

"You're welcome. There's plenty if you want more."

"Damn, it smells good in here, Miss Linds," Amy called, throwing the door open.

"Where've you been?" Lindsay asked.

"Around," she responded, dropping her keys and cigarettes on the coffee table.

"Well, that's obvious," Jason said, his mouth full.

Amy walked over to the table and glared at Jason for a beat. "You don't know me well enough to make that kind of remark."

Oh, boy, I thought. Here we go.

"I know *of* you," he retorted. She lasered me a look, obviously thinking I'd told him how often she'd messed around.

"You *wish* you knew of me," she spat.

"Come on, Aim, stop it." I urged.

"Whoa!" Jason threw his hands out in defense.

"Amy, just sit down and eat. It's gonna get cold," Lindsay whined. She brought Amy's dish to the table and set it in front of her.

Amy slunk down into her seat with an irritated expression on her face. Lindsay ignored her, and got her own plate from the kitchen and brought it back to the table. Turning to face us, she said, "Oh my gosh, you guys, do you even realize how bruised I am?" She lifted her shirt a bit to expose a round bruise on her side.

"What happened to you?" Jason asked. Amy rolled her eyes at Jason behind his back.

JASON

"From our snowball fight after Ballroom Dance," she laughed, looking at me. "Jason, your sweetheart pelted me pretty good in the side. That was fun, though, wasn't it?"

A sinking feeling of guilt and anxiety overtook me. I closed my eyes and bit my lip. "Wait a minute...." Jason started. You're in Ballroom Dance?" he asked me, scowling.

Lindsay's eyes grew wide as she mouthed, "Oh, no."

"Yeah, I thought I told you I was taking an exercise elective this semester," I said, avoiding his eyes and pushing around some chicken and rice on my plate.

"Ballroom Dance?"

"Jason, it's no big deal," I said coolly.

"What the hell are you talking about? You've been lying to me!" He abruptly backed up his chair and stood up.

"I haven't been lying to you. You never asked me specifically what courses I have," I protested, feeling my cheeks flush.

"It was her mom's idea," Lindsay offered.

"Uh, I'm pretty sure aqua aerobics and dance are two separate skills," Amy argued to Linds, her arms folded.

"It's just a dance class." I shrugged.

"A dance class where twenty other guys are putting their hands on you," he argued crossly.

"Wait, Rebecca, isn't that the class TJ's in with you?" Amy asked in a confrontational, snotty way. She seemed to be enjoying our feud. This was more evidence of Amy's disapproval of Jason, but I still couldn't believe she would give him more ammunition.

"Your 'old friend.' Now I get it." Jason stormed into my room to undoubtedly collect his things.

"Thanks a lot," I said to Amy. Her face lost part of its attitude. I went after Jason to no avail. He stalked off, hopped into his car, and sped out of sight. Amy stormed out too.

My stress-induced guilt left me with a headache and annoyance. Leave it to Amy to drive a wedge between Jason and me. I should've just told him about it, but I didn't exactly feel bad that I hadn't told him the whole truth. It would've been an argument regardless of the timing.

"I'm really sorry for spilling the beans," Lindsay confessed sadly. She came over to me and draped her arms around my shoulders, nudging my head with hers.

"You did nothing wrong, Linds." I hugged her back.

"Maybe I can try to call him and tell him signing up for dance was my fault?" she asked.

I shook my head, thinking about how I was going to get him to understand.

"Well, then I'm at least taking you out."

A little while later, we left for the bars. Lindsay wanted to get me drunk, so we chose Mom's, the party spot. It was packed. We spotted Amy across a sea of drinkers on the dance floor. She was standing near the pool tables, laughing with some guys.

"Looks like she's not coming home tonight," Lindsay declared.

"And guess who's here." I nodded my head in the direction where TJ and his roommates were huddled around the mid-section of the bar, where the action was, of course. They all looked pretty trashed. Lindsay got me a beer, and we headed over. TJ didn't notice us until we'd squeezed right beside him. Then he bumped into me while talking to Mason.

"Oh, sorry." He tilted his head and did a double-take. "Beck!"

"Hey," I said.

"Hey, yourself. What's up, Linds?"

"Hi, Tommy."

"So, what's the story, Beck? You need a drink?" TJ asked. His eyes were unfocused, and the smell of beer seeped from his breath.

"Got one!" I held it up.

"Hi, ladies," Trevor said in his husky voice. He turned to talk to Lindsay.

JASON

"So, what's goin' on?" TJ smiled and draped his arm across my shoulders. I shrugged and took a drink. "You ar-right tonight? Want me to beat somebody up for you?" he slurred.

"Sure," I said, taking another sip.

"Which one?" TJ scanned the bar with his finger.

"Oh, I know," TJ pointed his finger at Amy. "That one, over there. Your roommate, right?"

I gave him a stunned look, "How'd you…?"

"She was talking to me earlier. I found out she was your roomie. Said she felt bad cuz you guys had a fight about your boyfriend." He grinned broadly and turned to face me.

"Did she say anything else?" I asked.

"She said I was hot." He raised his shoulders.

I busted a laugh. "She didn't."

"I told her, 'I know.' She said I was hilarious, arrogant, and irresistible. I said, 'I know!' Then she asked me to come home with her."

Mason leaned in and added in a funny voice, "And he said, 'let's go!'"

TJ howled with laughter.

I had to giggle at their playfulness, "Forgive my slutty roommate."

"Naw, she's cool. We were hanging with her a little while ago. We've been here since four o'clock."

"Oh my God, TJ."

"One-D is bartending," he nodded repeatedly.

"Friend of yours?" I smirked.

"Absolutely."

"His name is One-D?"

"Nah. His name's Caleb, but a while back, his roommate caught him completely jamming out to One Direction. You know that English boy band? So, it just kind of stuck."

I smiled and shook my head.

"We're all gonna do a shot!" TJ announced suddenly, circling his finger around our group. "Hey, One-D! Jäger!"

His buddy nodded and set up seven shot glasses of Jägermeister.

"Not Jäger," Lindsay complained.

"Amy!" TJ called. She looked up, and he waved her over. She cracked a small smile when she saw us there, too. TJ passed out the shots to my roommates and his. "To the roommates. It's all good!" TJ cheered.

Amy and I shared a smile, twisted our arms together then drank. We hung out with TJ and his friends until the bar closed, and my issue with Jason was nothing more than a foggy blur.

CHAPTER 16

Playdate

"Rebecca? They'll be here in two minutes," my mother called from beside the living room window.

I heard her.

I understood what she was saying.

Still, I stood at my doorway in silent defiance.

Perhaps if I threw a tantrum while *her* friends were over, I could get out of playing with Melanie. But that wasn't my style.

I contemplated locking myself in my room and refusing to play but knew it would be worse for me later when I would eventually have to face my mother without the peer pressure of Marilyn Abrams.

My mother yelled up the stairway. "Rebecca?" She had that warning tone. When she looked up to see me at the top of the stairs, she was surprised to find me standing there.

"Get down here. No, wait a minute." She eyed my tank top and cutoffs, "I set out that cute yellow summer dress for you to wear today."

"You mean Rachel's dress?" I mumbled sulkily, too quiet for her to hear.

"Put it on and get down here," she threatened.

I gritted my teeth and stomped into my room to find Buddy lying on Rachel's crumpled yellow dress. He panted with a big doggy smile, winking at me as if he were in on my attempt to foil my mother's plans. I crawled up on my bed, eye-level with Buddy, and grinned at him.

"Good boy."

He licked my nose, and I caressed his silky, wavy fur.

Then I heard my mother's footsteps and shot up. I pretended to tug on the dress to get it out from under Buddy, pleading with him, "Buddy, get off! Come on!"

"What on Earth is going on?" She was beyond irritated.

"Buddy's on my dress," I cowered.

"Well, move him off of it!"

"Mom, there's somebody in the driveway," Ryan called from downstairs.

She rushed out of sight. Buddy got off the bed, and I reluctantly pulled on the ridiculous, yellow dress and flumped my way downstairs.

"Oh, thanks. What a lovely home." I heard as I walked into the living room.

"I apologize for the clutter."

"No, no, don't be silly." Mrs. Abrams said. And then, "Hello Rebecca." Mrs. Abrams sent a dainty, squinty grin in my direction.

She had short blond hair perfectly shaped around her tiny, pointed face. It even arched up on the frame of her shoulders. She wore a bright blue, crisscrossed, sleeveless blouse with white capris and a load of fashion jewelry, no doubt supplied by my mother.

"You remember Melanie?" Mrs. Abrams put her arm around a small, skinny version of herself with the same white-blond hair and pointed little face.

"Hi," Melanie whispered.

I nodded, barely able to turn up the corners of my mouth and smile. Buddy, realizing there were strangers in the house, dashed happily toward the doorway.

"Oh! Mommy!" Melanie exclaimed in a petrified voice while sneaking behind Mrs. Abrams as Buddy sniffed around her.

"Rebecca, put Buddy outside."

"But he was just out."

As Mrs. Abrams shielded Melanie, my mother withered me with a warning look. I took Buddy by the collar and led him across the living room and into the dining room toward the sliding door.

"Oh, thank you, Suzanne. Melanie is terrified of dogs."

"No problem, Marilyn. I'm more of a cat person anyway. We would've rather chosen a cat, but Robert's allergic," my mother said.

"Ugh, allergies. It's so difficult...." said Mrs. Abrams.

I slid the door open, led Buddy out, and closed the door behind me. Mrs. Abrams had been inside for only a minute, yet I felt disgusted already.

I took my time giving Buddy attention. *We would've rather chosen a cat?* "Did she hurt your feelings, Bud?" I stroked his head, "I'm sorry. I would've never wanted a cat more than you." I kissed his nose and got up.

From the side of our backyard, I noticed Ryan on the street practicing his moves on his skateboard. He had just done a pretty cool turn, but I wouldn't dare give him a compliment. He saw me watching him.

"What are you looking at?"

"Nothing."

"Shouldn't you be learning how to play dolls right now?" he sneered.

I turned and went back in for my doomsday.

We had club sandwiches for lunch. Melanie and I sat in the living room playing with her case of Barbies. If I had to play, I wanted to go into my room, but my mother suggested we'd have more space in the living room. I think she did it to keep a better eye on me. My knees were red from kneeling on our carpet, and because of the uncomfortable sundress, I kept shifting around.

My mother and Mrs. Abrams sat at the dining room table, eating fruit salad and drinking sun tea. They talked extensively about the upcoming fall catalog for the jewelry line.

Melanie had worn out her shyness and took advantage of mine, forcing me to move a Barbie a certain way, and put the baby down, then brush this doll's hair. Boring didn't even come close to the torture I was subjected to. Minutes stretched into hours of exasperation. Next, we had to play "Barbie wedding day."

"Now, your Lisa will get married to my Jonathan," Melanie said. "Put her wedding gown on." I obeyed. "She needs to walk down the aisle, but only after Belle goes first. She's the flower girl."

I rolled my eyes off to the side, wishing desperately that I had stayed with TJ. He was probably coasting down the block, heading for the pond. Or he'd be making up some new, annoying song while tossing the football. Or we'd be sitting around the picnic table with Grandma Lawson, listening to their family's classic stories, like when she and Grandpa Lawson went fishing, and he accidentally knocked both of them into the water.

"Suzanne, Rebecca's hair is just darling. What a great idea for the summer!"

I eyed my mother quickly.

"Oh, yes, it's growing on me a bit," she smiled. "We had it done at Armando's."

Unbelievable! She hated my hair.

She'd been so irritated with me earlier, yet now I was her darling daughter. I crinkled my forehead at her in frustration. She pretended not to notice.

Glancing out the window while walking stupid Lisa down a glossy white ribbon on the carpet, my stomach dropped. There on the field, two houses down and across my driveway, huddled TJ, Garcia, Pete, Bobby, Mikey, and Matthew, Bobby's younger brother.

I had forgotten about the game and felt nauseated. I stared outside, hopelessly watching TJ toss the ball back and forth to Garcia as Bobby threw his hands up at Pete in aggravation.

"I'm really hoping the girls will be in the same class this year," my mother announced.

"Rebecca!" Melanie's high-pitched voice jolted me from the football game. "She has to say her vows," she demanded.

I sighed, looked at my mother, who refused to make eye contact with me, and caught a glimpse of our deck out back, which gave me an idea. "Do you want to go swimming?" I asked Melanie tiredly.

Mrs. Abrams put down her sun tea. "That would be lovely, wouldn't it, Melanie? If Rebecca has an extra swimsuit for you."

We spent the rest of the afternoon in the pool, which was by far no picnic, but it was a heck of a lot better than playing Barbies by the window scene of a missed football game. Buddy spent the rest of the afternoon inside.

Melanie's swim proficiency was about a level one out of ten. She absolutely refused to get her face wet. I blamed that on her uppity mother. I had to limit my games to Marco Polo and a measly back float contest, which I obviously won. It was the longest day of my life.

Later that afternoon, Melanie changed back into her flowered pink shirt and skirt outfit. I hurriedly threw my tank top and cut-offs back on and rushed downstairs to send them off.

"Thanks again, Suzanne and Rebecca, for having us," Mrs. Abrams enthused, patting my shoulder.

"Of course! We'll have to do it again sometime." This from my mother.

"Certainly! Bye now."

We walked them out and waved.

"Bye!" I shouted joyfully. It was my first true smile all day.

"That was fun now, wasn't it?" my mother asked, grinning at me as I scanned the empty field across the street.

"Uh-huh," I answered apathetically.

My mother went out to the mailbox as I crept into the backyard, hopped on my bike, and sped from the driveway down the sidewalk.

"Rebecca! We are eating dinner soon, young lady!" She called after me, fury edging her voice.

"I'm not hungry!" I hollered back and sped even faster out of sight.

CHAPTER 17

Breaking a Sweat

With Valentine's Day lurking around the corner, Mrs. Mac had us learn the tango. TJ was terrible at it. It didn't help that he somehow rotated to Ashley twice. She was a rather large yet giddy girl with big, frizzy hair. When I finally rotated to him, he was giddy as well. He'd realized how awful he was at this new dance, and all I could do was laugh at him. Glancing to his left, he saw Lindsay and Trevor.

"Hey," he whispered, "Trevor likes Lindsay."

"Really?"

He nodded. I didn't say a word about how she really loved him instead.

Mrs. Mac pulled us in to demonstrate the dance one more time before dismissing us. "May I have a volunteer from the gentlemen?" She asked.

"Yeah, Lawson, show us." Freddie nudged him.

"Tommy Lawson?" she asked teasingly. The girls who had already danced with him that day shared a collective chuckle.

"That's ar-right. I don't want to make my fellow men jealous. Besides, I think I pulled a … groin muscle." He squatted uncomfortably, which got everybody laughing.

***

A few nights later, Lindsay almost tearfully begged me to accompany her to the Rec, claiming her thighs were getting fatter every day. I told her she was an obsessed beanpole but went with her anyway.

She was clearly in one of her moods. The why-do-I-still-not-have-a-boyfriend mood. It was nearly impossible for anyone to dig Lindsay out of a self-induced slump.

I decided to take on the treadmill while Lindsay did marathon training on the track. It was a pretty busy night, but I spotted one machine right beside Trevor, who had quite a sweat going on. His curly, black hair glinted with perspiration, and a trickle of sweat rolled down his dark, sculpted face.

"Hey, Trevor," I said politely, getting set on the treadmill.

"Hi, how's it going?"

"Good." I started with a slow jog.

"Are you here by yourself?" I knew immediately who he was referring to. He acted very casually about his inquiry, and I felt sort of bad for him because I knew Lindsay didn't like him in that way.

"No, Lindsay is on the track."

"Oh yeah?" he asked.

Wanting to change the subject, I asked, "Is Tommy working tonight?"

"He's around here somewhere," he said, looking over his shoulder while still running hard on his treadmill and sweating. Our conversation lulled for a minute as we both focused on what we were doing.

I was a second away from popping in my earbuds when I heard someone call me. I turned my head to see a guy from my finance class. He talked a lot and seemed very nervous every time I saw him. Plus, his eyes seemed to bulge out from his face, so he always looked surprised.

"Oh, hi," I stumbled. Trevor remained quiet. It was the only time I'd ever really wanted him to talk with me, but he didn't.

"Marc," he said, introducing himself while stepping onto the treadmill next to mine, "You're in Finance, right?"

"Mmm-huh," I said, picking up the pace so I'd appear too occupied to continue the conversation. I hated talking as it was, especially when confronted by an overly ambitious guy.

"So, how do you like it?"

"It's okay."

"Yeah, Fritz is a little over the top, though."

I didn't respond. The poor guy just didn't get it.

"What'd you think of his capital structure equation?"

"I don't really remember that."

"He wasn't making a whole lot of sense, considering the earnings per share that he mentioned. I think he left out some information, but…" he continued, rambling on and on.

I added a few uh-huhs, ohs, and yeahs here and there. Then I saw TJ's adorable smile pop up near Trevor. TJ nudged his head toward Marc. I rolled my eyes in response. He teased Trevor about something and laughed, all the while stealing glances at me and silently making faces.

"So, do you have a study group yet? Because you're welcome to join mine." This guy wouldn't quit.

"Um…" Out of the corner of my eye, I could see the twinkle in TJ's eyes, knowing he was loving this. "Do you really think you need one?"

"Sure, there are a lot of formulas to go over like…."

I couldn't take much more.

"We meet on Monday nights from eight until nine."

"Mondays aren't so good for me."

"Well, I could change the day if you need to. What's best for you?"

I sent a desperate, silent plea to TJ, and he didn't miss a beat. He zipped over to Marc.

"Excuse me, buddy," he said.

"Yes?" Marc responded, startled, turning toward TJ.

"You know we were actually having some problems with this machine earlier," he said, pushing the slow-down button on it.

"O-oh," Marc stammered, getting off and glancing down at the treadmill. I bit my lip and tried not to burst into giggles.

"See, the belt was jamming up under the front roller here, so for safety reasons, pal, I can't let you use this one. Sorry about that. There should've been a red tag on this one." TJ searched the machine over and pretended to get irritated. "Hey, Jeff! Get me a red tag for this treadmill!" he called down to his buddy at the desk, who tilted his head up in confusion.

"Again, I apologize. You know, if something were to happen, since I'm on the floor today, I'd get my butt chewed out and lose my job."

"Yeah, no problem...." Marc was deflated as he backed away.

"Hey, thanks for understanding, man." TJ slapped him hard on the back.

"Sure." He tripped a little. "See you in class, Rebecca."

"Bye," I called as he walked away.

TJ and I kept quiet until Marc was well on his way down the steps. Then TJ hopped on the "defective treadmill," grinning like a loon.

"You're bad," I laughed.

"Jeez, Beck, I think that's the first time I've ever seen you get hit on." I sighed out loud.

"That was an unpleasant but comical moment for me."

"You're welcome. I get the feeling you've done the 'red tag' line before," I said, eyeing him. Trevor coughed in a knowing way.

"That hurts, Beck," TJ said unconvincingly. "Man, that guy was trying hard. He had those spitballs collecting at the corners of his mouth. Did you see that? That was hilarious," he laughed.

Trevor let out a belly laugh and got off his machine. "Alright, I'm going home," he said, grabbing his towel and wiping down the treadmill.

"Come on, Trevor! That was *maybe* forty-five minutes. You're weak!" TJ teased. Trevor just bobbed his head and grabbed his water bottle, smiling. "Weak!" TJ yelled again as Trevor moved around us toward the stairs.

"So, how's the roommate situation? All good?" TJ asked.

"Yeah, you know," I answered casually.

"And the boyfriend situation? You guys all patched up? Want to talk about it?"

"What do you think?" I asked, leaning toward him.

"You're right, dumb question. Of course, you don't want to talk about it. So, are we gonna race or what?"

"Race?"

"Yep, endurance race. We go balls out until one of us quits or slows down," he said, one eyebrow raised. I gave him a "you're kidding" smile. But he was all ready to go.

"I've already been on this for ten minutes," I protested.

"Excuses, excuses," TJ said, throwing up his hands. "Are we racing or not?"

"Aren't you supposed to be working right now?"

"Absolutely."

TJ started jogging fast on the treadmill while looking straight ahead. He had a competitive smirk on his face. I took the bait and cranked it up a notch on my machine.

Just like he said, we were running balls out, trying to outdo each other. All of a sudden, I was nine years old again, running hard, playing, and getting sweaty with my best friend. It was such a great moment. My heart pounded out of my chest, and my sweaty face burned. After what seemed like four minutes of sprinting, TJ cracked me up by making loud noises with his breathing and panting. He moaned so loud that we got a lot of strange looks from other students working out. I tried so hard to block out his craziness but felt myself becoming weaker and slower with each laugh. Then he was laughing, too. Just as he started slowing down, he reached over and smacked the Reduce Speed button on my machine. I tried to shove his arm out of the way, but he kept lowering my speed.

"Ugh! Cheater," I gasped, out of breath as I slowed to a stop.

"Tie!" he panted. TJ winked at me, and he stopped, too. He leaned over, arms resting on his legs, his forehead dripping sweat.

"Whatever helps you sleep at night," I taunted breathlessly.

"I guess I should get back to work, huh? That was fun, though. Thanks," he said.

"Yeah." We shared a smile, and he walked away.

"You still got it, Beck!" he called, heading back down to the front desk.

CHAPTER 18

Something's Wrong

I reached TJ's house, dropped my bike in the yard next to his, and walked around to the backyard, where I heard muffled voices. I couldn't make out what was being said, but the tone was serious. When I peeked between a crack in the fence, I saw Mrs. Lawson sitting across from Grandma at the picnic table. TJ stood adjacent to his mom. She held onto his waist, and he had his arms around her shoulders, his face unusually sad. I had never seen him like that, and it made me instantly nervous.

I was about to turn around when Grandma called to me. I moved cautiously past the gate and closer to where they gathered.

"Hi sweet, Becky. I didn't think we'd see you today." Mrs. Lawson's face was tired and puffy. She squinted, trying to smile at me, but it just made her appear broken somehow.

TJ sent me a small, gentle smile. He didn't immediately come to stand by me.

"I'm gonna go check on Katie," Grandma announced. She rose from the table and disappeared into the house.

"Becky, do you want to stay for dinner? We're having homemade pizza," Mrs. Lawson offered.

"I don't know."

It was the truth. I didn't know if my mother was already on her way to capture me. I didn't know if my dad would be pulling up looking for me. I didn't know if TJ even wanted me there. The one thing I knew was that something was wrong. I was just about to give an excuse and escape on my bike when TJ spoke at last.

"Mom, maybe Beck and I can run to the pond real quick?" He let go of her and bent low to re-tie his shoelace.

"Alright."

"Come on." He grabbed my hand and pulled me toward the gate.

"Tommy?" Mrs. Lawson called. He turned around, and she locked eyes with him. "The sooner, the better, okay?"

TJ silently nodded, then we continued toward the front yard, our hands still together. He seemed very distracted but kept hold of my hand, almost as if he didn't know he had it.

TJ clenched his jaw as he stared down at our bikes. He took a long breath then let go of my hand.

I bent down to pick up my bike, "So who won?"

"Won what?"

"The football game."

"Oh, Bobby," he said matter-of-factly.

"Is that why you're upset?" I asked.

He looked down the street and clenched his jaw again.

Then he glanced at me nervously, searching my eyes, before looking away and mumbling, "Yeah."

"I figured," I said, although I knew that wasn't the truth. TJ would never be that glum about something as trivial as losing a football game to Bobby. It was something bigger. Something bad. He'd lied, but I wanted to believe he was upset by something meaningless.

"You didn't check on the eggs today, did you?" I asked, wanting a change of subject.

"Naw. Did you?" TJ asked, mounting his bike.

"I couldn't."

"Oh yeah, how was your playtime?" His face broke out in a slow grin. At last! A smile!

"Horrible," I snorted, wrapping my leg over my bike seat.

His smile stretched wider, "What did you do?"

"I don't want to talk about it. It was awful."

SOMETHING'S WRONG

"Sorry, Beck."

TJ started pedaling down the block as I took off after him.

After riding through the woods on the trail, we reached the pond only to find that mama turtle was busy patrolling the nest. She trundled back and forth in her dark green and orange coat in front of the nest, which we took as a sign that the eggs were fine, and headed back home.

Together, TJ and I ate pizza while he told me how awful Bobby's little brother was in the game. I sat up a little straighter as he talked about how Matthew could barely kick the ball ten feet, and he'd fumbled twice. TJ claimed it had been a mess without me.

We played War for a while. The game would never end, as we both had two aces for an eternity. I complained about swimming with Melanie. He didn't know her well but said he could see her being a pain.

My dad called TJ's house sometime later, attempting to get me to come home. TJ pleaded with him to let me stay a little longer. *E.T.* had just come on the television, and he didn't want me to miss it. He seemed almost desperate for me to stay.

We barely stayed awake for the final scene, but I did keep my eyes open enough to see Mrs. Lawson, weepy-eyed, watching us sitting side by side, my head on TJ's shoulder.

CHAPTER 19

Valentine

"Can you explain to me why your course schedule involves ballroom dance?"

My mother had found out.

"The aqua aerobics thing just sounded boring, like a geriatric course. And Lindsay wanted me to sign up with her. It's just for fun."

"Ballroom dance?"

"Yes, it's physical activity, isn't it?"

"Rebecca, you know how…." I stretched the phone out as far away from my ear as my arm would reach, not wanting to hear the scolding I was sure was on the line.

Once there was a lull, I replied with, "I should've just been honest, Mom. Sorry."

"You know you really should make plans to come home for a weekend."

I had never been allowed to have my own car, even though I had begged and begged for years to no avail. It was easier for her to see to it that I was where I should be if I had no mode of transportation. Clever. It had sort of backfired at college, though. She hadn't been able to get me to come home until Jason.

She continued. "Jason said he would gladly pick you up and bring you home."

Conversations with my mother were pretty routine. A suggestion (more like an ultimatum) would be offered. I would be given a few moments to think it over, and then she would instantly get angry with me for not deciding quickly enough, as if my second of silence had solidified my answer as being the opposite of what she wanted to hear. *Ugh.* I rolled my eyes at her over my phone, sure she could feel it.

"I'm not sure if that'll work. Jason wants me to visit him at U of I for Valentine's Day, so I won't be home that weekend."

"Yes, he told me about that. It's not the only possible weekend to come home, Rebecca."

"Got it." Eye roll. Oh, and could you please butt out of my relationship? Thanks.

***

After several sarcastic text messages and a few clipped phone calls, Jason and I made up.

"I apologize," Jason said.

"For what exactly?" I asked, trying to make him grovel.

"I jumped to conclusions which is a cardinal sin in my family. My father taught me better than that."

"Is that right?"

"Yes. I should've shown diligence in collecting all the evidence before expelling accusatory language."

Jason was typically not a humorous person. But he enjoyed getting a laugh out of me when he talked law—thinking that he was going to impress me and get me "hot," as he said.

As a peace offering, I agreed to spend Valentine's weekend with him. Amy let me take her car, so I could drive to U of I. I thought that was big of her to help me patch things up with Jason. She wouldn't admit it, but I could tell she felt a little guilty about pushing us into an argument.

When I got to his apartment, I was not only happy that his roommate wasn't lurking around, but Jason had a surprise for me. He buzzed me in, and once upstairs, I realized the door was cracked open.

"Jason?" I pushed through to see a room filled with pink and red candles. The soft, flickering glow stretched across the table and counter. "Hey, beautiful." He smiled.

"Wow!" I blinked, looking around, on one hand, delighted at his romantic gesture, and on the other hand, overwhelmed.

"I knew you'd be impressed," he said proudly, pulling me in and kissing me deeply for a few moments. I felt the surprising but welcomed flutter of butterflies in my belly. It had been a long time since we'd kissed that way. "And," he said, leading me toward his little kitchen table, "I made you dinner."

Two place settings had been prepared in the dimly lit dining area. There was even a bottle of wine set on the countertop next to two sparkling glasses. I was blown away at the scene he had set up and elated that it was all for me with no hidden agenda or people to one-up and impress. My heart did a little cartwheel. "That's so sweet." I wrapped my arms around his neck and kissed him again and again.

Jason did a superb job with the food. He'd made chicken marsala with fresh green beans and boasted about finding a recipe for the main dish. He'd even whipped up homemade sauce. My stomach growled. Everything was ideal, and I was relieved it would be a good visit.

Afterward, we exchanged Valentine's gifts. I gave him the Fossil watch he'd eyed over Christmas break. He really seemed to like it. Then he gave me a small, wrapped box, and I hesitantly wondered what it could be. Inside was a gold heart pendant on a chain. Looking at the box, I suppressed a sigh. It was from none other than my mother's jewelry line. And just like that, I sensed her eyes all over me again.

Faking a smile, I said, "Thank you, it's beautiful."

***

The next day was pleasant enough until Jason's roommate and stuck-up girlfriend arrived. I felt uncomfortable as soon as they walked through the door. Aaron was very cold and pompous, and his girlfriend was exactly the same. He tried too hard to impress everyone, always talking about politics and foreign affairs. I couldn't have gotten in on the conversation if I'd wanted to. The worst part of it was that Jason took on some of

Aaron's infuriating personality traits when they were together. He never caught on about how left out I felt or … how I felt about most things.

The night got even worse when we all went to his friend's house party. In a whole room full of pre-law, pre-med, arrogant snobs, I felt uncomfortable and completely out of place.

The night was dull and disappointing. Jason spent most of his time at the bar arguing with his friends. At one point, a girl in a snug red sweater dress tried to make conversation with me but left after a few minutes to talk to someone else.

Then like magic, I got a picture message: Amy with TJ and the gang at Mom's. My quick smile faded as swiftly as it had appeared. I ached to be with my group instead of where I was.

It was a long, sickening evening. I questioned what I was doing there and with Jason as well. *Would our relationship lead to anything but failure?* I couldn't fully admit my reason for hanging onto him.

The Rachel nightmare haunted me again that night. This time I cried out in the dream repeatedly until my voice became hoarse. The trail was more tumultuous and rougher. I kept falling, scraping my knees, getting up, and chasing her, again only seeing the back of her head.

I woke with a start and roved my eyes wildly around the room, expecting to still see the ominous trail. Then I got my bearings and spied Jason sleeping beside me. His presence did not comfort me; instead, I was suddenly desperate to get back to Eastern.

The next morning, as Jason headed to the shower, I got ready for the day and created an excuse in my head for an early departure.

After his first cup of coffee, I told Jason I needed to head home.

"Now?" he asked while sitting on the bed, watching TV.

"Yeah, I've got a lot of work to do," I said, packing and avoiding his eyes.

"I thought we were going to spend the day with each other," he argued, "Christ, I barely see you."

"I'm sorry. I've got to get going."

"Well, I'm going home next weekend, so I'll pick you up. We can go together this time," he stated simply.

The thought of going home was just about the last thing I wanted to think about at the moment. *Hadn't I been tortured enough from the previous night?* "Um, this coming weekend?"

"Yeah."

"I don't know if I can. You can just go without me." I zipped up my bag.

"Why? Why can't you go?" he pressed.

"I have a test coming up."

"Well, I don't know when I'll be going back next," he warned, glowering.

"That's okay." I threw my bag over my shoulder and walked to the door, Jason following. His roommate hovered in the kitchen, wearing a robe, and preparing his Keurig for coffee.

"Why wouldn't you just go home when I'm going? You know your mom's gonna be ticked."

I looked up at him, irritated. "I gotta go. Thank you, though." I opened the door.

"I don't get you." He swatted his arm at me as if shooing me off and turned to go back into the apartment. "That's exactly the point, Jason," I said to myself, walking away.

CHAPTER 20

Storm

A few days after Grandma Lawson's departure, I took Buddy across the street to the open field and threw his favorite purple frisbee around. He was so well-trained that I didn't have to worry about him running into the street. Then I raced him up and down to the "goal lines" a couple of times. We were both panting a bit, so we headed back across the street for a reprieve. TJ came riding down the sidewalk as we approached my lawn.

"Hey," I said, grinning.

"Hey, Beck. Whatcha doin'?" He hopped off his bike and rubbed Buddy's head, who panted and wagged his tail wildly.

"We were playing catch, but he needs a drink. You can come in."

We walked into my front hallway. Ryan sat in Dad's chair watching TV. He glanced at us with a vacant expression, then focused back on the TV.

"Hey Ryan," TJ said, rather unenthusiastically. Ryan barely raised his hand in a wave then let it fall back on his lap.

I went to get Buddy ice cubes for his water. My mother had just walked upstairs from the basement with a laundry basket full of folded clothes.

"Hi, Mrs. Winslow."

"Tommy." She used her fake smile.

TJ and I played around with Buddy for a while on the living room floor. He tried to encourage Buddy to chase his tail by demonstrating how to do it himself. TJ pulled his sock off and tucked it into the back of his shorts. He snarled and raced around and around in circles snapping at the sock, but of course, missing it. Buddy just sat alert and watched. I laughed so hard; I had to wipe tears from my eyes.

"Could you three dogs get your big butts out of the way? I'm watching TV," Ryan requested in his usual, insulting manner.

I frowned at him. He made a face and stuck his tongue out. TJ eyeballed him with a look of calm resentment but didn't comment.

***

Later that afternoon, the Lawsons treated me to Dairy Queen. It was pretty unusual for Mrs. Lawson to be home during the day and even more for her to take TJ and Katie for ice cream. They were much more of a cold-sandwiches-and-freeze-pop family than restaurant-goers. At the time, I was just happily surprised and didn't analyze the why behind the trip to DQ.

Mrs. Lawson was in an exuberant mood. She and TJ sang along spiritedly to "Bad, Bad Leroy Brown" from the front seat of her Caravan as we pulled into the DQ lot.

I ordered my typical strawberry sundae, no nuts, no whipped cream, just like my dad always did. We sat inside at a corner booth because of the steely gray clouds gathering over the parking lot.

Katie sang in a giggly voice about her vanilla and chocolate twist cone. "Dairy Queen, Dairy Queen, mma mma mma Dairy Queen."

"Hey!" TJ looked up with wide eyes and an expression of wonder, "I just thought of something. Do you think if Burger King married Dairy Queen, their daughter would be Princess Shakeburger?"

I laughed through my nose in a humoring way. TJ's mom grinned at him.

"No, she'd be Princess Chocolate Ice Cream Hamburger." Katie laughed at her cleverness. TJ and I giggled.

"Becky, honey, how's Ryan doing? I haven't seen him in ages." Mrs. Lawson studied me, warm interest in her eyes. I was taken aback, not by her consideration, but by the mention of my brother's name.

"Fine, I guess."

"Do you two get along pretty well?" she asked.

I shrugged.

"Hmm," she looked me over thoughtfully. "You don't really spend much time together?"

"Not really."

I didn't want to discuss my relationship with my brother. I thought he was a jerk. We didn't have anything in common, or so it seemed. All our interactions were based upon rude comments, arguments, and teasing.

I didn't even give it much thought. That's just how things were. Sometimes I imagined what it would've been like if Rachel were still alive. Would she be on my side, against Ryan? Would she have been like another mom to me? Or would she have just ignored me like Ryan did? I didn't really even need Ryan in my life. I had my two best guys, TJ and my dad. Ryan wasn't up to par by a long shot.

"Well, maybe it's just your age. You'll come to really need your brother someday. I'm hopeful that you two can have a great friendship, you know?" Mrs. Lawson encouraged me.

I raised my eyebrows at her skeptically. It didn't seem likely. *Me? Friends with Ryan?* I checked TJ's face to see if he shared my expression, but he just looked down in deep thought.

"What do you think you'll be doing at school this year? Maybe join some clubs or sports teams?" Mrs. Lawson asked. "Gosh, you impressed me so much with your gymnastics! You should be on the gymnastics team! I bet you'd just love it!"

"I don't know." I shrugged again.

Mrs. Lawson was acting weird. Nice, but weird. I felt like I was being interviewed.

Suddenly, there was a shattering crack of thunder, and my heart leaped momentarily in my chest. Katie yelped. TJ didn't even seem to notice. The sky angrily lowered its rolling purple ceiling.

"Oh! We'd better get home quickly and beat this storm!" Mrs. Lawson declared.

She herded us outside to the van, and we raced back.

When we got to my house, I thanked her, said goodbye to TJ and Katie, and then sprinted to my front door as pellets of warm rain crashed all around me.

CHAPTER 21

Field Day

I finally built up the nerve to call my dad and let him know I had seen TJ. I knew he would bring up our conversation to my mother. Dad seemed excited about TJ's reappearance and asked about his mom and Katie. I told him about her engagement. He was happy for her and told me to tell the Lawsons hello. My mother clearly didn't share the same courtesy when she called the very next day repeatedly asking about Jason.

"What did Jason give you for Valentine's Day?" my mother asked in an overly excited way.

"I'm sure you already know that."

"He said he wanted to give you something very special. Isn't he so thoughtful?"

She was being so obnoxious and going out of her way, *not* to mention TJ. I had to laugh at how ironic it was that I'd met up with him again in a class that my mother, in a backhanded fashion, chose for me.

"Did Dad tell you I called yesterday?"

"He mentioned it, yes. So, when are you coming home next? Jason said you had a test and couldn't come last weekend."

I wanted to reach through the phone and wring her neck. Each pry into my love life and each request for me to come home made me want to push the visit back.

My head ached at the end of our talk, and frustration about my mother and Jason set in deeper.

***

Ballroom Dance had become everyone's favorite class, especially mine. All the girls made it a competition to see who could dance with 80-year-old Mr. MacFarlane the most. Mrs. Mac chose TJ so often for demonstrations since he was the most outgoing student or because it was hilarious watching him attempt the dances. And yet, we actually had started a dance that even he looked good performing—the swing. Linds was very good at it, too. I had never seen her happier than when she was swing dancing with TJ.

As we were walking out, Trevor informed us about a sporting event the guys were scheming for the weekend.

"We're having a massive football game Saturday, and everyone's coming to our house after, so… we'll see you ladies there. One o'clock in the north quad."

Lindsay begged me to go with her and play football. I laughed at her and explained that catching would be involved, double-checking if she still wanted to go. Although I pretended to mind the prospect of going, it sounded like a blast. The conversations with both my mother and Jason had me feeling incredibly stressed and under attack. A game of football seemed like the perfect cure to relax a bit.

TJ pushed to get me out there and play. He'd organized a huge turnout with all his roommates, some people from dance, and a slew of other guys and girls. Teams were drawn, and Lindsay was heartbroken to find she wasn't on his team.

It was warmer than it had been for weeks but still damp and chilly, typical for early March. A cool draping mist hung low in the sky. We were all dressed in sweats, t-shirts, and yoga pants, except Lindsay, who was trying too hard to look cute in jeans and a pink, hooded sweater. I reminded her that we were about to play football in the mud, and Coach Teague would be furious if she found out Lindsay had put makeup on before we left. I'd barely touched mine, something my mother couldn't quite understand. Most days, I just wore a hint of mascara and lip gloss anyway. Lindsay was too stubborn to listen, though.

FIELD DAY

We were huddled in our teams, ready to start. TJ was captain and quarterback, of course.

"It's tackle, right?" asked a heavy guy with a white-blond buzz.

"No way," a girl responded.

"I brought the flags," TJ said, handing them out.

"Can't the guys at least tackle guys?" the big guy asked.

"How about, can the girls tackle the guys?" Taylor rebutted, unleashing a chorus of, "Oh yeah!"

"You can try," Brandon said.

"I should've brought my cup. Girls play dirty," Mason joked, grabbing himself.

Play started, and the rumble began. I was impressed with the athleticism of many of our players. They had speed, intensity, and flexibility. TJ was amazing. His focus, follow-through, and steady arm were almost unbelievable. The other team paled in comparison. It took me a few downs to regain my competitive drive, but I found it eventually and surprised everyone except TJ.

We were a team again, just like we had been so long ago. He threw to me often. I proved to be faster than most of the other players and, therefore, got a ton of yards before anyone caught up to me and ripped my flag. TJ was so excited, reveling in the game and literally bouncing up and down with joy at each touchdown our team scored.

Brandon was a wild beast. He not only tackled, but he clobbered all the other guys. Freddie got the brunt of his tackles since he was the biggest on the other team. At one point, Freddie shoved Brandon hard after a play as payback. After a brief halt in the action, the scuffle was over.

Lindsay tried to make some plays but didn't do a whole lot. She was a decent athlete, but her head wasn't in the game. Then she finally got the ball and ran it well until Brandon lunged for her flag. He ended up ripping the pocket of her jeans off, as well as a bit of her actual jeans. "Thanks for the nice piece of ass!" Brandon shouted at her as he charged away.

Lindsay was mortified. She laughed along with everyone at first but then wanted to go home. I tried to make light of it, but she wouldn't have it. Although she insisted I didn't have to, I walked her home. On the way, I tried to convince her to come back or just come out for the party. In the end, I headed back for the fourth quarter while she stayed behind, feeling sorry for herself.

By that time, everyone was pretty much dirty and stained. TJ's t-shirt was a disaster, and he had a gash on his elbow, but he kept playing anyway.

After our victory, despite the looks of the exhausted players, TJ said there was more fun to be had.

A large group of us, minus Mason, grabbed some food at Los Burritos and afterward trekked over to TJ's.

They were such a fun group. I even enjoyed hanging out with Taylor and Natalia since we had become pretty good friends during dance class. They were very easy to get along with. All of TJ's friends, although different, were congenial and comforting. Even Brandon had his nice guy moments. The roommates mostly made jokes or made fun of each other. They were genuine, hilarious, and a breath of fresh air compared to Jason's friends.

When we walked into the house, TJ was met by a screeching, happy little brunette who I assumed was Mason's daughter. She ran right up to him and was immediately scooped up and thrown around. He was too cute with that precious little girl in his arms. And although TJ was overjoyed to have her there, he remembered me at once and introduced us.

"Tana, this is Beck. Can you say hi?"

"Hi, Tana," I smiled. She looked me over shyly, then laid her head on TJ's shoulder.

"Okay, maybe later you'll talk to Beck," TJ said.

I also met Jenna, Mason's girlfriend, and Tana's mom. She was pretty with olive skin and long dark hair highlighted in three different shades. Mason and Jenna seemed like a cute but unstable couple, especially after already having a child together. They made fun of each other quite a bit, and their close moments quickly erupted into petty arguments. But Jenna was very friendly to me. She said she was so glad to finally meet me and that I was all Tommy talked about, which set my cheeks on fire.

We all drank and had a good time playing cards. TJ had already confided in me about Mason's cards obsession, and I got to see it first-hand. Mason was much more of an introvert when he was sober. But when he drank, he captured everyone's attention with his obnoxious humor. He was for sure a seasoned drinker, and the more he drank, the more he talked.

TJ held Tana almost the whole night, which turned him into a chick magnet. Tana even helped TJ play darts. He'd walk super close to the board, and she would stab it with a dart. Then TJ would toss her around in celebration and catch her again as she let out big belly laughs. Natalia was attached to him as well.

After a while, Jenna went upstairs to put the knocked-out Tana to sleep for the night. TJ was giving Natalia a tour when he called me over from the poker game at the table.

"Beck, did you ever see my room?" he asked while holding a staggering Natalia's hand.

"Um, I don't think so," I answered and followed them. TJ was no neat freak. I remembered his atrocious room when we were little. Now, clothes overflowed a hamper. Shoes piled up in the corner. Sports equipment, posters, and memorabilia were all over the place. His comforter was at least pulled up.

I looked on a shelf and saw a picture of his mom with a man I assumed was Howard.

"Aww, your mom."

"Yeah, and that's Howard with her. He's my 'wonder counselor.' Even with those big-ass ears," TJ chuckled.

Then I noticed something on his bookshelf. It was a kid-drawn picture secured in a dusty frame that I recognized at once. A little boy and girl gazed up at the stars while a figure roasted marshmallows above them. It was the picture I'd drawn for TJ. My mouth fell open as I stood there staring at it.

"Remember that?" TJ asked. I just looked at him, then back at the picture. "Beck drew that. Isn't it awesome?" he asked Natalia.

"¡Ay, qué lindo!" she said, squinting too close to the picture.

"She did that when she was like nine," he bragged.

"Tommy Lawson, were you always so cute, even when you were little?" she slurred, putting her hands around his neck, her long, loose brown curls sweeping over his bicep.

"Yeah, you know, all the chicks in first grade wanted to borrow my glue stick." He gave an exaggerated wink, and Natalia and I laughed loudly.

"I have to pee. Where's the baño?" she asked, moving toward the door.

"Here, I'll show you," he said and quickly led her out of the room.

I stood still, gazing at that picture, remembering again. I recalled how TJ had missed his dad so much and that it was one of the few times I'd comforted him instead of the other way around. I was so touched that he still had it. It looked weathered and dusty, but it was there in front of me, bringing me back to that heart-wrenching moment when I gave it to him. Out of the corner of my eye, I caught TJ smiling by the doorpost, seeing that I was still staring at our picture.

"That drawing is one of my most prized possessions."

"It is not," I said.

"Beck, I swear. I know it sounds cheesy, but I still believe that story you told me." He smiled. "Whenever I see a cloud with stars around it…" He looked at the picture, then smiled softly once more. We shared what seemed like a long moment looking at each other. My cheeks blazed, and my heart gave a surprised lurch.

Natalia came back into the room, and I suddenly felt out of place.

"Well," I said, looking away, "I've gotta go."

"You need a ride?" he asked.

"No, I'm okay."

"Beck," he scolded.

"Seriously."

The tension was broken up then by the sound of a fist slamming onto the card table, some barely audible swearing from Brandon, and a few moments of laughter.

"Amy is like one block away, and I'm meeting her, then we're leaving together, ar-right?" I mocked him while walking to the front door. TJ gave a satisfied smirk. Natalia giggled again and put her hands on TJ.

I waved goodbye to the roommates at the table and headed toward the door. As I pulled it open, I felt TJ right behind me.

"I had fun today," I offered, turning around and looking up at him.

"I know."

"See ya," I said and left.

CHAPTER 22

Crushed

The day after Melanie's visit, my whole world fell apart.

In the middle of a warm and breezy afternoon, TJ and I began another game of football with Pete, Garcia, Bobby, and Mikey. We were tied at seven. I had already caught a beautiful pass from TJ and ran it in for a touchdown. Bobby, of course, argued—I was supposedly out of bounds. After much deliberation from both teams, we let the play stand. Bobby cursed and took the ball to start up his offense. Garcia seemed to get bigger every time I saw him. Bobby was barely visible beyond Garcia's sweaty, meaty head.

Mikey pivoted forward and backward to try and lose me. TJ had been shadowing Pete. Bobby snapped the ball in his hands and jumped to the right. He shot the ball to the far-right side of the field. TJ and Pete charged toward it, but as Pete dove for it, it bounced out of his reach.

"Man! Pete, you gotta keep your eye on the ball. God!" Bobby hollered.

"Shut up, Bobby. Nobody could've caught that terrible pass!" Pete argued. Then they were at each other's throats.

TJ and I grinned, rolled our eyes in sync with each other, and moved to the sidelines to toss the ball around in the meantime. We were quite used to "Bobby delays," as TJ called them.

I saw Ryan and Scott on their skateboards in the street, approaching the field. *Oh, great,* I thought to myself. TJ's back was to them, so he didn't notice them until Scott spoke up.

"Ryan, isn't that your brother?"

TJ tossed the ball to me and spun around. I sensed that Ryan didn't want to back down in front of his friend.

"Yeah, Scott, you've met my little brother, right?"

Scott chortled to himself in amusement. "Didn't realize your brother was such a shrimp."

By now, Bobby and the others had quieted behind us, which could only mean they were listening in on Ryan's insults. I clenched my jaw as TJ kept his eyes glued on them.

"It's great that you could find other boys to play football with, brother." Ryan sniped.

"Leave her alone, Ryan," TJ said, calmly staring him down.

"Come on, just ignore him," I said as my nostrils flared with fury.

"You know what Mom's doing right now? She's on the phone trying to find girls that will be friends with you. She's been on the phone for hours." Ryan mimicked a high-pitched version of my mother's voice. "Hi, can my poor excuse for a daughter learn to play dolls with your daughter?"

Scott roared with laughter. I glanced at my team, that wouldn't stop staring at me.

"No, she can't because she's secretly a boy," he said, going on in his mocking tone.

TJ moved closer and locked eyes with Ryan. "You know what, Ryan?" TJ was livid with anger for the first time I'd ever seen. "You're just jealous."

"Jealous of what?"

"She's a better athlete than you, and you know it," TJ stated it as a simple fact. I watched them in cautious amazement.

"Oh man, burn," said Garcia.

"So, get over it, and leave Beck alone," TJ ordered.

He turned away to go back to the group while Ryan's fat face turned pink with embarrassment.

"At least my dad taught me the difference between boys and girls, but I guess your dad never got to that part, did he?" said Ryan.

The whole world stopped. The silence around us was deafening enough for Ryan to know he'd gone too far. My mouth fell wide open in horrid shock.

TJ turned his head with a jerk, revealing an agonized expression and rage burning in his eyes. In the next second, he rushed forward and clocked Ryan with a crushing blow to his face. Ryan fell backward into the street, covering his instantly bloodied nose and smashed cheek with a gasp.

TJ clenched his jaw in disgust at Ryan on the ground. Then he took a deep breath, and his expression changed to misery. He walked past his bike and, as though in a trance, sprinted all the way down the block. I could only stare in disbelief at what I'd just seen and heard.

Pete jogged a few feet to catch TJ but thought better of it and let him go.

Mikey jumped on TJ's bike and rode after him.

Scott, although stunned, helped the cowering Ryan to his feet and led him across the street to our front door and into the hands of my shrieking mother. Even Bobby walked home speechless.

CHAPTER 23

One of the Girls

In dance, the following Thursday, TJ was as lively and energetic as usual. We were still swing dancing, which set a great atmosphere for the class. TJ and Natalia weren't nearly as cuddly as they had been Saturday night.

As always, he led me onto the dance floor. For the entire rotation, TJ wanted to practice the Bow Tie move that Mrs. Mac showed us. We grabbed hands overhead and then stepped to opposite sides. We both ducked our left hands behind our own heads and pulled our right arms away. Then we let our right arms brush across each other's shoulders until we slid apart. TJ loved this move! Since he was in a talkative mood, it made getting the steps down more challenging.

"So, tell me one thing, Beck."

I braced myself, "About what?"

"Your boyfriend." His smile was guarded.

"What one thing would you like to know about Jason?"

"How did you meet? High school?"

I bit the corner of my lip, knowing how my answer would sound but figured I should just get it over with. "Our mothers are friends."

"Ah." He nodded, arching his eyebrows. I imagined TJ's every thought about this bit of news. Yes, my controlling mother had found my boyfriend for me. The son of her upper-class friend. He must've sensed my sudden distress and moved ahead with the conversation.

"One more thing about your boyfriend."

"No way, you said—"

"Hang on.... Does he know how good of a dancer you are?"

I grinned at that. "How good am I?"

"Well, I mean, you're not as good as me, of course." He fought back a smile. "But, you know, with some extra practice, you could give Ashley a run for her money." I snickered at his playfulness. "Did you just snort?" he asked.

"No, I didn't snort." I laughed as he flipped his elbows up way too high like he always did in his back step of the swing.

"Hey! Let's try a double loop-de-loop!"

"You're wired! What did you eat today?"

"A bag of Skittles," he laughed, flinging me around.

"Well, there you go." I shook my head, smiling.

"Hey!" he whispered noisily, "You know Linds invited me over on Sunday for dinner with you guys?"

My eyes bulged.

"Uh oh," he said, gritting his teeth. "What? Is that bad?"

I wrinkled my nose.

"What?"

"Oh boy," I said.

"She doesn't like Trevor, does she?" he asked, still gritting his teeth. I mimicked his face and shook my head. "She likes me, doesn't she?"

I nodded.

"Aww, shoot, Beck."

"Your arms are flying up too high, Tommy Lawson!" Mrs. Mac called.

"Sorry, Mrs. Mac," he yelled back.

"Are you gonna come over then?" I asked quietly as Lindsay and Freddie moved closer.

"I said I would already."

"And you don't like her at all?"

"Not like that, no."

"Now see..." I leaned in. "If you'd stop flirting with everyone, things like this wouldn't happen."

He dropped his jaw, his eyes smiling, "Well, thanks for noticing."

On the way out of class, he hollered at our group, "I'll see you ladies on Sunday." Then he took off jogging. I played dumb, so that Lindsay had to fill me in on the plans. I wasn't sure how to react to her.

***

On Sunday, Lindsay went all out and served Bulgogi, which is thinly sliced ribeye marinated in amazing sesame, garlic, green onion, and soy sauce over white rice. We were all very impressed with this mouth-watering meal. Lindsay attributed it all to her mom, but I could tell by her glow that she was proud of herself.

TJ played the invite perfectly. He was courteous to Lindsay yet made a great effort to act friendly to all of us equally. She showed him around our place while Amy and I followed along, putting in our two cents. He seemed impressed with our apartment, and especially how clean it was. It was easy for him to be so conversational.

TJ was good at making everyone feel comfortable. We spent most of the night hanging out in my room. He petted Scooter for a bit. It was amazing that Scooter was even visible because of her anti-male attitude. Amy said Scooter obviously had good taste. Although she had only known TJ for a short time, she absolutely loved him; that made me feel a little uneasy since she clearly disliked Jason.

TJ asked a ton of questions. "So, how long have you girls known each other?"

"Rebecca and I went to high school together," Lindsay explained.

"Right," TJ said.

"Then we met our favorite skank freshman year in Carmen Hall," Lindsay continued, batting her eyes at Amy.

"I don't know whom you're referring to, Miss Linds. I'm an angel." Amy folded her hands together in a saintly fashion.

"So, who's the housekeeper?" TJ asked. They pointed at me. I shrugged, acknowledging my title. "Who's the loud one?"

Amy said, "Hello! And Miss Lindsay is our chef."

There were a million other questions directed at the girls, then TJ looked over at my desk and some of my pictures.

"Ooh, he's a cutie, Beck," he said, holding up a photo of Jason.

That picture made me smile every time I looked at it. Jason was standing in front of the *Hamilton* billboard at the CIBC Theater in Chicago. The night had been a disaster. We'd missed the performance because of traffic, but it had turned into an awesome date anyway.

It was the closest we'd ever come to divulging deeper feelings. My eyes blurred over with a sudden thought, wondering if we would ever get to that point.

TJ set the picture down and continued to scan my other pictures. He smiled and held up my favorite picture of good old Buddy. "Aww, Buddy!" My face fell, glancing at Buddy's picture. "Is he...?" TJ seemed unsure how to ask the question.

"No," I said simply.

"That sucks, Beck. I'm sorry," he said, putting the picture down. I shrugged.

After a little more conversation not revolving around boyfriends or deceased yet beloved pets, TJ headed for the door.

"Linds, thanks so much for the delicious meal. Ladies, good hanging with you," TJ said, giving quick hugs.

"You are officially one of the girls now, Tommy Boy, so come over more often," Amy said.

"For sure," Lindsay agreed, unable to hide her intentions. TJ just smiled at all of us and then asked to see me for a second. I felt Lindsay's eyes on me as I followed him outside toward our parking lot.

"How did I do?" he asked skeptically.

"Perfect, no over-flirting, no worries," I said, shivering from the cold.

"Good, thanks. Oh, and you all can come to my place next Friday. Having a shindig," he said, shoving his hands in his pockets. "So, you could mention it to them sometime later, ar-right?"

I nodded, rubbing my arms in the ice-cold wind. "It's your birthday, right?"

His face broke out into a charming smile. "Yeah. You must be there." He moved to the driver-side door.

"No problem," I said through chattering teeth.

"Thanks! Hey, get inside, crazy. It's freezing out here!" He winked and got into his truck.

CHAPTER 24

Torn Apart

The day was sickening. My dad was called home from work early to assist with our crisis. He managed to make PB&J sandwiches for Ryan and me despite my mother's ranting.

"Oh my God, Ryan, has it stopped? We need to go to the emergency room." My mother moved the bloodstained rag of ice away from his face and examined him intensely.

I stared down at my PB&J sandwich with a nauseating feeling so strong I almost vomited.

"It stopped bleeding, right, Ryan?" my dad asked.

"Yeah," Ryan moaned.

"Look at this! Look at his face! You are *not* to see him *anymore*, you hear me?" She snapped at me bitterly, plunging me into sadness.

"Calm down, Suzanne," my dad coaxed.

"Calm down? Do you see what he's done to our son, Robert? Look at his face!"

"I would like to hear the whole story before we get ahead of ourselves. I can't believe Tommy was involved. He would never have done this unless Ryan did something first, am I right?" My dad eyed us suspiciously, wanting an answer.

"You're blaming *Ryan* for getting what will be a black eye and broken nose?"

"It may not be broken, Suzanne. Please, I'd like to hear what happened," he stated in a calm voice. "What did you say, Ryan?" He looked him over, knowing Ryan's smart mouth had to be the cause.

After a minute of silence, Ryan confessed, "I was picking on Rebecca."

"And?" My dad motioned for him to continue.

"And I said something pretty bad." He grimaced as he shifted the rag to a cooler side.

"Here, honey, let me help you," my mother offered, coming to his aid.

Just then, my dad's cell rang. He answered it after only one ring. "Hello? Hi, Janet."

We all looked toward the phone. The scowl was suddenly back on my mother's face. I was sure she wanted to yank the phone out of my dad's hands, but she somehow restrained herself.

"I know. He'll be all right. There's no need to.... Yes, I'm getting it out of him right now, too." Ryan studied the ground. "Well, it seems they're both to blame. I appreciate that." He paused, then said, "I think that would be a nice idea. Sure, Janet." Another pause. "Hi, Tommy. It's alright, son. I know you are. Okay. Just a second." He pointed the phone at Ryan.

"What?" my mother asked.

"He wants to apologize, and I think Ryan should do the same."

"He can't talk now, Robert."

"For five seconds, he can." My dad forced the phone into Ryan's hand. He held it to his ear.

"Hello? Yeah. Well, I shouldn't've… Sorry. Alright. Bye." He clicked it off.

Anxiety flooded over me again as Ryan hung up the phone. I hadn't gotten a chance to talk to TJ, to tell him it was okay, or ask him how he was. The furious expression he'd worn glaring down at Ryan was all I saw when I closed my eyes. I needed to see him.

"Well, now that's a step," my dad remarked.

"What did he say? Is he alright?" I begged.

"Tommy? Is Tommy alright?" My mother's shrill voice cut the air.

"You didn't hear what Ryan said!" I cried. "I want to go see if he's okay."

"Absolutely not!"

"Not tonight, kiddo," my dad said rather forcefully.

"You are *done* seeing him."

"Suzanne, you're being irrational."

"Because my son was assaulted right outside our house? You treat this as if nothing has happened!" she cried furiously.

"Boys fight, Suzanne. It happens," he insisted.

"Boys fight? Ryan didn't even touch Tommy! You call that a fight? He was assaulted. I knew that family was—"

"Please," he cut her off. "Tommy means a lot to Rebecca, and we're not going to end her friendship with him over one incident. It'll all turn out fine."

"Why do you always insist everything's fine? Just like Rachel was fine, right?" she spat.

"Oh, wonderful. Are we there again, Suzanne? Are we going to go down that path now?"

"Everything is fine, Robert. Right? Ryan's nose, Rebecca's hair, her hobbies, her friends. *It's not* fine!" she yelled.

"Why are you so adamant that it's not? If you would look a little closer, Rebecca *is* fine!"

Ryan and I stared at each other as if we were being pulled toward a pit of alligators in a game of tug-o-war. At least, we finally had something in common. We shared a hopeless look across the table as our parents tore each other apart in front of our very eyes.

It was the worst fight they'd ever had, and my heart ached all night as I cried myself to sleep, my arms wrapped tightly around Buddy.

CHAPTER 25

Birthday Bash

Once again, I had a boatload of work to do in classes for the week. A research project in one class, exams in another, and a huge paper in another had me feeling stressed.

Everybody was feeling the pinch. Of course, Amy still went out three nights during the week.

In addition to my obligations, I helped Lindsay create an ocean life thematic unit for her practicum class that she was stressing over. I worked primarily on drawings and graphics, and she handled the content. The display turned out to be magical, and Lindsay burst with praise and gratitude.

Jason and I spent the week bickering about me coming home and seeing me in general. His relentless requests about going home together made sense. I understood his need for me. I *wished* I wanted to see him more.

I persuaded Jason to come down the following weekend, and that pleased him for the time being. Amy would be out of town anyway, so that would help ease the tension. I'd noticed that Jason tried to hold me tighter when I pulled away. So, I decided I'd just relax and let things happen. I'd try to be more open with Jason and see where it would take us.

TJ was having quite an effect on me. My mother sensed it too. But I wasn't talking to her that much. I analyzed everything she said even more than usual. When I'd mention something about TJ or anything remotely fun, she would nag me about not messing up my grades. It was just easier to say very little about my life in general or something cute about Jason. Then she'd shut up. Mentioning him in conversation was my only way out of her constant criticism.

Still, I could never break out of the cycle I was locked in with her. She kept bugging me about what I should be doing, and I didn't want to discuss anything with her.

Even with all of that business going on, I locked myself in my room one night and drew a little present for TJ's birthday. He was becoming more and more important to me, just like when we were kids. And we were spending so much time together. He wasn't attached to technology like most other college students but did send me some goofy texts from time to time, mostly from the Rec Center when he was bored.

With my newfound confidence in drawing, thanks to Lindsay's raves and TJ's pride in the drawing I'd done for him years ago, I created a drawing for him. I sat down with a pad and paper and thought about what I could draw that he would love, even years from now. I pictured him tossing a football to his students as a future PE teacher. So, I drew a caricature of him as a coach with all kinds of sports equipment flying around him. It actually turned out pretty cute. I was sure TJ would love it.

***

That Friday, we got to the party late because Lindsay took forever to get ready, and Amy couldn't find her keys. I gingerly told Lindsay not to get crazy when I let it slip that it was TJ's birthday. She insisted on stopping somewhere to get him a card or some liquor.

Amy piped up, "You know he's not your boyfriend!"

Then Lindsay didn't speak to Amy for the rest of the night. Amy called Megan and had her meet us at TJ's house. Megan and TJ had already made out before, so that didn't help Lindsay's situation at all. I thought it was for the best, though. If anything, it would help Lindsay see the reality of her one-sided crush.

The house was jumping, packed like I'd never seen it. There were so many bodies that even with the windows open in forty-degree weather, it was stifling. Trevor greeted us as soon as we came in. He handed us cups and pointed toward the keg. Lindsay didn't want beer, so Trevor guided her to his private stash of hard alcohol. She seemed to loosen up with him a bit after that.

As we passed through the living room and headed toward the beer, we found TJ doing a keg stand in the kitchen. Amy thought that was awesome. She wanted to be next in line, so she tried to finagle a chance by flirting. When he got down, beer was soaked into his hair, and it dripped everywhere. TJ shook off like a dog and gave everyone in the kitchen a nice sprinkle, causing shrieks and laughter. He wiped his eyes and glanced up.

"Beck!" TJ hollered and threw his fists up. He stumbled over to me and flung his arms around me clumsily, dampening my clothes with beer.

I just shook my head at him. "Thanks for comin', Beck," he mumbled through an adorable smile and unfocused eyes.

"Happy birthday TJ. Are you okay?"

"Never better, Beck, benetter never," he tried to explain. I laughed loudly. He finally let go of me then assessed my empty hands. "You need a drink. Want a beer? Or whatever you want."

"Beer's fine."

He pulled my arm toward the keg and playfully pushed Mason's cup out of the way. Mason faked to punch him.

"Beck needs a beer," TJ explained, filling up my cup.

"Oh, I see. How are you, Beck?" Mason nodded at me.

"Good Mase, how are you?"

"Can't complain. What the hell are you doing?" he barked at TJ, "It's all foam."

"What are you talking about?" he asked Mason.

"Gimme this." Mason took my cup and chucked the foamy beer through the window screen. I covered my mouth to avoid busting out. "Pay attention," Mason ordered. He pumped the keg a few times then poured the beer, so it ran clear down the side of the cup.

"Hey, thanks, bro," TJ said happily, slapping him on the shoulder.

"So, Beck, are you in?" Mason asked, teasing.

"In what? A card game?"

"Yep. Poker. Two minutes." He handed me the cup.

"Sure, I'm in. You got enough cash this time?" I joked and took a sip.

"Aww, man! She's got your number, Mase," TJ laughed and threw his arm around me again.

"Stashed in cash." Mason nodded, smiling.

Amy seemed to be making friends, especially with Brandon. Lindsay was practically drinking from the bottle of Jack Daniels that Trevor shared with her. I grabbed the picture I'd made for TJ that I'd stashed by the door when we'd come in, snuck into his room, and set it on the shelf next to the old one I'd made all those years ago. I knew he would see it in the morning when he was sober.

Trevor was trying very hard to be sweet to Lindsay, but she was just becoming too drunk. Megan came by after a while with a bottle of tequila, sliced limes, and a saltshaker. It was a special gift for the birthday boy, she said. She was dressed skimpily in a low-cut, skin-tight top, painted on ripped jeans, and tall, black leather boots. She strutted right up to TJ and gave him a birthday kiss. Then she asked if he wanted to do a body shot.

"Hey! Good call on the stripper!" Brandon called out, sending our group into a fit of laughter.

The next thing we knew, a whole crowd started throwing back tequila shots. TJ did a body shot off Megan, which he seemed to enjoy. After a few of those, Trevor confiscated the bottle to save TJ. I thought that was a good move, seeing that TJ was already wasted. Megan quickly became drunk and couldn't keep her hands or tongue off him. This caused Lindsay to drink even more to the point of puking outside their house. Poor Trevor knew he didn't have a prayer then.

I walked Lindsay home, thinking the cool air plus the long walk would help to sober her up. Also, I didn't want to spoil Amy's fun and make her leave. She had disappeared with Brandon. TJ and Megan were nowhere to be found, so I waved goodbye to the rest of the crowded house, and we started our long journey home.

Lindsay didn't do too badly, considering her state. It was 2:00 a.m. by the time we finally stumbled in with aching feet and cold noses. Lindsay barely avoided stepping on Scooter in the hallway then crashed onto her bed. I washed up then lay awake for a while, replaying the night's events in my mind. I knew Lindsay had feelings for TJ, but I didn't see that connection. Also, I couldn't shake off the image of Megan molesting TJ. Then I just became annoyed with myself for even allowing that thought. I shook my head, turned over, and finally dozed off.

CHAPTER 26

Escape

"Rebecca, get up. It's 10:15."

I blinked a few times and saw my mother's shadow in the hallway. As I rolled over and squinted at my digital clock, I remembered why I'd had such a rough night's sleep. I recalled many of the terrible comments from the day before that had come from my mother and Ryan. The sick feeling came back to the pit of my stomach. I wished for my dad to be home but knew he wouldn't be. Couldn't I just stay in bed all day?

I knew my mother wouldn't allow me to see TJ even though Ryan had hurt him beyond belief, even though he had stood up for me, even though TJ had called and apologized, even though my dad thought it would be fine, and even though he was my best friend. She didn't care. None of it mattered.

"Rebecca, get up," her eyes scolded me as I stared back with a look of sad resentment. "Melanie and Marilyn Abrams will be here in half an hour. You need to wash up, get dressed, and make your bed. Now."

I couldn't believe what I was hearing, "What?"

"Melanie is coming over. Now get up." She opened one of my drawers and pulled out a pair of daisy-flowered shorts and a yellow top to match.

"Why does she keep coming here? I don't want her here!"

My mother issued an angry look. I'd never expressed such strong disagreement with her before. It was surprising to me even, but I didn't apologize.

"We are not discussing this; get dressed." She turned on her heel and marched out of my room and downstairs.

ESCAPE

I made up my mind then. I would *not* sit there in the front room playing Barbies again with someone I had nothing in common with—someone my mother had chosen as a friend for me. I got up, put on her stupid outfit, and tried to calm myself down. Then I walked Buddy downstairs and grabbed a bowl of cereal. Ryan came up from the basement and stopped when he saw me. His upper cheek was puffy and bruised near his eye. We swapped a knowing look but didn't say anything. He silently climbed up the steps and disappeared.

I ate my cereal like an inmate on death row, coldly awaiting the arrival of the white-blond-haired princess.

A few minutes later, my mom called from the front room window, "Oh, here they are! Rebecca, be polite. Come on." She walked out the door to greet them in the driveway.

My heart racing, I slid open the sliding door and zoomed it closed, then silently tiptoed to the garage and pulled my bike from the side door. I waited on the side of the house, listening to make sure it was safe to take off.

"Don't you look adorable, Melanie? Rebecca was so anxious to see you today."

The door shut. I imagined my mother calling for me at that second. In a mad rush of adrenaline, I jumped on my bike and took off as fast as my legs would pedal. The warm breeze slapped me in the face. I blinked furiously, trying to block the stinging wind as I stood on the pedals to charge even faster.

By now, my mother would be looking in every room, calling "Rebecca, Rebecca," in a light tone she'd strike just for Marilyn when I knew she wanted to scream her head off. At first, she would be confused until she saw the side door of the garage ajar and my bike missing. Then she would be outraged and make up an excuse to Mrs. Abrams like, "She must've run over to the neighbors," or "She's sick on my bed. Perhaps another time."

I was shaking from the catastrophe I had just created and would have to face eventually. All I could do was ride faster and farther. My bike seemed to steer itself to TJ's block. I saw him down the street, leading the lawnmower toward the side of the house. Shards of grass lay along the edges of the sidewalk.

TJ must've heard the humming of my tires and turned in my direction. His golden hair shone with perspiration. He dropped his mouth open when he saw me. I rode closer, the sweat beading around my hairline and on the back of my neck.

"Come on!" I gasped, waving him on.

He must've sensed my urgency and called into the house, "Mom, I'm going for a ride." Then without waiting for a reply, he lifted his bike off the sidewalk and mounted it. I whipped my head back behind me in worry and again sped toward the trail.

"Beck, hold on," TJ pleaded, trying to catch up, "What's going on?"

I ignored his question and kept peddling.

"Did your mom let you come over here?"

"No," I breathed.

"Is Ryan okay?"

"Who cares? He's a jerk." I zoned out as I flew down the street, turning on a dime to get to our secret spot.

"Slow down!"

"I can't!"

"Why not? What happened?"

"I'm not staying there! I hate it!" I choked out, my eyes welling with tears.

He stopped asking questions, and we said nothing. He knew I had to escape, and he let me. TJ simply came with me to let me have my moment of losing control.

We zipped through the trail, my heart hammering in my chest. "Beck, slow down."

ESCAPE

"We've got to check on them. They might be in trouble. They might be all gone," I cried, pretending to worry for the turtles. That would distract me enough for the moment.

"Beck, please slow down."

I forgot the drop-off.

I only wanted to get to the pond or anywhere else—to get out of sight. I forgot how the path narrowed and how the left side disappeared three feet below.

It happened so fast.

I was speeding toward the pond one second, and in the next second, my back tire dropped off the side of the trail. My bike and I came crashing down on my ankle, smashing me into the mud and rocks, my ankle pinned under my back tire.

"Beck!" TJ yelled. I heard a thud as he threw his bike down to find me.

Pain seared into me. I shut my eyes and grimaced, trying to pull the bike off my scratched and twisted ankle.

TJ hopped down into the hole with one hand on the dirt ledge above. "Beck, are you okay?" He searched me over breathlessly. My whole body was sweaty and throbbing. I could only whimper in pain and clench my jaw.

"Oh no. Here, I've got to pull your foot out."

"No," I said.

"Beck, come on, I gotta get you home."

"No!" I cried. My lip quivered. My ankle pulsed in agony, but the thought of going home was worse.

TJ looked helpless. "Please, Beck." He gently raised the end of my bike off me. As it moved, a shiver of pain snaked through my leg.

"Ahh," I moaned, my eyes filling with tears. I fought them back. He bent down to pull me up, and I prepared my body for the jolt of pain coming.

I gripped down hard on the rocky moss beneath my left hand, trying to prop myself up. TJ hung low, pulled my right arm firmly over his shoulder, and slowly heaved me up onto my right leg.

I groaned again loudly, trying to rebalance, beyond devastated. All I wanted to do was run away—from my mother and Ryan, away from the aggravation that surrounded me at home and pulled my spirit down. I only wanted, like always, to be with TJ, to be free and comforted and welcomed. Now, I was in a terrible mess.

"I'm sorry."

We hobbled out of the drop-off, then TJ scooped me up and trudged with me in his arms quickly down the trail, leaving our bikes behind. We walked a few yards with my hands wrapped tightly around his neck. I buried my sweaty head into his shoulder and cried silent, miserable tears. My ankle felt as if it would explode with every bounce of TJ's trot.

"I'm sorry. Just hang on."

He was so strong for his age yet strained every muscle trying to hold me up. We were nearly at the end of the trail, halfway to his house, when he slowed to a stop.

"I gotta put you down for a second," he panted. I nodded into his shoulder. TJ slid me off his arms and onto my right leg. I kept my arm pressed on his back. He breathed hard, his hands on his knees. His orange t-shirt was soaked down the center of his back. Then he took a giant breath and looked up at me like his heart had broken. I bit my lip as tears streaked my face.

"Okay, I'm gonna carry you on my back. Just hold your leg out, and I'll grab it. Wrap yourself around me."

I moaned and nodded. My ankle was swelling right before my eyes. TJ grabbed behind and held my leg. I hopped on his back with my other leg with all my might. He caught me, and I curled myself around him tightly. I forced my injured leg away from him. Again, I flung my arms around his shoulders and dove my sobbing face into his warm neck with the constant surge of pain pounding through my body.

"Just a few more minutes, Beck. You'll be ar-right," he breathed heavily and marched on.

ESCAPE

We had made it to the corner around his block. TJ's breaths got faster and shallower; his pace slowed with every step.

"Pete!" he shouted suddenly. I picked my head up to see Pete riding toward us. "Get my mom quick!" Pete tore down the street and up the driveway of TJ's house. Mrs. Lawson came out straight away. She hurried toward us.

"Oh, my goodness! Tommy? Becky? What is it?" She pulled me off him and into her arms, her eyes scanning over me. She saw my ankle, which was purplish and swollen, and cradled me closer.

"My sweet Becky. Oh no," she soothed. "Tommy, go run and grab an ice pack from the freezer."

"I'll get it," Pete offered and ran into the Lawson's home. TJ was still trying to catch his breath. Seconds later, Pete and Katie came out with the ice pack.

Mrs. Lawson set me on the front step, then carefully lifted my swollen, dirt-smeared leg and set the ice pack down gently on my ankle.

"Ouch," I cried.

"I know, sweetheart. I'm sorry, but it has to be done."

TJ slumped down beside me, drenched and still out of breath.

"Katie, grab the phone for Mom and bring it here," Katie ran in promptly to get it. Mrs. Lawson repositioned the pack as she crouched over the cement, still holding my leg up on hers.

She grabbed the phone from Katie and dialed. I started crying again in agony, knowing whose number was being called. After a second, she said, "Suzanne, it's Janet. She's here, and she's hurt her ankle badly. I think it may be broken. Yes, all right." She hung up and handed Katie the phone. "Sweet pea, get a cold, wet rag for Becky." Mrs. Lawson pushed the hair out of my eyes and wiped my tear-stained cheeks with the backs of her hands. "Sweetheart."

TJ squeezed my hand and covered it with his other hand. Katie handed Mrs. Lawson a cold, wet cloth, and she smoothed it over my face and neck, cleaning me up.

Before I knew it, my mother's car came racing down the street and stopped in front of TJ's house. Ryan was sitting in the front seat. He looked out at us, then turned his head away. My mother frantically flew out of the car, on the verge of tears.

"Dear God. Rebecca, what happened?" She knelt beside Mrs. Lawson, moved her eyes over my ankle, and pulled at my bloodstained elbow.

"She fell off the drop on the trail," TJ said.

My mother hoisted me up, anger billowing in her eyes. "Let's go! Maybe we'll get a two-for-one deal at the emergency room," she said roughly. Ryan stepped out and opened the back door.

"I'm so sorry, Suzanne. Please call and let us know how she is."

My mother ignored Mrs. Lawson, set me in the back seat, and slammed the car door. I turned to look out the window, and through bleary eyes, saw TJ standing solemnly on the first step, staring at our car as we sped away.

CHAPTER 27

Apology

Amy stumbled in just after dawn, waking me up in the process. She never liked to be alone, so I knew she'd come bounding into my room to tell me about her night. Lindsay was still sleeping off her hangover while Amy raved about the great night she and "Tommy's roommate" had. I explained that his name was Brandon. She laughed it off and continued rambling.

"He's got a killer body. My God! It was so good," she ranted before coming up for a breath. "So, when did you take off? I sent you like five texts."

"Huh?" I said, reaching toward my nightstand for my phone. It was gone. "Oh no," I moaned, searching my bed.

"You lost your phone."

"Crap."

"Well, it'll probably turn up. So, what did I miss?"

She was oblivious to my worries as I tore my room apart. "Lindsay got sick," I blurted, lifting up my pillows futilely and rummaging through the pockets of my discarded jeans.

"Nice. So, is she over Tommy boy or what because he and Megan…?"

"Yeah, I don't know, Aim," I said shortly and went looking in the front room.

"Alright," she yawned, "I've got to go get some real sleep now. Good night." Amy slithered out of my room and into hers, then shut the door.

I continued to search around the apartment for my phone, knowing I wouldn't find it. After being up for a half-hour already, I wasn't tired anymore. I figured I should probably work on my paper. So, I sat down at my computer desk in my room and outlined a rough draft.

About two hours later, I was making good progress when I heard a soft knock on my door.

"Beck?" A worn-out-looking TJ in a baseball cap and jacket called quietly. He peeked his head through the crack of my open door. "Oh, I wasn't sure you'd be awake."

His eyes were exhausted but smiling. He'd obviously had quite a night.

"Hey," I answered with a surprised but broad smile. "What are you doing here?" I turned my chair to face him.

"Can I come in?" He gestured to sit on my bed.

"Of course." I got up and removed a stack of books.

"Oh, don't—"

"It's no big deal," I sat beside him.

"You know your front door was open."

"Amy," I explained.

"You look cute," he remarked, grinning at my pajamas.

"Uh," I snorted, "Thanks, and you look like you've had better days."

He grinned, his eyes nearly shut, "Yeah, for sure. I wanted to give you this." TJ pulled my phone out from his coat pocket.

"Oh, thank you," I gasped, reaching for it.

"Mason found it on the table. There's a very good chance that uh, that he had a few conversations with your boyfriend last night."

My eyes grew wide. "Really? Great."

"Sorry."

I could just imagine Jason talking to a drunken Mason. Whenever Mason drank too much, he was unintelligible and hilarious. I would be stunned, however, if Jason had found any part of their conversation amusing. When I quickly scanned my texts, I gasped to see the evidence of Mason's and Jason's interactions.

> "hey baby is this a booty call"

APOLOGY

> "Who is this?"

> "who do u want it to be"

> "Where is Rebecca?"

> "who is rebecca"

> "yor Jason right"

> "You're a clever one."

> "im mason"

> "I'm losing interest in this conversation."

> "Where is Rebecca?"

> "we should call ourselves the Ason brothers get it"

> "Right. Please give my girlfriend her phone back, asshole."

> "oops u spelled it rong ... its Ason but since yor into aholes...."

Then Mason signed off with a blurry selfie of his ass.

"Oh, God." I covered part of my face with my hand and dropped my phone onto my bed as if it had burned me. How in the world would I explain any of that to Jason?

"You should really utilize that lock screen feature, Beck," TJ offered, barely able to hold back his amusement.

When I glanced up at him, we both burst out laughing.

"Look, I..." he started. "That's not the only reason I wanted to come over here," he said in a suddenly uncomfortable tone. "I saw the picture."

"Oh yeah?"

"That was really neat, Beck. It's like, the coolest drawing I've ever seen." He shook his head. "Honestly though, seeing that this morning kind of made me feel like a jerk." He stared at the floor.

"Huh?"

"I just want to apologize for being a crummy host last night. You know, especially after you made me that present." His eyes quickly flashed to mine and then down again.

I screwed my eyebrows together as I regarded him. "TJ, it was your birthday. You're supposed to get wasted and crazy. I don't need you to play host."

"Yeah, that's not...." He seemed unsure how to explain what he meant. "I just feel bad about not hanging with you. I don't want to be that guy, ya know?"

I was still trying to decipher his apology when it hit me. "Oh my God, is *that* what you're apologizing for? You're crazy!" I threw my pillow in his face and giggled. He looked up in surprise and smiled.

"Are you really apologizing to me for sneaking away to get some action on your birthday?" I laughed again but felt a tinge of pink rising in my cheeks.

"Well, no, I...."

"God, I've never seen you like this," I said.

"Nothing happened with Megan." He shook his head as his own cheeks reddened.

I didn't need his explanation. Of course, I didn't. But it was relieving to hear.

"I just didn't want you to think I was scum. I want to be better to you than that," he professed with sincere eyes. I was truly surprised at his vulnerability, realizing that he meant it.

"Better than what? TJ, it's almost impossible for you to be better than you already are to me and even more impossible for me to be mad at you."

"Do you know how important you are to me?"

I leaned closer, bumping my head against his. "We're all good, okay?"

His expression changed, and he relaxed, "Ar-right."

"Do you want some water or anything?" I offered.

"No, I've gotta run. Mason's in the truck." He stood up.

"He's in your truck?" I asked in disbelief.

"Yeah, we're heading home for the weekend. What are you doing? You want to come with us?" he asked. I smiled to myself over his flighty invitation. "My mom keeps asking when she'll see you."

"No, I can't." I gestured to my paper, "But thanks."

"Aww, that sucks," he said, following my gaze.

He was almost out the door. "Gimme a 'we're all good hug,' and I'll get outta your hair." He smiled, holding his arms out. I crawled inside the warmth of his embrace and felt completely at ease for a moment. "You know, you're ar-right, Beck." He squeezed me harder once more and then went off toward home.

CHAPTER 28

Broken

A creaky step near the foot of my bed told me I had company. We had come home from the hospital the evening before, me with a cast wrapped from the ball of my foot to just below my knee, and Ryan with a copy of a CT scan. There proved to be nothing wrong with him after all, except his smart mouth. My mother argued with Dad that they should send the bill directly to the Lawsons. She made it blatantly clear how *disgusted* she was with my behavior and said again that I needed to be done seeing that family.

"Perhaps Rebecca doesn't enjoy Melanie's company and a forced friendship," my dad suggested. "And there is no chance I'm sending a bill for an unnecessary procedure to a widow with two children." Right on schedule, my mother ignored him for the rest of the night.

My ankle was fractured in two places. I would have to stay off it for six to eight weeks and be imprisoned in the house for the rest of the summer.

I'd opened my puffy eyes to see my dad trying to sneak a goodbye kiss. He gave me a sympathetic smile and sat on the side of my bed.

"How'd you sleep, kiddo?"

I pouted at him. *How do you think I slept?* My leg was propped up on pillows, and three others supported my back, head, and neck. I hadn't been able to turn or angle my body any other way. The bed was so crowded with pillows that my mother banned Buddy from sleeping with me. He seemed so confused and alarmed that each time he'd try to jump up on the bed, she pulled him down. Eventually, my mother took him into her room and closed the door. She must've gotten tired of his whining, though, because, at the first glimpse of morning light, he was back in my room beside my bed.

"I'm sorry. You'll get used to it," he said, trying to comfort me.

I shrugged my shoulders, twisting the edge of my bedsheet between my fingers.

"Are you in any pain?"

"No, not really."

"Well, I'll call and check on you later, kiddo." He leaned over and kissed my forehead. Then he got up and slapped his leg. "Come on, Buddy! Want to go outside?" Buddy sprang up, tail wagging, and pranced out the door, following my dad.

I stared, unfocused at my new cast, my splintered ankle beneath it, and then examined my crusted, sore elbow. It was stupid of me to forget the drop-off. TJ tried to warn me, but I hadn't listened. It was stupid of me to think I could outrun what was waiting for me at home.

My mother walked past my room and down the stairs. I stared at her shadow in the hallway as she passed. It was tall and elegant, poised, and cold. With my summer canceled, I could only imagine how delighted she was.

I would be trapped at home for weeks. I shut my eyes in tired frustration and nodded off to sleep again.

***

A startling ding shattered my sleep in my sun-drenched bedroom mid-afternoon. I had already managed to eat a proper lunch at the dinner table; my mother said it would be good for me. After an arduous effort, held up on her forearm, I hopped back up the stairs and collapsed onto my bed. She timidly lectured me on trying to have a good attitude, but all I could bring myself to do was sleep and stare at my cast. I woke with a jolt when the doorbell rang, then heard the creak of the front door, muffled voices for a minute, and another creak and click as the door shut.

"I'll give it to her, Mom," Ryan said in an eager voice.

"Let her sleep."

"Well, I'll put it in her room." I heard Ryan's footsteps coming up the steps and getting closer to my room. I thought for a moment to close my eyes and pretend to sleep but decided against it.

Ryan walked cautiously into my room with an envelope.

"Hey," he said and paused to look at me for a moment.

"Hey," I answered, eyes half-open.

"Tommy brought this over with your bike. Mom told him you were sleeping." He handed me the card and stood as if waiting for me to open it and share it with him.

I set it on my lap, gazing at it wearily for a while.

"Want anything?" Ryan spoke at last.

I was startled at his uncharacteristic effort and turned my head to find his eyes on mine.

"No thanks."

With that, he left my room.

The day carried on that way, with me in a state of sleep-induced depression. I ate dinner and quietly watched the Sox with my dad and Buddy. By the following morning, I'd mostly snapped out of my miserable state thanks to another bizarre encounter with my brother.

My mother was on the phone with Aunt Colleen discussing an upcoming visit while I sat at the dining room table numbly watching TV beside my unfinished bowl of Apple Jacks.

"Here, I thought you could use this," Ryan said, pulling up the chair next to me and sitting down.

"What?" I asked suspiciously.

He set down a thin book. *Do it Yourself Doodles and Drawings*. I looked him over.

"It teaches you how to draw really cool stuff. Look." Ryan flipped around to some pictures he'd drawn from the step-by-step illustrations. There were all different types of animals and insects. He stopped on a fly that he drew. It looked identical to the sample next to it.

"See? It breaks down all the steps."

"Did you really draw that? That's good."

"Yeah, thanks. I figured you might want to draw or something. I'm done with it so, use whatever you want." He shrugged his shoulders and scooted past me through the sliding doors to our backyard.

I scoured through the book, fascinated with its contents. In addition to the fly, my brother had drawn a lion, zebra, T-Rex, and grasshopper. They were amazing. Each was sketched with geometrical shapes, then rounded off into limbs and backs, claws, and faces. Apparently, he had more talent than I knew about. I stopped at a blank page with a box turtle and smiled as I looked it over, then snapped my head up at the memory of the turtle's nest. I'd wanted to see if they had hatched yet on the day of the accident. I thought about TJ as if I had just remembered some wonderful plan set for the afternoon. But I hadn't even opened his card yet.

"Come on, Buddy, help me upstairs," I beckoned him to me. He carried the book gently in his mouth as I forged up the staircase.

Two minutes later, I'd reached my bed and the card shut in its envelope on the nightstand. I pulled the drawing book with its newly moistened cover from Buddy's mouth and thanked him with a kiss. He lay by my bed, cleaning his paws as I opened the card.

It had three bright blue balloons on the front and read "Get Well Soon" in big bubble letters. I opened it. The printed message wrote: "It sure is sad, things sure are blue when you're not feeling quite like you. Get well soon."

Below it was squiggly cursive words from Mrs. Lawson: "Becky sweetie, I'm sorry about your ankle – get better. Love, Mrs. Lawson & Katie" with a heart around the message. On the opposite side of the card was a roughly horrid drawing of what appeared to be me in a bed with a cast around my leg. I laughed at how awful TJ's drawing was. Under the picture was a sloppy handwritten poem.

Don't be sad, don't feel blue,
Because you can't put on your favorite, smelly shoe.
Don't be mad and just sit on the grass,
Cuz you're still faster than Garcia with your leg in a cast.

He had drawn a tongue smiley face. And then...

Love, TJ.

His ridiculous poem lifted my spirits, and I couldn't stop staring at: *Love, TJ.*

It had only been two days since I'd seen TJ, but it felt like a month. I changed into a cutesy outfit since all my cut-offs were too tight to get around my cast. Then I tossed my crutches to the base of the stairway and hopped downstairs, banging away at each step as I went. Buddy was near to panic, thinking I was hurting myself. He actually barked at me, which I took to mean, "Be careful!"

"What are you doing?" My mother walked over. She had on cleaning gloves and held a rag. Even when she was working around the house, not a hair was out of place. Her hair was a beautiful, deep chocolate color, but in direct sunlight, it glinted hints of red. It hung loosely on her shoulders and mirrored her deep, brown eyes. I had my dad's hazel eyes that turned green or brown, depending on what I was wearing. My mother and I only shared the same pouty lips.

"Rebecca, don't jump down the stairs. You could seriously injure your good leg, and then where would we be?"

"Sorry."

"Where do you think you're going?" she asked, eyeing my wardrobe and one shoe as I stooped to grab my crutches off the carpet. I looked up at her, my hope deflated.

"I wanted to thank TJ for the card."

She shook her head.

"I don't think that's a good idea." I waited for her to explain why knowing it was coming. "You are not going three blocks on crutches."

"What if you drive me over there?"

"No. Besides, I'm sure he'll come looking for you anyway." The annoyance in her tone was undeniable. "Plus, Aunt Colleen and your cousins will be over in two days, so why don't you help me dust the pieces in the china cabinet?"

I hopped over to the loveseat and plunked down.

She grabbed a can of cleaner, then sprayed a small coat on the rag she was holding and handed it to me.

"Don't I need gloves?" I asked, looking over at hers as I started smoothly rubbing the plates with the rag.

"No, I just need them to protect my rings and bracelets and manicure." She stiffly smiled at me.

"Oh. What's a manicure?" I asked, handing her the polished saucer and picking up another.

"It's a hand and nail treatment. You know, when I get my nails shaped and painted."

My mother's hands glided the rag delicately over the picture frames and relics in the cabinet. The silver frames shimmered, catching angles of the morning sun streaming through. The photo of my parents' wedding day was my favorite to examine. The old-fashioned church altar and gorgeous, snow-white, flowing gown. She looked like a princess. My mother's face was poised and tight but content. My dad looked great in a sleek, black tux and dimpled, cheerful smile.

"I love how handsome Dad looks there. Don't you?" My mother smiled faintly, looking over her shoulder at the frame I was still admiring.

"Yeah. He looks good."

"He takes good care of me," she said almost more to herself.

I set down the frame I'd been working on and picked up the next one.

"I'll take that one, please," my mother called out, reaching across my body to extract the white ceramic frame holding Rachel's fourth-grade photo. It was the last official photo of her before she'd died. I watched as my mother's eyes froze hypnotically as she gently wiped the picture down, smoothing Rachel's identical chocolate hair, dimpled smile, and deep brown, brilliant eyes. The same eyes she had. I looked away and grabbed one of my own photos to polish.

She let me handle *my* frame myself, and my jealousy for a girl I would never know reared its ugly head again. I was nonexistent once more.

We were nearly finished when the doorbell chimed, and Buddy jumped up, excited to see who it was.

"I'll get it," I said, propping myself up on a chair to grab my crutches. I began trudging toward the door, then pulled it open to see a delighted-looking boy with golden hair and eyes like the bluest sea.

"Hey, Beck!" He smiled as though amazed to see me in front of him.

"Hi, TJ!"

Relief washed over my heart, and I smiled shyly at his enormous grin. And in that one instant, just like whenever else he was around, all was right with the world. My damaged heart healed up, and my ankle was as strong as ever.

"So, you ar-right? Aww, cool," TJ said, bending low to get a close-up of my cast. "Can I knock on it?" he asked, looking up at me mischievously.

"Yeah, if you want me to kick you in the head." We laughed. I was about to invite him in, but TJ interrupted me.

"So, come on out, Beck, I've got a surprise for you."

"O … K," I said slowly. "Mom, I'll be right outside," I called, then shut the door behind me.

I hobbled down the walkway to the driveway where three rolling, oversized, flat scooters and Katie's basketball stand were all positioned. I wrinkled my nose in a smile and approached the scooters.

"See, I had this great idea, Beck. It's scooter basketball, and even you can play."

"Where'd you get these?" I motioned to the scooters.

"From Pete's dad. Come on, Beck, it'll be awesome." TJ slid two scooters toward me. I dropped my crutches in the grass and lowered myself onto one scooter, then propped my left leg on the other one.

"Cool, huh?" TJ eyed my enthusiasm.

"Yeah."

We played all afternoon, carting sideways, forward, and backward, tossing the ball and bouncing it to each other. TJ's long arms made shooting the ball in the hoop look effortless. It was a little harder for me to maneuver with two scooters, but I held my own and made a great many assists.

An hour flew by. Our backs were sore, and our arms were tired from shooting and pushing off the cement. We had indentations of gravel bits in our hands which were dry and dusty. TJ's shirt clung to his body with sweat. I was hot, sweaty, good, and dirty.

After a little break, TJ came up with more ideas for fun.

He told me he was going to push me down the street on my scooters; then, he'd jump onto his own scooter to see who could coast the longest. TJ had just pulled our scooters out onto the street, had me sit, and put his hands on my shoulders when my mother opened the front door.

"What do you think you're doing?"

TJ and I froze in surprised panic. "Hey Mrs. Winslow, I was just–"

"Get the scooters off the street." Her eyes drilled into us.

"Sure," TJ said, helping to lift me up. He dragged the scooters back onto the driveway.

"Oops." He smiled at me.

TJ had a blast walking with my crutches. He said he couldn't wait to go out and buy a pair. He lunged himself forward and threw his feet up in the air. After five minutes of that, he tried turning my crutches upside down to walk on the grips like stilts. I was enthralled at how much fun he was having. After his eighth attempt, he managed to walk a couple of steps. Then he fell with a thud, and I let out a howl of laughter. He laughed along with me. Soon, my dad pulled up in the driveway as TJ cleared out the scooters to make a space for him.

"Hey, Tommy!" My dad yelled out the window.

"Hi, Mr. Winslow. How was work?" TJ asked eagerly.

"Same old, same old, not bad." Dad winked.

"Hi, Dad!"

"Well, well, well, look who's in a better mood." He raised his eyebrows and smirked at me. "You have quite a remarkable effect on my daughter," my dad directed at TJ. They both looked at me and smiled. "She always seems to feel better when you're around."

I felt my face grow hot with a burst of embarrassment. TJ must've sensed it and looked away.

"Alright, take care, Tommy. We're probably eating soon, kiddo."

"Okay."

My dad walked into the house. For the first time ever, there was an awkward silence between TJ and me. He walked over to me, crutches in one hand, as he extended his other.

"Come on. I'll help you up."

I grabbed his hand and thrust myself up, then took hold of my crutches. I glanced nervously into his eyes and was intrigued by a hint of sadness within. He looked me over for a minute and opened his mouth to speak but closed it too soon.

"Hey!" His eyes suddenly flew open wide with another idea. "Tomorrow, I'll pull you from my bike with a rope attached to your scooter. It'll be awesome! Oh, and I checked on the eggs for you. It looks like they're all still okay."

"Yeah?" I felt butterflies in my stomach, thinking that I had not yet thanked him for the card or anything else.

I knew I had to. "TJ, thanks," I said.

"Sure," he said casually.

"No, I mean, I'm glad you checked the turtle eggs, but thanks for everything else. Really." My eyes scanned the street as I said it, feeling too embarrassed to look at him.

He bit his lip, then smiled at me, "No problem, Beck. I'll see ya. We'll try the scooter trick after the game." Then realizing in an instant that I couldn't play football, he added, "You wanna ref?"

"Sure!"

He headed home, and I left the scene of a brilliant summer day in tremendous spirits as I nursed my way through the front door.

CHAPTER 29

Comfort

"No, no, no," Mrs. Mac called out. "This is a one-two-three, one-two-three rhythm. Got it?" Mrs. Mac corrected one of the guys.

We were learning the Viennese Waltz, Lindsay's new favorite. She'd finally seemed to accept the fact that she and TJ wouldn't work out. Even though she was bitter, she slowly became her talkative self again. I even saw her laughing with Freddie during the first dance.

TJ was pretty bad at the waltz. He kept commenting on my skillful dancing. I rolled my eyes at him, but deep down, I knew I was good. Mrs. Mac used me for a lot of demonstrations, despite my lack of volunteering. TJ told me that everybody noticed me and that Gabriel was tired of being shown up. He was Latino and had a flair for dancing. Gabriel was light on his feet and twisted and pivoted with lots of hip action. All the girls liked dancing with him. Lindsay especially loved Gabriel, as together, they would gush over all the attractive men in class.

"So, how was home?" I asked, getting off the topic of my great dancing. "You've recovered?"

"Oh yeah, it was great. My mom threw me a little party. You know, cake, ice cream, strippers with whipped cream, the whole bit."

"Wow, that was really sweet of your mom," I said, playing along.

"Yeah, she's great. You know that she and Howard are swingers, right?" He continued but cracked a smile. I shook my head, grinning. "But really, I went fishing with Howard, played some cards, and sang karaoke."

"You won't give up the singing, huh?"

"Beck, it's my livelihood."

"Mmm-hmm. What was that song you always used to sing? Sunshine or something?" I asked.

"'Walking on Sunshine,' Katrina & The Waves!" TJ said and started singing loudly.

"That's enough." I smiled, then turned my head and sneezed twice.

"Gesundheit," TJ said. "Hey, what about you? Have you been home lately?"

I looked up at him and searched for what I could say. But I just felt so uneasy whenever I heard the dreaded "Why haven't you been back home?"

I was aware of being out of the norm, having not been home since Christmas. The confused looks and questions from whoever asked made me uncomfortable.

Unlike everybody else, though, TJ didn't hassle me with a million questions about my absenteeism.

"So, that's a no then." He smiled sweetly. "Do you want to talk about it? Wait a minute; survey says: 'dumb idea, Tom.' Sorry, Beck, I forgot with whom I was speaking," he teased.

"Well, no, there's nothing to say. I just haven't been home in a while." I sniffled, feeling my immune system weaken.

"That's okay." He looked earnestly at me. "You don't have to explain to me, remember?"

Although he claimed I didn't need to explain anything, I read his face and realized I was shutting him out. I didn't want to go there. I never did. I didn't want to take him down that rabbit hole of emptiness, of feeling not good enough, of feeling Rachel's eyes watching me from her photo all the time and taking me over. But this was TJ, and I wanted to give him a tiny piece.

"I just don't feel comfortable there anymore." I sniffed again. Being with him at Eastern made home seem removed.

"I'm sorry to hear that." TJ burned his eyes into mine, seeping sympathy.

I quickly covered my mouth as I sneezed again and shivered. "Bless you. Uh oh, you're getting sick?" I shrugged. "But, um, Beck, I need you to do something for me."

A tired giggle passed over me at the flighty TJ having difficulty once again remaining in one conversation. "Sure."

"Great. Thanks a lot. Wow, I didn't think it would be that easy. So, ar-right that'll be awesome," he ranted. I gave him a quizzical look.

"I need you to come to my mom's wedding with me. Otherwise, I can't go." I looked at him in confusion. "Seriously. My mom said, 'Either Becky's coming with you, or you're not invited at all,' and then she stormed out of the room."

"She did not."

"I swear."

"Your mom would never say that to you."

The room got noisier as everyone switched partners. "Sorry, we can't switch right now. She's infected and contagious," he told Casey and Brooke, who were approaching as he twirled me away. TJ always found opportunities to avoid rotating when I danced with him. It made me feel protected in a warm way. He never even bothered to ask me if I was okay with it. It was cute and expected that he always wanted to dance with me.

"Okay, she didn't exactly say that, but she *really* wants you to be there, for real."

"When?" I began imagining a weekend escape from school, Jason, and my mother. Plus, I would be with the Lawsons—the family that so long ago had meant more to me than my own. Talking about going home usually stressed me out and made me clam up. This time, I was all too eager.

"In three weeks, the weekend after spring break. Please, I'll give you a dollar."

"Yeah, I'll go," I chuckled.

"Really?" He beamed.

"Yeah, I'd love to." I shivered again.

"Awesome, it's a deal. But I'll have to owe you that dollar. You promise you'll come with me?" he asked.

"I promise. Keep your dollar."

***

I was exhausted after class. My head spun with thoughts of my projects, reports, and spring break approaching. I also had to find a way to tell my mother and Jason about the Lawson wedding.

My head ached, and my ears popped with each stretch of my jaw. I went to work just for a bit and then went home sick. By Thursday, the virus consumed me and left me so sleep-deprived that I couldn't relax and rest.

My mother called me, and I couldn't even attempt to sound normal due to my congestion and exhaustion. She flew into a panic over my illness, drilling me about my symptoms, and demanded that I go to the health services building immediately. I should've taken it as comforting that she was so worked up over my sickness. She always freaked out whenever Ryan or I got sick. I understood why—Rachel had died of the flu after all—but it just made me annoyed at her overbearing control.

To add even more unpleasantness, Jason got upset with me, stating that I was faking at being sick to avoid him. Later on, after he realized I was truly under the weather, he emailed me a virtual bouquet of flowers and apologized. My mother must've let him know how sick I actually was. The virtual flowers only proved my point that she was way too involved in our relationship. The only part of my life that she knew or cared about was Jason. It didn't help that our moms knew each other and constantly gossiped. Jason's mom was very wealthy and influential in their little circle of friends, so of course, my mother had to make sure everything was perfect between the two of us. She couldn't bear to have Jason and me at odds with each other, or it would cause tension with her stuck-up friend group.

Later Thursday afternoon, I tossed and turned on the couch, having given up on my bed, and missed my classes that day, including Ballroom Dance. Lindsay was a real friend and made me soup when she got home. She was so sweet and nurturing and even bought me a vaporizer that she filled up and turned on. Every so often, she sneaked back in to readjust the angle of the steam. It was very thoughtful but also disruptive. I still couldn't sleep and was going out of my mind when I heard a knock on the door.

"Hang on!" Amy yelled, bounding down the hall toward the door. Had I been able to sleep, her loud mouth would have woken me a hundred times over. She turned the lock on the door and opened it.

"Hey, Amy."

"Tommy boy! What a pleasant surprise."

TJ came in and stared at my spent self. "What's the diagnosis, Beck?" he asked.

I shook my head miserably, my eyes closed.

"That was a killer party you had, Tommy boy. I had a blast!" Amy yelled from the kitchen, opening and banging drawers.

"Oh yeah?" TJ answered blankly. He took off his coat and sat down on the chair nearest the couch.

"Quite the fiesta. Miss Rebecca, where the hell is our packing tape?"

"Aim! Please, shut up," I whined.

"Fine, I'll ask Lindsay," she said, slightly put off, and went toward her room.

"Uh," I moaned and rubbed a tissue on my nose. TJ examined me with a soft expression.

"What can I do for you? Have you been to the doctor?"

"Health circus ..." I rolled my eyes.

"That's a good one. They give you anything?"

"Of course, Robitussin."

"Ah, yes, of course. The cure-all for flu, ingrown toenails, and genital herpes," he teased.

"Mmm-hmm. I just need to sleep. I can't sleep, and I know I'd feel better if I could just freaking shut down, you know?" I vented. "I'm so frustrated." I rubbed my forehead again in exhausted aggravation.

"Okay." He stood up, sounding as if he was leaving, but instead said, "Scoot over for a second."

I moved the tissues off the couch and scooted down. Then TJ took off his shoes and climbed onto the couch. He laid down, gesturing for me to lie beside him. I just stared at him with a tired smirk.

"Come here." He smiled, patting the couch. "I don't smell bad. I showered and put on more deodorant even after dance." I still looked skeptically at him. "Look, give me ten minutes, Beck. If you're not sleeping by then, I'll leave. Now please, come here." TJ motioned with his head.

He looked so adorable, and I had no strength to argue with him. I smiled and collapsed onto him with my head in the crook of his shoulder and chest. He felt so soft and comforting. Although I was moderately congested, his warm, woodsy scent put me instantly at ease. I giggled to myself, admitting that he knew me too well. He then began petting my hair and smoothing it out of my face. My eyelids got heavy.

With each breath of his, my body rose and fell in the same motion. As I breathed more deeply, I became drowsier. TJ caressed my shoulder in soft, slow strokes. After that, I was asleep.

***

Something woke me after a while. I sat up momentarily and noticed TJ. His eyes were shut, his face calm and perfect. I sighed and smiled, thinking I had never really seen him sleep before. He was always up later than me at campouts, and he definitely woke before me. It was getting darker, yet not wanting my TJ nap to be over, I set my head on him gingerly and fell back to sleep.

A long while later, I woke up. It was pitch-black in the front room except for the light from the TV shining on us. I moved a bit and shifted my head. Amy was laughing about something, and I could hear Lindsay typing in her room.

"Hey," TJ said, sounding awake. He was petting Scooter with one hand as she laid below us on the carpet, purring noisily.

"Hey." I squinted, then shot up, blinking again, confused about the darkness. It hit me at once. *TJ is supposed to be at work for the evening shift.*

"You okay?" he asked, sitting up a bit.

"Don't you have to work?" I asked, grabbing my phone and seeing that it was just after eight o'clock at night.

"Don't worry about it," he said.

"Come on."

He smiled at my reaction. "Beck, really. José is covering for me. He owes me anyway." I looked at him for a second, but he didn't flinch.

"You're crazy," I said, falling on top of him again. I couldn't believe he'd stayed all that time for me. All for the trouble of an incredibly boring, most likely uncomfortable nap with me. "You're telling me you're cool with me passed out sleeping on you, probably drooling...."

"Definite drool," he interrupted, stretching his right arm to nest behind his neck.

"For like..." I tapped my phone again to see the time. "Five hours instead of working and earning money?" I asked.

"Absolutely. For you? Absolutely." His eyes pierced mine. My heart skipped suddenly, and all I could do was stare at him.

"Hey," he said excitedly, turning back into the erratic TJ. "Did you ever notice your TV will automatically switch on and off between Spanish and English?"

"Uh, no."

"That was awesome!" He continued propping himself up a bit. "*Seinfeld* was on, and George had this totally deep voice in Spanish. It was hilarious!" I giggled at his playfulness. A few quiet moments passed. "Well, seeing that you're going to survive, I gotta get moving. I'm gonna use your bathroom first, though." He got up and walked down the hall.

COMFORT

I sat there, staring after him. He was right. It had taken less than ten minutes to put me to sleep. I was still a little sick but definitely revived.

When I glanced at my phone again, I noticed texts from my mother wanting an update about my health status and Jason checking in on me. *I shouldn't have been so harsh with him,* I thought. *It really wasn't his fault he was away from me at a different school and couldn't physically be with me.*

But in the end, it was TJ who had made me truly feel better. I couldn't figure out how he had this power over me—this positivity to make any situation better.

Being with TJ was better than any vitamin supplement.

"See ya, Amy, Linds," he called, coming back down the hall.

"You know," I explained as he looked at me with his head cocked, pulling on his coat. "My dad used to tell me that you had this amazing effect on me. That no matter what, you always made me feel better. It's so true. Thanks."

He beamed down at me, then reached out and stroked the side of my cheek gently with his fingertips. My stomach fluttered.

"Good. I need you well. Ashley was on me today like flies on crap. I can't handle that again, ar-right?" he said with a straight face.

"Sorry," I laughed.

"Just get well," he warned and walked out the door.

CHAPTER 30

Sidelined

One of Garcia's three younger sisters rode her tricycle up and down the sidewalk the next day, smiling and dodging in and out behind me and my cast during a battle of a game. I smiled and played along the first couple of times in a peek-a-boo fashion until I missed a touchdown by Pete, then I quit playing around to focus on the game.

Garcia's oversized tank top was drenched and clung onto his back. His black hair sparkled with droplets of perspiration in the sun's glare. His massive arms wiggled in the air above his head, ready to deflect the ball as Bobby launched it.

I cringed during several missed plays and wrung my hands together that I couldn't join the fun and take up my position. Matthew played on Bobby's team, and Mikey played my position with TJ and Garcia. Matthew improved throughout the game; however, he was even more obnoxious and self-centered than his brother, Bobby. On one play, he intercepted the ball from Mikey and scored a touchdown. After that, he chanted about how great he was and taunted Mikey. Mikey was livid. He looked as though he could spit fire but said nothing. Garcia mouthed off to Matthew as TJ whispered something to Mikey, causing his face to crack into a smile.

With the game over, Garcia and Mikey took off immediately, complaining about the brothers. TJ slapped hands with Pete and left Bobby and Matthew to boast to each other. He dragged his feet to my patch of grass and grinned at me through a red face, his chest puffing in and out.

"Good game," I said, trying to be positive.

"Yeah. We could've won if you'd played," TJ said. I shrugged. "Man, it's really hot out here!" He wiped his forehead.

"You can jump in the pool if you want," I suggested.

He looked delighted, then paused to look at me. "What about you? Hey, we can use your cast as an inner tube!" His eyes bulged at his bright idea.

"No thanks."

I reached my hand out so he would help me up. Then I led the way to my backyard and pointed him toward the pool. His eyes lit up, unable to hide his glee. He yanked off his shirt and shoes and dove in. I watched TJ's head bob up and down and in and out of the shimmering crystal water, almost able to feel its chilling sensation on my skin. Then I looked down at my ball and chain literally plastered to my leg and slumped into a nearby lawn chair under the patio umbrella.

TJ popped up and glanced where I had been standing, then scanned the yard to find me on the patio. His face turned sympathetic for a moment. I returned his gaze and asked, "How's the water?"

His face twisted mischievously, "Not good. It kind of…." He sniffed. "Smells like Ryan's feet. There's a bunch of bugs." He pointed around and added, "And a couple dead birds way in that corner, and it feels like my skin is melting off me! I gotta get out of here!"

My whole body jiggled up and down with laughter. Then he pushed his arms off the deck and effortlessly jumped to his feet. He fiercely started shaking his whole body side to side like Buddy. Blasts of water spun off from his hair and shorts. I laughed uproariously. And the harder I laughed, the harder he twisted himself. I howled as he stumbled, still whipping from side to side, then lifted one leg and shook himself sideways back into the pool. My eyes watered, and my stomach ached with delight.

***

After TJ's dip in the pool, just as he'd promised, he set me up on a rope contraption to pull me on the scooters with his bike. His idea worked better in his head than the actual result. A couple of times, I felt a rush of wind as I rolled along the smooth surface of the pavement, but mostly the rope would burn my hands, or he would slow down too fast as I would coast past him with a mixture of excitement and terror.

Ryan and Scott rode by on their skateboards during one attempt. Ryan shook his head as he passed us. Scott seemed confused and simply continued his conversation with Ryan.

The experiment was finally over when my mother stood at the door, horrified. She barked, "No more!" We looked at each other with guilty expressions, then untied the rope from his bike.

"Well, I should go anyway," TJ said.

"Yeah. Auntie Helen is probably wondering where you are."

"No." He looked away. "My mom's home today."

"She's been home a lot this summer, huh?"

He continued to fiddle with the rope. I watched him carefully. I was about to ask why but he didn't seem to want to talk about it. His chin quivered slightly as he got the rope untied, and when he paused to glance up at me, his eyes were cloudy and lost. It was over eighty-four degrees in the sun, and we were standing on scalding black pavement, yet a shiver went up my spine.

"I got to tell you something, Beck," he whispered and glanced around nervously. His eyes, on the verge of tears, met mine.

Then he opened his mouth and said in a rush, "I forgot to check on the turtle eggs." I said nothing, and he went on. "I'll go check on them now, ar-right?"

TJ got up and threw his leg around his bike seat.

"So, see ya."

In a flash, he darted from view, and I swallowed hard to push the lump back down my throat. I didn't want to know what he had been too afraid to tell me.

CHAPTER 31

One on One

I recovered steadily over the next few days but took it easy and stayed away from the bars and parties that weekend. Then it was my turn to play nurse and entertainer since Lindsay had caught the virus. She'd taken good care of me during my sick days, so I tried my best to return the favor.

Even though Linds felt ill, she was in good spirits, thanks to her cooperating teacher. He had written Lindsay a nice letter about how great she had been that week with the students. It appeared, too, that Lindsay was over the TJ situation. She thought it was very sweet of him to check in on me and stay with me that day. Her eyes lingered on me as if she were trying to get a hidden message across. I shrugged it off as TJ just being himself.

In dance, I was getting used to all the attention TJ caused for us. He was by far Mrs. Mac's most charming student and could really brown nose. She ate it up. He was getting mildly better at the waltz but still looked slightly ridiculous doing it.

The more time we spent together, the more I felt like that lively little kid from so long ago. I was carefree and easy with TJ. I didn't have to second-guess my actions or analyze his comments as I did with Jason. I didn't have to pretend I was someone else like I had become accustomed to being with my mother for years.

But of course, a vacation can't last forever. Jason was coming down for the weekend.

I couldn't help but feel removed from him, and I was getting more and more anxious about the two of us. I was never fully comfortable with him. He had his ways to make me feel special, but mostly I felt as if I had to watch what I would say. Whatever mood he was in at the time determined how well our visit would go.

***

That Friday evening, with Lindsay feeling back to normal, we met up with some of our neighbors to play an intramural soccer game. TJ helped because of his connections with the Rec department. It was exhilarating to get out and play. Lindsay and I realized dance plus frequent visits to the Rec Center helped us stay in shape. As we were packing up the equipment, I felt eyes watching me and turned to see that adorable boy with golden hair leaning up against a maple tree.

"You ladies looked pretty good out there," TJ called.

"Oh, my God!" Lindsay clapped her hands to her chest, "Tommy, you scared me, jeez."

"Sorry, Linds." He smiled, coming closer.

"You looked like a stalker," she said, and we all started laughing.

"So, what are you doing, stalker?" I asked.

"I just finished reffing a basketball tournament. I figured you gals would be done, and I could save you a trip returning the soccer balls and pinnies. You hungry?" He pulled out a bag of cheddar fries and planted himself at the foot of a tree.

"No thanks," Lindsay said. "I'm gonna head home. Are you gonna hang for a while or what?"

"Yeah, I'll see you at home," I said. I slid down against the tree beside TJ.

"Remember when we'd sit on my porch and eat these?" He tilted the bag so I could take a handful.

"Of course, and you would always wipe your fingers on your shorts, so you'd have patches of orange grease," I added. In a flash, I saw him in a memory: disheveled golden hair, shoving handfuls of cheddar fries in his mouth. Greasy, orange fingers. His grin of pure contentment.

"Man, those were the days! Do you ever miss it?" he asked.

"Cheddar fries? No."

"Wow, am I really rubbing off on you that much?" He bumped my shoulder. I giggled, my mouth stuffed with fries. "See how much you sound like me?" Then he got a little more serious and asked, "Do you ever miss the old days?"

Do I ever miss the old days? Days of just being a kid and riding my bike and hanging with my best friend? Days before the Rachel nightmares began? Do I ever miss tossing Buddy his Frisbee and playing ball with TJ? Thinking that the world had so much still to offer for me?

That question made me so sad so quickly that I took a minute to answer him, letting my shyness hide the composure I was trying to gain.

"Yes. I miss those days, all the time, really," I said softly. I couldn't meet his eyes as I disguised my sorrow. I noticed he was still watching me, so I elaborated, "It was nice without all the stress and deadlines, you know?"

"For sure. Hey, how did your reports go?" he asked.

"Fine, boring. Don't you ever have papers to write?"

"Not really, or if I do, Trevor can be bought pretty cheap," he laughed.

"No, you do not have Trevor write your papers for you," I scolded.

"Nah, but I did pay him to edit a few. That kid is addicted to cash. What class was your paper for?" he continued.

"Finance."

"Is that your major or is it just like Business Administration?" he asked, shoving another handful of cheddar fries into his mouth.

"Business admin," I stated cautiously, wondering where the conversation was heading.

"Huh."

"What?"

"Nothing." He cracked a smile, fishing in the bag for another handful.

"Yeah, right. What?" I wasn't letting him get away with that.

He smiled bigger. "Nothing Beck, it's just…." I peered at him as he paused, licking the cheese off his fingers. "It just seems unusual for you, that's all," he finished. I stared at him as he went on, "I mean, I wouldn't think you'd be interested in a business or finance career, ya know? Is that what *you* want to do?"

There was something about the way he emphasized *you* that immediately brought my mother to mind. "Rebecca," she had said, "you have to set yourself up for a myriad of opportunities. You know, in this economy, we can't take chances. You need a stable major, and this will make you very marketable."

I was sure he saw my thought bubble.

"Are you into that? Or is it just a necessity for you to major in that?" he asked.

Honestly, I didn't know what I wanted to do. I wasn't by any means dying to be an accountant, have a corporate job, and analyze spreadsheets all day in a cubicle. My scores were excellent in all my classes, but did I actually enjoy them? Probably not. It was a gentle nudge on his part to get me to really think about my aspirations, and he knew he had planted a seed since he knew me so well. It was something else for me to think about.

"Now, let me ask you something," I countered.

"Shoot."

"Why weren't you ever in college sports or looking to go into the NFL or something? You easily could've been."

"Want to see why?" He pulled up his right sleeve and exposed a thin scar on his shoulder. "I tore my rotator cuff junior year and had to have surgery."

I gave him a surprised, pitying look. "Ouch. That's awful."

"Really bad timing near the end of high school when all the scouting begins. It took a long time to recover, too. But I think things happen for a reason. Like living in Carlyle when we met Howard. He changed our lives."

"You said that before. How?"

"I kind of got into some trouble for a while. Started going down a rough path."

"What do you mean?"

He looked at me for a minute, debating his answer. "I just got mixed up with some bad choices."

"I didn't know that," I said apologetically.

"I didn't want you to know that." He stared into my eyes. I took in a deep breath. "Then, there was Howard. He set me straight. He's had a big impact on me." TJ grinned. "Anyway, it's all good now. I'm where I'm supposed to be. Let's have a round." He jumped up, retrieved a ball, and kicked it out onto the field.

I sat for a second, then smirked and took up his challenge. Although I was sore and sticky, I had a great time battling him. TJ was in awe of how quickly I destroyed him on the soccer field. Although he gave quite a lot of effort, he couldn't steal the ball from me without fouling me, which made both of us laugh. I dodged him easily with my footwork and even "broke his ankles" a few times to his disbelief, sprinting past him to score. After I scored fifteen times to his four, he called it a tie.

As he walked away with the equipment, he yelled, "Where are you gonna be tomorrow night?"

"Jason'll be here," I replied.

"That's cool. Bring him to Mom's. I've got a surprise for you. Besides, I've gotta meet this guy."

CHAPTER 32

Sunset

That evening, I pleaded with my dad to let me take Buddy for a walk. After much persuasion and showing him sample runs with the leash and crutches, he agreed and then immersed himself in his sports channel. I grinned, knowing that my mother would've been furious with my dad for letting me try the walk.

Buddy and I strolled up the block aimlessly. When I realized I was now a master with my crutches, I veered off the path and headed to TJ's.

The slight chill in the air brought welcomed relief to the additional two blocks I would have to hop. Buddy pranced alongside me, sniffing here and there. The sun was an orange and pink circle, illuminating rosy, golden shadows over the sidewalk. I knew TJ and Katie would be thrilled to see Buddy. Thankfully, I was getting close since Auntie Helen's house came into view and then TJ's.

Auntie Helen sat in her screened-in porch with two yellow parakeets. Buddy got excited, sniffing around Auntie Helen's home.

"Is that you, Rebecca?" she called out.

"Hi, Auntie Helen."

"Oh, I heard about your fracture, dear. Are you alright?" she said, inching toward the screen door to get a better look at my cast.

I climbed a few steps to get closer to her and said, "I'll be okay. Thanks."

Buddy tried to climb onto her porch, but I pulled him back onto TJ's grass.

"Such a handsome dog." She smiled. "I find it's too difficult to take care of a dog anymore. I used to have so many dogs. But I have my Pollys now." She stroked a fluffy, yellow bird on its breast feathers and smiled a squinty smile at me. The sun was sinking low on the horizon.

I knew how much Auntie Helen liked visiting, but extended conversation made me uncomfortable. "I'm gonna go see TJ now," I said.

"Of course, dear. I'm sorry." Her voice was tender and sorrowful. She gave me a pitying look. "Well, you come visit Auntie Helen sometime. It's going to be lonely around here soon."

With that, she turned and scooted back to her chair to sit.

I stood staring at the back of her floral printed blouse, trying to make sense out of what she'd just said. *Lonely around here? What is she talking about?* A brief and violent drop in my stomach started a world of uncertainty and worry. Buddy nudged me toward TJ's front steps. Something was wrong. Everything was moving in slow motion. I knew I would finally find out what TJ had wanted to tell me earlier. The sun disappeared behind me.

CHAPTER 33

Boiling Point

Early Saturday afternoon, a clean-cut Jason rapped on my apartment door. He had just gotten his hair trimmed, and I could tell he was trying to look cute. I appreciated his efforts and gave him a big hug and kiss. I hadn't seen him in a while and was surprised at the genuine smile on my face he caused. The fact that Amy was away for the weekend helped me feel more comfortable with him in the apartment. Amy hadn't taken Scooter with her, and it was interesting to see her hiss at Jason and then run off to hide in Amy's closet.

Jason had bought me a general weekend pass for the train to downtown Chicago.

"What's the occasion?" I asked.

"Because I like you a lot." He kissed my cheek and lifted me up, so I could wrap my legs around his waist.

"*Now* I remember."

It turned out he was scheming plans for us when we would both be home for the next weekend, which was my spring break. That was the reason for the train pass.

After grabbing fast-food dinner, we talked about our plans for the night, and I asked him if he wanted to go out to the bars.

"Yeah, that should work. My cousin Paul is actually here this weekend, so we should meet up with him."

"We could go to Mom's," I offered. "And hey, you know what? You can meet TJ tonight," I said, trying to sound casual.

"Wow. I can't wait," Jason answered sarcastically. "Is that his real name? TJ?"

"No, his name is Tom."

So, why do you call him that anyway?"

"It's just what I called him when we were little," I said more quietly than I had planned to.

"Well, you're a grown-up. It's juvenile."

I didn't say anything but felt my stress level rise. I sighed and closed my eyes, willing Jason to be at ease.

"Is that the only reason we're going out? To see TJ?" He frowned at me.

"No, you just said we should go out and meet your cousin. Besides, hanging out at the bars is the only thing to do." I shrugged.

My stomach turned, and I suddenly didn't feel like going out at all. If Jason was already throwing in rude comments, I wouldn't know what to expect after a handful of drinks. My only hope was that TJ could win him over, or maybe not even show up.

Jason's cousin and his friends were already out at Mom's and planned on staying there for a while. I begged Lindsay to go with us, and she agreed. I tried to talk up Jason's cousin to her, even though I'd never met him.

Jason downed the rum and Cokes quickly. He remarked how they were cheaper than at the bars on his campus, but the way he made it sound, I wasn't sure if that was a good thing or not. As the evening wore on, he was feeling pretty good. He and his cousin played pool for a while, one of Jason's talents for sure. Lindsay got bored just watching them. She kept eyeballing me in annoyance over the situation, especially with Paul. Lindsay had earlier identified Paul as "definitely not dating material" soon after meeting him.

More and more people filtered in, making the scene lively. I was in the middle of a conversation with Lindsay when two large hands from behind me covered my eyes.

"Ar-right, Beck, you ready for your surprise?" TJ asked in his unforgettable way.

I could just imagine Jason's reaction if he looked over and saw TJ touching me. Without waiting for an answer, TJ turned me around. I couldn't even begin to guess what he was about to show me, but it made me very nervous.

"Ar-right, one, two, three, ta-da!" He pulled his hands away.

Before me stood a tall, slightly darker-haired female version of TJ. I blinked a few times, trying to process who it was.

She smiled and said, "Becky, it's Katie!"

My eyes grew wide, and then joyful relief washed over me. "Oh, my God, hi!" I said, hugging her.

I was amazed at how tall she was. She stood a good six inches taller than me. It was unbelievable to think this beautiful seventeen-year-old was the same little girl who would sit on the front lawn playing Barbies. "Wow," I said again, looking at her. TJ now stood smiling beside us.

"Wow, to you! You're gorgeous," she said in a cute southern accent.

"Uh," I laughed.

"Were you scared, Beck?" TJ asked, giggling.

"Yeah, a little," I confessed.

"That was awesome! What did you think I was gonna do?"

"I ... don't ... know."

"Alright, stop yapping," Katie said, pushing TJ away lightly. "Becky and I have to talk." She pulled at my arm.

"Hold on a second. I have to introduce you guys." I turned to Lindsay. "Katie, this is my friend, Lindsay.

"Hi," Katie said cheerfully.

"Linds, this is TJ's sister, Katie."

"You totally look alike," Lindsay said, smiling big.

"Jeez, I hope not!" Katie stuck her tongue out and laughed.

"And that's Jason." I pointed toward him. "Jason, come here for a second."

"Hold on, I'm making a shot," he said, not looking up. After what seemed like the longest setup ever, he hit the cue ball and knocked in a stripe. Then he sauntered over with stick in hand and a tight expression on his face.

"Jason, this is Tommy," I explained. TJ shot me a funny look. I never called him Tommy. "And Katie, his little sister. This is my boyfriend, Jason."

"Hi." Jason shook their hands formally.

"Hi," Katie replied.

"Hey, nice to meet you, Jason." TJ shook his hand. "I've heard a lot about you." Typical TJ, trying to make friends.

"Is that right?" Jason asked. He turned toward me, giving me the slightest trace of a smile.

"You look like you know what you're doing over there." TJ nodded toward the pool table.

"You game?" Jason asked.

"Sure, in a little bit. Thanks," TJ said.

Jason took a sip of his drink, set it down, and strode back to the table to play some more. I let out a huge sigh of relief.

Katie, Lindsay, and I talked and danced near the pool tables. Katie wanted me to introduce her to boys because Tommy wouldn't. She was a riot and so cute and peppy. It was apparent, too, that Katie was no stranger to alcohol. She had no trouble chugging beers, especially for a seventeen-year-old. And she was so proud of her fake ID that belonged to her friend's sister, who looked a lot like her. Lindsay and I just laughed at her.

A while later, Paul and his friends left for Stix. Jason told them we would swing up there later. Freddie was talking Katie's ear off and buying her drinks. Trevor was standing quietly beside us. Brandon, of course, was talking to and teasing a group of ladies.

It was an odd experience seeing Jason and TJ there challenging each other at pool.

It made me a little uneasy. They seemed evenly matched, although Jason should've had a huge advantage, having grown up with a pool table in his basement. Yet TJ was very precise at any sport involving aim. With both of their competitive natures, I wasn't sure how it would end.

TJ tried to make conversation, asking questions, but Jason only gave him brief responses and asked him nothing. I was sure that TJ sensed Jason wouldn't be happy losing. As TJ took his shot, his expression intensified for a second, then he missed the pocket with only two balls to hit in.

"Dang it," TJ grunted at himself.

Jason saw the opening and wouldn't give TJ another turn. He raked the balls in, then nodded to TJ.

"Good shot, man," TJ said, cupping him on the shoulder. "I'm gonna get a drink."

Jason stood and set up the table again. I gave TJ a smile.

"What?" he mouthed. I grinned and shook my head. He and I both knew that he had thrown the game. It was like watching him pretend to drown in my swimming pool. No one else caught on but me.

"I don't know why you're looking at me like that, Beck," he said, leaning over with his money on the bar for a drink. "You need a beer?"

"No thanks, I'm good," I replied.

TJ then jerked his head to the corner where Freddie sat close to Katie, his arm around her shoulder. His eyes tightened in a scowl, but then he laughed and snapped his fingers to get Katie's attention. "Hey, maybe you should start dancing again. You're looking a little tired!" he called.

Katie shooed his advice away playfully.

"No, really, your leg is probably asleep!" he yelled.

I decided to come to his rescue, "Katie!" I gestured, waving my arm. "Come here for a second."

She excused herself and walked to my side. TJ then went to have a little talk with Freddie. I made up some question about Auntie Helen. She took the bait and babbled for a while. Jason waltzed over and ordered another drink.

Then things got worse in a heartbeat.

"Becky, I'm so excited that you're coming down for the wedding with us!" Katie shrieked and hugged me, jumping up and down. As soon as she said that, I knew my night was over. Jason's eyes burned through me.

"What?" he said.

I faced Jason.

"It's their mom's wedding at the end of the month, and she wants me to be there."

"What? So now you're going to some wedding with this guy?"

"It's not a big deal. They're old family friends."

"Well, she thinks it's a big deal. And if it wasn't, why wouldn't you tell me about it? Huh? Am I right?"

"No!"

"So, you don't go home to see your parents, or me, but you'll go somewhere with him? What the hell is that, Rebecca?" He flinched. I could see the hurt in his eyes behind his rising anger.

"Jason," I said calmly, trying to control my breathing and figure out what I could possibly say, but then Lindsay came back from the dance floor, grabbed me in her excitement, and started grinding on me. I swear, Jason almost had steam coming out of his ears. TJ then slid up next to him, unaware of the catastrophe in the making.

"She's great, huh?" He nudged Jason, referring to me.

"You know what? Let's say you try to find your own girlfriend!" he replied, turning to face TJ. Lindsay kept trying to pull me this way and that, dancing. TJ was stunned but kept his cool. Trevor must've heard some commotion and moved closer.

"She's just a friend of mine," TJ stated calmly, raising his hands.

"You might just be dumber than you look, thinking I'm gonna fall for that bull."

My heart raced. TJ bit the corner of his mouth. Trevor bumped shoulders with Brandon and nodded in our direction. I broke away from Lindsay and stood between TJ and Jason, breathing hard.

"Jason, I need to talk to you," I said forcefully.

He disregarded my comment. "You know, from what I've heard, you don't quite have the 'stamp of approval' anyway," he sneered at TJ.

"You might be right about that."

"Jason, stop it," I warned.

Brandon now stood beside us. "Is there a problem over here?" he raised his voice to be heard.

Jason ignored him.

TJ didn't take his eyes off Jason. He didn't even blink. More and more people turned to see the unpleasant development.

"And just for the record … *my girlfriend's* not going anywhere with you, so do yourself a favor and stay the *hell* away from her!" Jason yelled in TJ's face.

"Would you stop it?" I pushed Jason back away from TJ.

"Is this asshole bothering you, Beck?" Brandon bellowed, shoving his huge chest up to Jason's. Jason was dwarfed beside him. A crowd had formed, and the bar got quiet.

TJ finally moved and pulled Brandon's shoulder back, "Bran, lay off," he said assertively.

"Get the hell out of my face!" Jason snapped. Brandon's eyes popped.

"Bran!" TJ pushed him. "Back off, seriously!" TJ ordered.

There was only one other time in my life that I had seen TJ look so fierce. I was close to losing it, so I grabbed Jason's arm. "Let's go. Now! Lindsay, come on," I yelled. But she was already right beside me. I pulled Jason's arm, but he shook away from me and headed out the door. I was mortified. I couldn't even look back at TJ or anyone else as I followed Jason out the door.

The silence outside the bar was deafening. As soon as we reached Jason's car, I grabbed his shirt and turned him around. "What the hell is wrong with you?" I screamed with tear-filled eyes and gritted teeth.

He glared at me the same way he'd glared at TJ. "Me? What about you? You never tell me anything. Ever. You barely call me or text me. You won't even go home to see me, your *boyfriend*, remember? Now, I find out you're going to some freaking hillbilly wedding with that asshole? You're out of your damn mind!"

"He's not the asshole. You are!" I cried, finally boiling over.

"Perfect! Now you're gonna take his side?"

"What side? What are you even talking about? TJ didn't do anything!" I protested.

"Did you tell your mom about this? Of course not. Why would you ever include anyone in on what's going on in your life, Rebecca?"

I stood there, shaking, a scowl on my face, but I had no retort.

"You don't even allow me a chance to get close to you." He shook his head. "Well, here it is. You make your choice right now, me or him."

"You are not going to give me an ultimatum," I seethed.

"There is *no way* you're going to that wedding," he threatened, his eyes explosive.

"That is not for you to decide," I said.

"Oh, no?" He laughed sarcastically. "Well, it looks like you just did."

He threw his driver-side door open, shot inside, and sped off, leaving Lindsay and me stranded. I was stunned as hot fury filled my throat and eyes. The night quieted around us until silence stung my ears again.

"O … K, now what?" Lindsay said.

I covered my face in my hands and started walking down the street toward the apartment.

"Rebecca! What are you doing?" Lindsay called. I didn't answer. "Let's just go back in there and ask Trevor for a ride home."

I got further away and wiped my furious tears aside, trying to smother my anger and keep warm.

"Slow down! You know you're too fast," she called and then caught up to me. "You alright?" she asked. I shook my head and kept walking, refusing to speak the whole way home. The cool wind whipped around us. Lindsay complained most of the way and, since I was unresponsive, she managed to have a conversation with herself. I tuned her out and kept moving, concentrating on putting one foot in front of the other, willing myself to make it home before I fell apart.

CHAPTER 34

Sinking

I pulled myself up TJ's steps with heavy legs, my cast an anchor. I was breathing hard but didn't know for sure why or how to stop it. After staring at his screen door for what seemed an eternity, Buddy barked, obviously confused as to why we weren't walking in. I didn't move.

The door swung open, and Katie emerged looking triumphantly at a quivering Buddy.

"Ooh!" she squealed and threw her arms around Buddy's neck.

Mrs. Lawson appeared over her shoulder, peering down with surprise then contentment. "Becky! And Buddy! What a nice surprise to see you both. Come in." She ushered me into the living room.

I stared open-mouthed at a crowded room filled with boxes upon boxes. Brown, large and small, sturdy, labeled, taped-up boxes. I thought I might be sick. I closed my mouth and swallowed hard in between rapid breaths.

"How are you doing? I've been meaning to come by. I swear I have," she rambled on and on about my leg and how sorry she was and did I need to sit down, etc. But I couldn't speak, move, or understand a word she said.

I blinked hard and stared again. The boxes were still there.

Mrs. Lawson continued speaking, but still, her words were drowned out by the banging of my chest as I glanced from one cardboard box to another on all sides of the room.

My head hurt, and my right leg shook like mad under my weight. Katie crawled into an empty, oversized box with Buddy. I caught snippets of words: "So busy ... Crazy ... mess." I was ushered toward a chair but couldn't sit. My ears rang loudly in my head. I kept breathing faster

SINKING

and faster, and then....

TJ appeared at the end of the kitchen, facing me with horrible surprise. We stared silently at each other, then he glanced nervously from his mom to me to the boxes and back to me.

"What's wrong?" Mrs. Lawson spoke at last. TJ shook his head quickly, sending an urgent message to her.

I looked up at her. Sorrow and disappointment filled the room. Her eyes closed slowly, then opened again as she shook her head at him.

"Tom-my."

He clenched his jaw and blinked furiously. I couldn't take it. I hobbled back out the door with my crutches.

"Becky, honey," Mrs. Lawson called.

I made it down to the last step.

"Beck, wait," TJ called.

He followed me off the porch, his eyes glassy and disturbed. I longed for the adorable smile that melted my heart, but it didn't come. We said nothing for a moment. I forced myself to look into his eyes, knowing he couldn't lie again.

"Beck..." His lip trembled. He took a deep breath. "I, I wanted to tell you, but I couldn't, and then your leg, and...." There was another long pause. My stomach dropped another foot. "We have to go live with my grandparents. We're moving downstate."

I swayed on my crutches. My eyes begged him to smile, to make a joke. *It was a joke, right?* He squirmed on the spot, opened his mouth like he was going to say something, then, with a last glance of anguish, shut it. That was it for me. I charged away from his house and back toward mine.

"Beck!" he called.

Somehow, I made it home. I hurtled myself upstairs in a sinking state, threw my crutches angrily aside, and crashed onto my bed face-first, gasping for breath between sobs.

CHAPTER 35

Fallout

Amy and Lindsay walked on eggshells around me for the next few days. Lindsay had obviously caught Amy up to speed with respect to Saturday night's disaster because she said a few choice comments about knowing Jason was a jerk, but I never responded. Since Jason had left us outside the bar, my nightmares had been constant. The trail, Rachel's robotic walk moving ahead. I could never stop her, see her face, or talk to her. I woke up unnerved for three mornings straight and stayed out of sight from virtually everyone. I felt like a zombie.

Jason left me a text message explaining that we should talk. I didn't respond at all. He did call once after that, but Amy answered my phone. She said, "Rebecca doesn't want to talk to a complete and total loser. If she does ... trust me, you're at the top of the list." Then she hung up. That sealed the deal that our relationship was finished.

Surprisingly, my mother didn't try to call me. I assumed I'd hear from her, advising me to give it another try with "sweet Jason." But she didn't. Maybe Jason hadn't mentioned his idiotic, drunken behavior to his mom yet.

Although his reaction was beyond inappropriate, I had to ask myself, *was he wrong about the situation? Probably not.*

True, I didn't tell him things.

Maybe I should've.

But maybe I never wanted our relationship to work. Maybe I only wanted it to be enough for my mother's sake. What does it show your love interest when you won't go home with them but rush at an invitation somewhere else with a different guy?

I honestly couldn't blame him for being angry. Regardless, I wanted nothing more to do with Jason. Ever.

I had been taking long walks and gone jogging a few times a day since that Saturday. Ordinarily, I would've gone to the Rec Center, but I didn't know what to say to TJ. It was difficult for me to even think about him without getting upset. I couldn't imagine what he thought of the explosion at the bar and Jason especially. TJ didn't call or text me, which he didn't often anyway, but he didn't even stop by.

I worked myself into a panic, worrying about how to fix the damage Jason had caused. By Tuesday afternoon, I couldn't hide anymore. I literally had to face the music.

I got to Lantz Gym early and sat outside on the steps where TJ always entered. I hoped that he would take it as a peace offering that I was waiting for him. My nerves were peaking when I caught a glimpse of him and Trevor striding down the sidewalk toward me. Then I became even more anxious, though I should've known better. TJ saw me from far away and gave a slight smile. Trevor bounced up the steps ahead of him.

"Hi," Trevor called and walked right past me into the gym.

"Trevor," my voice didn't carry well.

TJ got closer, and I started breathing heavier. I wanted to run to him, wrap my arms around him and cry on his shoulder, but I didn't. I lowered my eyes to the ground, convincing them to keep dry. TJ stood in front of me.

"Hey, Beck, thanks for waiting for me."

I looked up at his piercing yet gentle blue eyes and wanted to melt, but I kept my composure and looked away. He sat beside me.

"You ar-right?" he asked quietly, turning his head toward me.

I shrugged and finally spit it out. "I'm so sorry." My eyes filled with tears. I pulled my knees into my chest and wrapped my arms around them.

He kept his gaze on me. "Beck." He didn't speak again until I looked at him, "You've got nothing to be sorry for, really," he stated.

TJ took a deep breath in and out. Then he squinted at me and said, "You want to ditch?"

Is he serious?

"Come on." He stood up, smiling.

"Where would we go?"

"Well, let's sneak into Stevenson and grab some lunch. Come on!" He winked at me and started walking toward Stevenson Hall.

I exhaled deeply, then got up and followed him. "Are you always hungry?"

CHAPTER 36

Nightmare

TJ tugged on my arm and pointed ahead to the pond that was strangely silent and misty. I looked all around and noted the marshy reeds and the algae-skimmed surface that seemed eerily still.... TJ moved his lips to tell me something but didn't make a sound. I searched for the turtle eggs hoping we weren't too late, but there was nothing there where we had left them. No sign of life at all. A chill rose up the back of my neck, and I turned around to face TJ.

He was gone.

I called in rapid whispers, knowing I wouldn't find him. I scanned every part of the trail and saw my sister, Rachel, ahead of me, but I never caught sight of her face. Still, I knew it was her. I begged her to help me look for TJ. Then a golden shadow in the pond caught my eye, and I let out a muffled scream.

TJ was bobbing up and down in the sick, murky water. Lifeless. Gone.

"No!" I bolted upright in my bed with tear-stained cheeks. My eyes darted madly around the room. Then I calmed down, realizing it was just a dream. Everything was fine. Until I saw my get-well card on the nightstand lit by the morning sun. TJ. He hadn't drowned, but he was leaving all the same. My poor heart plummeted as my mother raced into my room.

"What happened? I heard screaming." She checked me over, whipping my covers off and rubbing a tissue on my face. Buddy hurried to my bedside.

I sat up and refused to look at her, my eyes landing on the get-well card. The same sinking sensation from my dream filled me. Tears welled in my eyes and gushed down my cheeks. She sat down on my bed and folded her hands together.

"Hmm." She sighed, looking at TJ's get-well card. Even though she was calm and tried to look sympathetic, I knew she was not devastated by news of the move.

"I know you're upset, and I'm sorry about that. But this might turn out for the best, Rebecca," she said matter-of-factly.

I pulled my lips apart in disgusted shock, wanting to hit her or push her away.

She fluffed my pillows and tucked the sheets around me once again. "The Lawsons will be better off with his grandma and grandpa, and you will get to make a lot of new friends now. Try to be positive." She eyed me. I flared my nostrils and narrowed my eyes at her. "Why don't you come downstairs and eat? I'll make waffles." She got up and walked down the hall, but I didn't follow.

I didn't go eat, get dressed, wash up or "try to be positive." I didn't get out of bed the whole day.

***

The next few days went on in the same way. Alone with my thoughts, I absentmindedly sketched in the back pages of Ryan's drawing book. The drawings came easily as if I was meant to have this new skill that Ryan had helped me uncover. I drew turtles, Buddy, and TJ. Then I stared at my sketch of him. *What will happen when he's gone?* It seemed he already was. I had nothing left to hold onto. The only person who knew my heart was leaving.

My dad convinced me to come down for pancakes early one morning before he went to work. My mother's hairdryer buzzed faintly from her bathroom. He wanted to let me know that he knew Tommy was a good friend and assure me that everything would be okay, but he changed the subject when my mother came down.

She told me I needed an attitude adjustment and that nice girls wouldn't want to be my friend if I didn't change my tone.

NIGHTMARE

Also, she was working on forming a weekly playgroup with a few other moms from my school. With no opportunity to dash off on my bike or head to TJ's, I was defeated. I gazed vacantly at the china cabinet while my mother lectured on. Rachel eyed me from her photo. As I was shooed off into the distance, my sister's life took over. Before long, I would be gone forever, living like Rachel would've, unable to find my way back to myself.

CHAPTER 37

Ditching

Lunch in the cafeteria at Stevenson Hall was just as TJ said it would be. He knew someone who worked the line, and sliding in and eating for nothing was as easy as him saying, "Hey Tyler, how's it goin'?"

Within minutes, we had two free meals in front of us. Not that dorm food was anything to gush over, but it was free. Also, we hadn't exactly ditched for the food; I knew he wanted to talk.

"How often do you do this?" I asked as we scanned the cafeteria for a seat.

"Eat? A lot. Probably every four hours or so."

"Yeah, no, sneak dorm food."

"Not much, just like once a day. Is that bad?" He laughed as I rolled my eyes at him.

As soon as we sat down, TJ turned serious. "Do me a favor, Beck," he said with penetrating eyes. I nodded. "I need you to let me know if and when you need me to get out of the way. I don't want to create issues for you." He looked very sincere and almost sad.

I didn't respond at all, just continued to study his gaze.

"I only want you to be happy." His eyes locked onto mine, and I felt as if all the air had been sucked out of my chest.

Then in the same serious tone, while keeping his eyes on mine, "And I want you to pass the salt," he said without even blinking or giving a hint of a smile.

My mouth spread into a huge smile. He smiled, too, and we enjoyed the rest of our lunch, never really addressing the Jason incident. I appreciated that bit of courtesy. He knew I didn't want to talk about it, and even though TJ must've had a ton of questions, he remained patient.

When we had finished eating, TJ walked me to Coleman for work and said he was going home to Carlyle after his classes on Wednesday for spring break. *Spring break. Ugh.* I would be going home, too—the last place I wanted to be. With the horrendous incident on Saturday taking up all my thoughts, I hadn't prepared myself for spring break.

And even though TJ kept mumbling about something, trying to keep the conversation going, I couldn't focus on anything but the rising panic in my chest. I'd completely neglected a plan for spring break. Having a week with my mother to discuss my separation from Jason was too much for me to process. Of course, I would have no car and no chance to escape. It suddenly dawned on me that I wouldn't see TJ for a while either. A sense of helplessness overcame me, and a flood of emotions brought me back to the day TJ had left eleven years ago.

CHAPTER 38

Gone

My dad kissed me goodnight one evening shortly after my world imploded and handed me a note from TJ.

"I stopped at Tommy's after work," he said. "They're leaving tomorrow. We're going to stop by bright and early to say goodbye."

He didn't give me any chance to agree or disagree.

"You know, Mrs. Lawson lost the campground that she and John started together. That's why they're moving. They're going to live with his grandma. Janet's been out of work for a while now and put all her money into their business, and now she has nothing left."

Hearing that, I felt even worse, but I finally understood. All the pieces fit. I looked up tearfully at my dad.

"That's why, kiddo," he soothed. "She lost her job. It's not to hurt you. Now, go to sleep. I'm waking you early."

I nodded, and he left the room.

TJ was leaving tomorrow. I stared at the note in my hand. When I opened it, I read two scribbled words: "I'm sorry." A rush of anxiety hit me that I had been wasting my time. I hadn't seen him in four days, and he had already apologized, but I hadn't. I had to tell him sorry for hiding from him and stop wasting time before he would be gone for good.

I reached into my nightstand drawer and pulled out my sketchpad. Almost instinctively, I started sketching TJ and me. It was the pose from a picture we'd taken a year ago in his tent, hands on our chins, laying on our bellies. My favorite picture. I even added a figure roasting marshmallows in a cloud above us. When I finished, I tore out the page, laid down my pencil, and after smiling shyly at my work, drifted off to sleep.

GONE

***

True to his word, my dad had me up, dressed, and in the car by 8:15 a.m. The Lawsons had probably been up for two hours at least. I knew TJ had. He could never sleep past the first crack of light. My hands shook as we turned the corner to TJ's block.

A large "Move Yourself" truck was parked on his street. Mrs. Lawson hopped down from inside the truck when she noticed us. She seemed to breathe a great sigh of relief. I hoped she wouldn't cry but prepared myself for the inevitable.

"Hi, Janet," my dad said politely.

"Oh, Bob, thanks for bringing her by! Tommy told me he wasn't leaving until he saw Beck again. Oh, my darling, Becky." She squeezed me for a while and calmed my racing heart. "I'm so sorry we have to leave like this. We love you very much." She wiped her eyes.

I heard the screen door slam and snapped my head over to see the boy with golden hair grinning on the top step.

"You're here," TJ said. I gave him a sheepish smile but felt guilty. I could see by the look in his eyes that he did, too.

"Janet, let me help you with a few of these." My dad went into the house to grab the last remaining pieces.

TJ jumped off the top step. "Hey, Beck."

"Hi."

He walked slowly over to where I stood. "I'm sorry." I stared back at him as he went on, "I should've told you." He was silent for a minute and then said, "Hey!" I had to smile. TJ always seemed to revel in a bright idea that sidetracked him. "I got you something. I think you're gonna like it."

He clutched the top of my hand over the grip of my crutches and nudged me over to a muddy cardboard box sitting in the sun alongside his house. He picked it up and took off a makeshift lid to reveal a tiny spotted turtle. I gasped in delight. "This was the last one around. Not sure what happened to the others, but I figured you should have him."

"Wow, thanks."

He took the box to our car as my dad, and Mrs. Lawson came out with a load. Katie followed with her pillow and a rag doll. TJ set the muddy box carefully in the back seat of my dad's car.

"You gotta name him, Beck. How about Bruno?"

I laughed, then brought myself back to reality. There was no chance that my mother would let me keep him. And worse, TJ was about to disappear.

"We're leaving in a minute," my dad whispered into my ear as he passed by with another bundle for the moving truck.

My chin quivered. I reached under the seat and pulled up the sketch for TJ. With tears in my eyes, I gave him the picture. He smiled his adorable smile.

I couldn't hold back my tears. "I'm sorry I ran off," I burst out all at once and wiped my eyes. "I don't want you to go away."

He looked at me softly, then put his arms out for me and hugged me tighter and longer than ever before. "I don't want to go either, Beck. You know you didn't really run away, though. You kinda hobbled away," he teased. I sniffed loudly, still hugging him. "Did you just blow your nose on me?"

"No," I laughed and pulled away. He was laughing, too.

"Now, you be safe driving, Janet," My dad said, signaling TJ was about to leave.

"Oh, we will, Bob. Thanks again for everything." TJ's mom hugged my dad while tears ran down her face.

"Tommy," my dad said firmly, shaking TJ's hand as a goodbye.

I wiped my eyes quickly.

Mrs. Lawson jogged over to me. She grabbed me and kissed my forehead. "Becky. We'll miss you so much." She released me and walked back into the house, covering her face.

My dad waved to Katie and got into the car. It was my signal to get inside, too, but my legs wouldn't cooperate. I wished I could've told TJ

GONE

more as we stood frozen in our goodbyes, our parents having left us alone. I wanted to beg him not to leave, ask him to take me with him, or say simply that he was the best friend I would ever have. I wanted to tell him nothing in my life would be the same again, confess that I loved him so much, but I couldn't say it.

He seemed to understand as he always did. He pulled me in close again. "You're my best friend." I nodded. "You'll be okay. Bye, Beck."

"Bye," I muffled on his shoulder. Then he slowly pulled back, looked into my eyes one last time, and pressed his lips to mine in my first, precious kiss.

As I stood there mesmerized, my head swimming, he backed away, looked at my lips, and smiled his adorable smile.

I managed to grin back at him as he sang "Walking on Sunshine" and retreated to the steps of his house.

I got in the front seat, and Dad put the car in gear and drove off. I watched TJ's house fade as we headed in another direction. Sections of green parkway grass sped past as I stared back at him, unsure what was to become of me.

Then he was gone.

That chapter closed the best part of my childhood. Everything changed after that, and I was completely lost.

FUTURE

CHAPTER 39

Spring Break

"So, hey," TJ said sweetly, standing on the sidewalk outside Coleman Hall. "Try to have a good break."

My emotions got the better of me. All my anxiety since Saturday night, compiled with the realization that TJ was somehow leaving me again, broke me in two. I knew I wouldn't be able to fake it and put on a happy face for him.

"Please do something for me?" I heard myself beg as my throat burned with sorrow. *Why did it feel like I was losing him again?*

He furrowed his brow, taking in my sudden change of emotions. "Anything," he said, looking me over carefully.

I paused for a few moments. "Just please come back this time, okay?" As soon as I said it, a stream of tears overcame me. He was absolutely stunned. Deep sobs seeped through my heart and exploded all around us. TJ's mouth opened in surprise as he moved closer. Concern flooded his face.

"Losing you was the worst time of my life," I managed to choke out. "I don't want to go through that again. I really need you." I surprised myself by saying it, then wiped my eyes. TJ's expression broke into a sympathetic smile. He seemed to swell with pride and confidence.

He came closer to me and held my face in his hands. "I promise I'll be back." He smiled so sweetly and kissed my forehead, then hugged me tightly as he sighed out loud, "Ah, Beck. How am I supposed to leave you now?"

I took full advantage of his warm offer. My arms clung to his waist, desperate to hang on to him. I breathed in and out deeply to slow my grief from boiling over again. My eyes were closed, allowing my senses a break for healing. He just stood there with me, cradling me as if we were the only two people in the whole world that existed at that moment. Even though crowds of college students walked this way and that, we were in a separate place. After what seemed like forever, I pulled myself back together, knowing I would see him again, knowing he had to go temporarily, and knowing I had my own issues to face. I would put on a cheery smile and wish him a pleasant vacation. And I would be okay. As long as I could see him again, I would be whole once more.

TJ sensed my pulling away from him. "Hey, if you need anything or want to get away…." He backed up, examining me, holding my arms to get a good look at my face. "Reach me in any way, call or text, and I will come get you in the next second ar-right?" He bent his head, searching my eyes. "Really."

"I know you would. Thanks."

"You know what? Let's all meet up next Saturday to camp out at Lake Katherine. It's just a few miles away. Bring the girls."

"Sure," I smiled for him and sniffed away a final tear.

"Ar-right." He grinned back, relieved.

***

Thursday's dance class was calm and eerily quiet without TJ. A lot of students had skipped out early for break. Mrs. Mac had us do the Hokey Pokey just for laughs since she said we were all half-dead.

Lindsay and I finagled Taylor to agree to drive us home on Friday for spring break. We were on her way, so she said no problem. We also needed a ride, seeing as I was no longer on speaking terms with Jason. Lindsay was ecstatic to be going home because she had been promised her sister's car during break and for the last few weeks of school. Everyone had smiles on their faces and a spring break attitude as they packed up their gear. Everyone but me.

After dropping Lindsay off and pulling up to my driveway, I felt a surge of dread. I didn't belong in this house. I couldn't even look at it with sweet memories of Buddy or TJ because it was not my childhood home. I forced myself up the flagstone walkway and waved goodbye to Taylor.

Watching Taylor's car zoom away, I wished to be anywhere else. I had half a mind to sprint down the driveway and vanish like I'd done in January when my mother had been so overcome again with the loss of her perfect daughter Rachel that she couldn't see she was losing me, too.

Standing awkwardly on the flagstone path, I surveyed the landscaping and extrinsic features of the house. This house never felt warm to me. It was nothing like our house on Foxgrove. It was beautiful with a stone fire pit, ridiculously priced patio décor, and a private lake in the back bordering the ten other posh houses in the elite subdivision. At the front of the house, perfectly sculpted shrubs and rose bushes accented the greenery of the path, making it look inviting, but I still could not find the energy to make my way to the door.

Am I supposed to knock? Ring the doorbell? Walk in? What an odd situation to be standing at the entrance of my home and feel confounded as to how to enter it.

Then the door opened, and my mother stood before me. "Rebecca? Welcome home." She held the door open, and I turned sideways to enter. Of course, she didn't pull me into a hug. That wasn't her style. She did wear a real smile on her face, though. It was … nice for a change.

"Hi, honey!" My dad appeared behind my mother and grabbed me in his arms, squeezing me tight.

"Hi, Daddy."

"It's been a long time," he commented, still squeezing me.

"Yes, too long," my mother piped in. She moved toward the great room and scolded my dad for not fully allowing me in the house.

The house was exactly as I had remembered it—with its stainless-steel appliances, quartz counters, recessed lighting, and a huge kitchen island atop dark hardwood flooring. It was like a model home in an upscale subdivision. I headed down the hallway to toss my things in my room. There it was hung in the hall: Rachel's class photo.

I felt braver now, staring at her. Before this semester, I couldn't even look directly into her eyes because I felt that she knew I was faking confidence. It was like she knew how fragile I was. How pathetic I was to keep chasing her. This time I stared her down a little. "Leave me alone," I whispered and pulled away.

I turned into my bedroom and looked around, trying to get a sense of myself in it. I felt like a guest checking in to some unknown space. It was, of course, clutter-free and clean. Part of me wanted to rip the covers off the bed and fill the empty spaces or furniture with something—clothing, knickknacks, accessories—anything to make it feel like me. I sighed and tried to put my happy face back on. I had to think positively, or I wouldn't make it through the week.

My mother had made chicken scampi with garlic bread, a favorite family recipe. She was as polite as I expected her to be with occasional conversation about my ride home, courses, and the girls.

My dad did most of the questioning, but my mother made an attempt to talk, too. I wished so badly that I could just stop analyzing the situation and enjoy the company of my parents for a change. My mother seemed as if she were trying, at least.

My dad filled me in on the opening of baseball season and the goings-on in town. He had received another promotion and had a lot on his plate. Now he was the director of sales for HVAC Standard Supply Corporation. He said it was a nice position for him. I wondered how many more hours each week he had to put in for his position to be good enough for my mother. He seemed pleased with his advancement, but I was crestfallen at his news. A promotion meant more work and more responsibility. *When will it ever be enough for her?* Both my father and I had gotten caught up in the desire to please her, no matter the cost. While I was just beginning to ponder a different life for myself, my dad was stuck.

I felt sick to my stomach and attempted to remove myself from the table.

"Why don't you sit and talk with us for a while?" my mother asked. She was suddenly trying too hard.

"The Sox are playing, kiddo," my dad suggested, nodding toward the TV.

"Robert, she's just come home from a long school year being gone, and you want her to watch television?" She looked at my dad as if he were a fool.

"That's okay … I don't really ever watch TV," I said.

"How do you usually spend your free time?" he asked, trying to make conversation.

I shrugged, "I'm busy with schoolwork, or I go to the Rec Center a lot. Just hang out with Amy and Linds."

"So, is there anything going on that you'd like to talk about?" My mother said, folding her hands and trying to be casual. I eyed her and knew she was referring to Jason. Here it was, finally, the Jason discussion. All the warmth I had been coated in up to that point was pulled off me like a blanket yanked from a sleeping child.

I took a while to respond and let my stubbornness show on purpose. "No," I said simply, staring her down.

She pursed her lips in dissatisfaction but didn't push the issue.

"I'm really tired. I'm just gonna go to sleep," I said, getting up and excusing myself. My dad followed me to make sure I had everything I needed. He told me it was good that I was home, and "they" were glad to see me. I dreaded the nightmare about to overtake me as I went to sleep in a bed that didn't feel like mine, suddenly missing Buddy terribly.

***

On Saturday, I managed to survive the mall excursion my mother had planned for us. With the hustle of seasoned shoppers and marble floors shining the way into each specialty shop, she was truly in her element. Of course, my mother bumped into several acquaintances that she introduced me to each time. They gushed over "Suzanne's beautiful daughter," and I played along as best I could but felt uneasy helping to put on a show of appearance.

As usual, I didn't add much to our conversation. The bright interior lights of the mall, along with chic merchandise, helped to distract my mother enough from having a real conversation with me. She spoiled me with a bunch of new clothes and jewelry that I said I didn't need. My mother really did have a knack for accessories. We spent a good chunk of time gazing at the sparkling pieces in several jewelry stores. I could tell she was having fun for a change, so I told myself to smile and accept each new gift. It was refreshing to see her feeling comfortable beside me for once, even if I wasn't.

That evening, it was my dad's turn to spoil me. He got us Sox tickets. At the ballpark, he bought matching Sox hats. I teased him a few times, calling him a nerd because of his child-like excitement about the game. It was incredibly cute, though.

Just like old times, my dad and I sat side by side scrutinizing the game, shelling peanuts, and eating hotdogs. We cheered loudly when our third baseman hit a home run and booed even louder when our outfielder got hit by a pitch.

We huddled together under blankets when the temperature dipped. I pressed my head against his shoulder, relishing this great evening with my dad. It gave me hope that my visits home wouldn't have to be so intimidating.

The next morning, unfortunately, turned out to be what I was expecting. Lindsay had family obligations to take care of, and with my dad on a golf outing, I had to spend the day with my mother. Only this time, she had used up all her conversation topics and cautious interactions with me.

Perfect.

SPRING BREAK

Once again, she kept herself busy, this time with chores that didn't need to be done—straightening her jewelry catalogs and rechecking order forms. She smiled at me, but her eyes squinted a little too much. It was painfully apparent that we had nothing to talk about.

After a rough morning, she dropped subtle hints about Jason. I stated as clearly as I could that I was not going to discuss my former relationship with Jason any longer. She wouldn't back down, however, as she unbelievably suggested I call and have him come over. I tried my best to convince her without getting worked up that Jason and I were completely finished. Then I was horrified to find out that she had called him and left him a message, asking him to come by.

That was it.

I couldn't cope for another second.

I boiled over and screamed at her as if I was watching the scene from somewhere else. When I'd had my say, I ran to my room, shoved my things in my bag, and bolted from the house, almost knocking her down as I fled out the door.

I ran with the same sense of sickening hopelessness as I'd had when I'd run from the visit with Melanie Abrams so long ago. I raced down the block and kept going until most of my anger had subsided and my tears dried up.

I didn't know what to do. I held my phone in my hand but willed myself to make it through without asking TJ to come save me.

I needed a plan.

I didn't know where I was going but knew I couldn't be at my parents' house.

I thought for a second about seeing my brother downtown. But we barely spoke anymore, and I was sure he would get my mother involved.

As I searched in my wallet for a clue as to what I could do or where I could go, my fingers flipped through receipts, cards, and cash until I stopped on the Metra Rail weekend pass that Jason had given me. With a sense of determination, I walked the additional eight blocks to the train station and boarded the third car heading into the city.

Once I calmed myself and made it downtown, I called Amy to see if she wanted some company over spring break. She said yes. So, I bought a bus ticket to Peoria, a twenty-minute ride away from Amy's small town of Dunlap, and spent the rest of my spring break at her house with her family.

CHAPTER 40

Camping

Amy was definitely a lifesaver. She took me in, welcomed me into her family, initiated me into her group of crazy friends, and even went back to Eastern early for me. We waited at our apartment for Lindsay to get back from break, then headed off to camp out with TJ and the guys. I was more than ready to have some fun and get back to normal. Plus, I couldn't wait to see TJ.

We were late arriving because Lindsay couldn't navigate her way to Charleston, even with the help of GPS. Then Amy insisted we stop at the liquor store to buy some hard stuff to speed the night up. Lindsay, being the teacher, brought marshmallows, chocolate, and graham crackers for s'mores. Amy teased her about being pathetic, but I knew she would end up downing the s'mores eventually.

It was a perfect night for camping out. It had been a warm day, and the air was crisp and dry for April. The skies opened up, and an ocean of stars appeared above us.

We pulled up next to TJ's truck, and I breathed a sigh of relief that he was really there. A handful of tents were already set up and scattered around the campsite. A small group gathered around the fire, and an uproar of delight greeted us when Amy put the car in park.

"The party's here, kiddies!" Amy called out the window.

"Hot damn! It's about freaking time!" I heard Brandon's familiar yell. Amy trotted over to the gang.

As soon as I climbed out of the car, I turned my attention toward the fire, and a golden-haired boy with the most adorable smile I'd seen all week met my gaze. In that one second, I had complete clarity. My heart flipped inside my chest, and my mouth parted in stunned realization that I was in love with TJ. *Of course, I was. How could I not be? How could I have just figured that out?*

"Ouch! Rebecca! What the heck?" Lindsay smacked into me as I stood frozen in the realization.

"Sorry, Lindsay," I muttered, pulling my face away from TJ's stare and fumbling with our bags.

Now what? For some reason, what should've been the most natural and expected transformation of my heart—acknowledging a love for TJ—made my pulse quicken and my stomach turn. *What am I supposed to do? Run over to him? Pull him aside and confess my feelings? Risk losing his friendship in an awkward one-sided monologue?*

Tortured. My gut was immediately tortured.

"Thank Jesus, females are finally here," Mason's girlfriend Jenna sang out from the campfire. "Becky, come sit by me." She held up a bottle of beer and waved it as a beacon.

That was my short-term answer: liquid courage. Although I'd sworn to take it easy after one rough night of drinking with Amy, I needed to relax and figure out how to manage this new explosive feeling for TJ. The alcohol would simply buy me some time.

After small talk, a few beers, and some deep breaths, I loosened up. We were all snacking, drinking, and laughing around the campfire. TJ's friends were a total riot. They made me feel so welcomed. Jenna was animated and quick. She and Mason almost seemed like brother and sister from the way she snapped at him. Mason was already pretty loaded.

"Bustin' out the big guns," Brandon commented on our liquor choice as Amy pulled out a monster bottle of Jack Daniels from her bag.

"We can share on one condition." Amy waved the bottle teasingly at Brandon.

"What's that?" Trevor asked.

"I'm not singing any damn camp songs," Brandon interrupted.

"We play Never Have I Ever," Amy cheered.

CAMPING

"Oh God," Lindsay complained. I gave her a reproachful smile.

"Fine, I'll get smashed." Brandon snatched the bottle, poured some JD into a plastic cup, and sat down.

"What's Never Have I Ever?" Jenna asked.

"It's this drinking game where you say something that you have done before or that you haven't done before, and whoever's done it has to drink," Lindsay tried to explain.

"Say that again. I don't get it."

"Like I would say, 'Never have I ever been horseback riding.' Then whoever has done that takes a drink. You have to tell the truth by drinking when you're supposed to," Lindsay finished.

"Let's just play. She'll figure it out," Amy said.

TJ sighed uneasily from across the campfire. "I'd rather not play this game. It gets people in trouble."

"What?" Amy laughed.

"Tommy, I think that's the first time I've ever heard you not wanting to play something," Jenna said, pulling her chair closer to the fire.

"Come on, Lawson. You clean up at this game," Brandon persuaded.

"Exactly my point," he mumbled quietly.

"You got some skeletons in your closet, Tommy boy?" Amy pressed.

"Come on, Tommy, you're among friends," Jenna said.

"Okay, I'm starting then, but I'm not actually drinking." He poured some Coke into a plastic cup. "Someone should be sober enough to drive Mason to the ER later if he falls in the fire. And it's Jenna's night off." He winked at her. "Never have I ever suggested playing Never Have I Ever," and he raised his glass to Amy, but he didn't drink. She was the only one who did.

"Yee-haw! My turn!" she shrieked.

"Start off at a PG-13 level, okay, Aim?" Lindsay begged. "I'm bad at this game."

"Fine, fine … never have I ever … seen porn."

Laughter erupted.

"PG-13 porn all the way," Mason commented. Everyone else followed except Lindsay, who didn't drink.

"Yes, you have," I told her.

"When?" she asked quizzically.

"Whenever Amy's on her laptop?" I giggled.

"Oh, yeah! Yay, I get to drink!" she said happily.

"You dork," Amy said.

Then it was Brandon's turn. "Let's see, never have I ever ... made out with a chick." He looked sneakily at Amy just to see her reaction. All the boys lifted their cups, then Amy smiled and drank, too.

"Nice!" Mason saluted.

"Oh yeah!" Brandon hooted along with the sudden outbursts from our circle. TJ looked at me, shook his head, and grinned. I just rolled my eyes.

"With who?" Jenna asked Amy, leaning over Mason.

After a second or two and Amy's explanation of, "One time when Megan and I were drunk and getting drinks from strangers, it was my turn.

"Never have I ever done a tequila shot," I said, winking at Lindsay. She raised her cup to thank me.

"Never have I ever kissed a boy," she said and drank happily.

Then Brandon called out, "Come on, Trevor, drink!" The guys exploded with laughter.

Trevor grinned with one side of his mouth. "Never have I ever gone fishing," he said, and everyone drank but Lindsay. TJ gasped in mock horror.

Jenna was next. "Never have I ever flashed anyone before," she said. I automatically looked at Amy, who looked at me and burst out laughing. It was rare that I would come out from my comfort zone, but Amy somehow could get me there. Force me, I guess. A few shots of courage and a handful of cups of "I don't give a damn," and we had made a whole bunch of bad choices in one night in Amy's hometown. I had nothing but love for her, feisty as she was. We raised our glasses to each other, drank, and giggled. TJ smiled at me. I bit my lip and looked away as my face caught fire.

Mason waited until it was quiet. He seemed to be searching for words. "Never have I ever been caught ... by myself," he toasted our group and drank. We all hit the ground, laughing.

"Ugh! Mason! That's disgusting," Jenna complained, but he kept chugging anyway.

TJ finally broke his laughter, "Ar-right, PG-13. Never have I ever been out of the US before."

"Oh, come on, PG-13 is bull," Brandon growled.

Trevor and I were the only drinkers on that one.

"Trevor, thanks for playing," Brandon teased. There was more laughter from the group. "Alright, never have I ever made out with five chicks in the same night. Bottoms up, Lawson, you loser!" Brandon shouted.

Lindsay's eyes bulged. "Giddy-up!" Amy hollered. I just watched for TJ's reaction, feeling flushed from the alcohol and imagining what it would feel like to kiss him. TJ bit his upper lip irritably.

"Are you for real? You made out with five girls in one night?" Lindsay asked, astonished.

"No, I didn't. He's exaggerating," TJ muttered feebly.

"No way," Brandon egged him on.

TJ just shook his head, an air of annoyance on his face.

"So jealous," Mason said quietly. He shook his head. I giggled and TJ, seeing my reaction, did too a little.

"Forget you! You're jealous!" Jenna snapped, smacking him on the arm.

"No..." He paused, looking confused. "So nervous. I said, so nervous."

"What are you nervous about? You're an ass."

Trevor and TJ were dying with laughter.

"Alright, forget it. We know who should've drank, but it's my turn," Amy started. "Never have I ever had a one-night stand." She drank proudly.

"What happened to the parental guidance?" TJ asked. He took another drink from his cup. Brandon drank, too.

"Never have I ever...." I stopped myself and tried to focus. The dancing fire seemed to wave and swirl toward me. I closed my eyes for a moment and opened them, clearing my vision. "...gotten a speeding ticket," I finished. There were a handful of drinkers.

Lindsay was next. "Never have I ever been French kissed," she said proudly. We all drank to that.

"Never have I ever messed around in a car," Trevor said and raised his glass with everyone but Lindsay. I felt TJ eyeing me.

"Put that glass down, Trevor!" Brandon teased.

"Okay, okay. Never have I ever ... kissed anyone in this circle before," Jenna said. She took a swig, moved in, and planted a kiss on Mason. He took a second to react but then got a little handsy with her. He started moaning and slobbering on her, on purpose. I heard the clunk of plastic cups as Brandon and Amy saluted each other.

"Liar!" I heard TJ call out. I looked up at him. TJ gave me a sly smirk while he stared at the cup resting on my lap. He held his drink up as if to toast me. I stared at him for a second, feeling my cheeks get hot. How could he know? *I was just imagining kissing him. I imagined it? Didn't I?* Then a smile spread across my face.

"Oh," I said simply. We drank together. Suddenly I noticed eyes on us.

"Hold up..." Trevor said.

"You've kissed?" Lindsay looked affronted.

"Beck was my first kiss," he said proudly, not taking his eyes off me. I had already kissed him. Of course. I smiled at him for a while, putting the pieces of our first kiss together in my head. It was a little fuzzy because of the alcohol, but I still remembered his soft lips and sweet smile. And that he had sung his TJ theme song afterward.

"You get any tongue?" Mason slurred, jabbing TJ in the shoulder.

"Naw, not when you're ten. I think that's eleven and up," TJ laughed. We all waited for a minute. "It's your turn, pal." TJ nudged Mason.

CAMPING

"Yep," Mason said. "Never have I ever taken a dump in a trash can!" He threw his drinking arm straight out, then back in, and finished his cup. We were all hysterical. Jenna was mortified.

"Oh my God!" Amy screamed.

"Oh, man!" Trevor howled.

"This guy…" TJ started and then laughed harder than I'd ever seen him laugh.

"What is the matter with you? You're a pig!" Jenna spat. "I'm going home."

"Hey, Jenna, come on," TJ said while still cracking up. "It's okay. Come on." He grabbed her arm to encourage her to stay. She stopped for a second then sat down.

"Sorry," Mason said, "and so was that trash can."

TJ held his stomach. "Uh…" He wiped his eyes. "Never have I ever been camping before." He looked my way, and I smiled at him in return.

"Thanks, Tommy," Lindsay said.

"No problem, Linds," he said. Everyone drank.

"Okay," Amy said, thinking. "Never have I ever shacked up over spring break," she called.

"Any spring break or this past one?" Trevor clarified.

"It doesn't matter!" Brandon yelled.

"Uh, this one."

I dizzily watched her sip from her cup, but I didn't drink. I noticed TJ had his elbows on his knees and hands folded, examining me softly. He had a more serious expression on his face. Was it concern? Fatigue? Or something else that I couldn't exactly hope for.

"Oh, yeah, right, Lawson!" Brandon argued. TJ rolled his eyes at Brandon. "What, you took a weekend off? Since when?"

"Since, whatever." He shook his head uncomfortably and took a tiny sip.

"Where've you been, Brandon? Tommy hasn't seen any girls in months," Trevor added as Jenna fidgeted.

"I hear you're a big stud in that dance class, Tommy boy." Amy winked at him. He smiled broadly. I grinned too, thinking of how even Mrs. Mac had a crush on TJ.

"Yeah, he is," Lindsay added. "With all those girls chasing you, why is it that you don't have a girlfriend? Do you just not want one? You can pretty much have any girl you want. You don't want commitment?" Lindsay asked earnestly.

Ugh, Lindsay was getting too personal again. I thought she was over it, but maybe she'd just hidden her feelings for TJ.

I was sure it was tough on her when she had to see him all the time and dance with him twice a week. Guilt flushed through my cheeks, knowing that I was breaking a cardinal friendship sin—being in love with the same guy your friend liked. Still, Lindsay had a knack for quieting a room—especially when she was drinking. There was an awkward silence for a minute.

"He's into the spice of the month," Brandon offered.

"Yeah, it's because he's a player," Amy said.

"No, he's just holding out for Beck," Mason announced, then poured more JD into his glass.

"Mae-sin!" Jenna snapped in a surprised whisper.

"What?" he asked dumbfounded, setting the bottle down.

Although I was a bit out of it, those words and reactions rang in my ears for what seemed like minutes. *Would I dare to hope? Could that be true? Did TJ really want me that way?* I found it hard to breathe for a minute. Plus, my focus was getting fuzzy. I looked at Jenna, who was staring hard at Mason then my eyes sunk to the fire.

"God, don't you ever shut your stupid mouth? You're so obnoxious!" She stormed off toward the gravel path.

"What?" he asked again.

My eyes moved up from the fire to meet TJ's. He closed his mouth, grinned sweetly, and winked at me. Mason stumbled to his feet, knocking his chair into part of the fire.

CAMPING

"Whoa!" Trevor cried, jumping up as did TJ. They moved the chair, laughing at their wasted friend.

"Tommy, I'm sorry, bro," Mason clapped him on the back. "I didn't mean to...."

"It's ar-right, man. It's all good," TJ replied pleasantly.

"I gotta go talk to...."

"Yeah, you do. Good luck with that." TJ thumped him on the back. Mason stumbled off in Jenna's footsteps, calling for her until he, too, disappeared from sight.

After another bit of silence around the fire, it seemed the game had ceased. Lindsay let her obvious discontent seep out as she folded her arms, scowling.

"Well, I think I'm hitting the sack." Amy stretched, grazing Brandon's arm. She giggled as she led him into the furthest tent and quickly zipped it up.

"A-my!" Lindsay followed. "Can you at least toss out our bags?" she called irritably. Two seconds later, my bag was shoved outside along with Lindsay's. "Thanks a lot," Lindsay moaned.

My head wobbled on my shoulders, and I repeatedly swallowed, blinking heavily. I felt nauseated and dizzy.

"So, uh," Trevor began, trying to start conversation.

"You ar-right Beck?" TJ asked, interrupting him. I tried to stand up and balance myself, still swallowing. "Uh oh," he said, coming over to me.

"I'm okay. I just need to lie down. I think," I reassured myself, trying to straighten the ground by spreading my arms out in front of me. It wasn't working.

TJ stopped me near the tents, unsure of where to place me for the night. "Do you want to stay with me?" he asked quietly. At this, I closed my eyes and gave a muffled laugh at the mere ridiculousness of this question. It was like a dream. Being there with TJ, knowing my love for him, and getting to stay beside him all night. It was absurd how obvious my answer was. However drunk I was, I gathered that he didn't understand my perspective or my laugh. I opened my eyes at him as much as I could and nodded. "Ar-right," he whispered.

We crawled into TJ's favorite tent with the clear, plastic dome roof. The same tent we used in his backyard all those years ago. He smoothed his sleeping bag out flat and grabbed a blanket. I stumbled out of my shoes and eased myself onto the sleeping bag as TJ unrobed a bit. I felt hot and dizzy all at once, as if my whole body was simmering. I had to cool down, or I was sure to be sick. Without considering my location, I quickly stripped down to my camisole and panties while breathing slowly. I collapsed onto the sleeping bag and ran my hand lazily across my forehead.

"Wow. Um, are you ar-right?"

I fanned my hand side to side with my eyes closed. I could feel the tent spinning but knew it was only my drunken self. He then inched up beside me and helped to smooth the hair back from my forehead. I looked at him for a few seconds and felt relieved that I was away from home but mostly glad to be back with TJ. I inhaled slowly and deeply while staring at him, trying to sober up. Although my eyes weren't focusing so brilliantly, he looked gorgeous. The way his body hung loosely over me, his hair tousled, and warm concern in his breathtaking eyes, it was almost too much.

"I'm glad you're here."

"You too, Beck. Listen, though. You can't lie down yet. You'll be in way worse shape. Trust me. Sit up and stay awake as long as you can. Okay? It'll help."

I nodded and sat up but slouched a bit, teetering forward and backward slightly.

Although I was plainly drunk and feeling nauseated, I still felt a sensation of joy at being in a tent with TJ. Images of our childhood campouts flashed in my memory. I grinned with my eyes almost shut, thinking back to the last time I had camped out with TJ. He always had corny ghost stories to tell.

CAMPING

"Hey."

"What?"

"Tell me a ghost story."

His grin matched mine, "Sure." He folded his legs and repositioned himself. "Let's see…." His eyes darted around as he invented his tale. I was amused already. "On Halloween night long ago," he began with a contorted face. "Red Neck Randy crept up into his attic to find … the most gruesome…." He snapped his fingers, startling me. "Costume ever."

"Red Neck Randy?" I smiled idly.

"Shush. Randy reached into a dark and musty chest hidden in the shadows, raised its lid hastily, and saw it. The costume. That of a dead, mangled rooster. Ouuu!!!!" He howled.

I jumped a bit and smiled at his silliness, then gazed at him through two barely open slits as he continued. And in a drunken state with half-open eyes, I finally saw what I had been unable to really see before. He was all that I needed. I was sure of it. I could think of no one who was a better fit for me or who was as accepting of me. I loved him so deeply. How dense I'd been not to see it before. My heart leaped, remembering the campfire confession.

"Suddenly, Red Neck Randy heard a crash of thunder," he continued.

"TJ?" I cut him off.

"You're interrupting my story, Beck," he warned.

"Is it true?" I asked, barely awake, swaying involuntarily as my body began shutting down for the night.

"Red Neck Randy? Absolutely," he laughed. "Sorry. Is what true?"

I stared into his smiling, crystal blue eyes, urging my own eyes to beat imminent sleep. "What Mason said." We locked eyes for a moment. "Is it true?"

I blinked heavily. After a few seconds, he grinned in a soothing way as my blinking became longer and longer. Then he leaned in and gently pressed his lips to my forehead. I couldn't fight to stay awake any longer. I closed my eyes and slumped onto TJ's shoulder, sleep overtaking over me.

CHAPTER 41

Breathing In

A gust of cool air swirled into the tent. I heard a loud zip and felt TJ crawling around on the covers next to me. He mumbled something about it being freezing. I slowly propped myself up and felt an invisible weight crush the top of my scalp. Instinctively, I cupped my palm around my forehead.

"Morning, Beck. Here."

I peeled my eyes open to realize he was holding a bottle of water in front of me.

"Oh, thank you," I croaked. I carefully sipped for a few seconds then gulped the cool water down. Instantly, my entire body was rehydrated.

"You ar-right?"

"Yeah. Thanks. What time is it?" I asked. He didn't answer. I looked him over. He opened his mouth, gritted his teeth, and flared his nostrils glancing side to side as if he were trying to get out of trouble. Like, trouble from waking me at an irritatingly early hour!

"Uhn!" I moaned, pulling the pillow from behind me and hitting him with it. "What's wrong with you?"

"The sun's up," he stated simply like I knew he would.

"TJ, the sun's always up. *We* rotate."

"It's light out. We shouldn't be sleeping."

I put my hand on my forehead. "Yeah, well, when I close my eyes, it's still dark." I grinned, lying back down.

"I've actually gotta get going."

I turned back toward him. "You're leaving?"

"Yeah, I've gotta work the first shift at the Rec."

I looked around the tent, "What about your camping stuff?"

"Oh, that's ar-right. Trevor'll get it. Don't worry. You can sleep some more," he teased me.

"You have to go right now?" I couldn't hide my disappointment. I heard myself sound like that little pouting girl who was told to come home after a day with TJ. I never wanted him to leave me.

His eyes lit up. "Well. I guess I've got *some* time." Then he flashed his eyes mischievously. "Scoot over," he ordered and lay back down next to me. He grabbed a corner of the blanket and shivered as he nestled closer.

Lying beside TJ allowed me to stare into his brilliant eyes, even more brilliant than I had ever noticed. They were the most amazing shade of blue with a depth, brightness, and intensity that made my heart lurch forward a few times before I had to look away and regain my composure. TJ was never lost for words with me, but this time was different. I was the one who broke the ice.

"Thanks for taking care of me last night. I'm sorry about that. I didn't do anything embarrassing, did I?"

"Naw, you were good." He swallowed still, studying my eyes. "You're a good drunk, Beck. No puking, crying, loud, lewd behavior. Nothing like Katie. She's the worst. She cries every time she's hammered."

"She cries?"

"Yeah. It was refreshing to look after you. You just got a little dizzy. And hot." He flashed his lids downward, reminding me of my intimate attire. I blushed, realizing that I had stripped down in front of him last night.

He quickly confessed, "I didn't take your clothes off. At least … not literally." When he didn't meet my eyes, I swear I grew a deeper shade of red.

"I know. Sorry about that."

"Um, no sorries, please. I really didn't mind."

I took in a long breath. It could've been the outdoor air, but more than that, it was that TJ had allowed me to really breathe whenever I was near him. He was like a portable oxygen tank for me somehow. Thinking that made me smile.

"What?"

"I don't know how to explain this, but … I can physically breathe better when you're with me. How do you do that?" I shook my head at him. "How am I able to finally breathe these relieving breaths whenever you are by me?"

My comment faded into silence as my eyes peered into his.

He licked his lips, "See, now you have the opposite effect on me. I can hardly catch my breath when you're around."

My heart skipped, and my mouth opened. He looked intently at me for what seemed like forever. Our feet absently bumped into each other's. I studied his lips, wishing so desperately I could be brave enough to lean in and kiss him. How was I just figuring out this undeniable attraction?

"Being here with you, can I confess something?" he asked.

I felt dizzy all over again. What will he tell me? What if Mason was right?

He didn't wait for my response. "You remember," he began, and a huge grin warmed his face. I pursed my lips and gave an internal giggle at how easily distracted he could get. "When we camped out that one time when it was super-hot, and you woke up, and I told you," he started cracking up, "that I spilled lemonade in the tent?"

"Oh no…" I wrinkled my nose.

"When really Katie peed all over." He shook with laughter.

"You're crazy, shhh, you're gonna wake them up," I laughed quietly.

"Oh, God!" He wiped his eyes.

"Why didn't you tell me?"

"Cuz Katie was crying that Mom would never let her camp out with us again if she knew."

"You're a good brother."

"Yeah, sometimes." He chuckled, then grew serious. "So, whatever happened to your brother? What's he up to?" He propped his head on his elbow.

I suddenly felt uneasy, like I always did when it came to my family, and stopped smiling. "He's okay, I guess. I don't really see or talk to him much."

"No?"

"He lives in downtown Chicago and works for a day trading company." I shrugged, hoping to end the conversation.

"You didn't see him at all over spring break?" he asked. I shook my head lightly. "Ar-right," he said sweetly. "So, do you want to tell me about spring break? Was it okay? Did anything happen? Did you have fun? Did you relax, have a good time? Did you get arrested? I should just stop asking, huh?"

Then I felt guilty.

I opened my mouth to say something, but nothing came out. TJ definitely deserved that conversation, but I just couldn't stomach such a heavy talk at that moment.

Being there, camping with my friends, relaxing, laughing, and snuggling with TJ was an incredible high. I didn't want the memories of my fight with my mother or talks of Jason spoiling our time. It was too much information. I would tell him in private, in my own way.

Later.

"Beck. You can tell me anything. You know that, don't you?" He paused. "I know how you are, but it is nice sometimes to let the air out of your tires, ya know?" I grinned slightly at his ridiculous analogy. "It's not good to let things build up. So, when you're ready to let it out, just tell me, ar-right? I can take it."

I nodded, sensing once again that he could read my thoughts.

"I'm sorry. I will. Just not here. Not now. Okay?"

"Here's what we'll do then. I'll tell *you* what *you* did over spring break," he said with wild eyes. I gave him a smirk and laughed at this silly notion.

"On Friday, you and Lindsay chartered a plane to pick you up and take you home, but since it was only fifty bucks more, you decided to fly down to Panama City. You stayed there for two days, laying out. Raul, the cabana boy, tried to convince you to stay longer, but you had grown tired of his yellow Speedo and were about to be busted for stealing a box of tiny paper umbrellas, so you hitchhiked back home."

I chuckled here and there at his amazing tale. He was having a blast telling it.

"On Monday, you spent the day watching reruns of *Full House*. On Tuesday, you created a new kind of chili. You had Jason come try it out, and he ended up in the hospital for the rest of the week. Wednesday, you went to the mall with Linds. She had a second interview at Dollar General," he continued. I stifled a big laugh, trying not to wake the gang.

"On Thursday, you helped campaign and draw posters for the sixth annual pogo stick championship in Springfield. Then on Friday, you joined the circus as a trapeze artist. You were amazing. They had never seen anything like it." My eyes were lively, watching him in delight. "You ran home to tell your mom about it, but she thought it was a big waste of time and suggested against it."

At that detail, my face smoothed into an intense stare. TJ continued his story, "And you were so disappointed, thinking how great you'd be and that she wasn't on board. So, I signed up with you for the trapeze, and we brought Brandon to be the bearded lady." I faked a smile for a split second, although I could tell he faked one as well.

I turned away from him and set my head back on the pillow, thinking about what he said. I'd offered him no real evidence of my unhappiness within my family, and yet, he knew. He knew how hurt I was by my mother's constant lack of support, and it pained me to know it.

BREATHING IN

"You're right. She wouldn't be on board," I confessed, sitting up. "Why is that do you think?" I pleaded, searching his eyes. He waited a second, then shrugged.

"I don't know, Beck." After a long pause, he spoke again. "It's not ... hard for me to see you, to know you. And it bothers me that *some* people like your mom don't *know* how to see you or don't *understand* how perfect you are."

His eyes were so soft as he gazed at me. He gently tucked a strand of my hair around my ear. I shivered at his touch.

"I'm far from perfect," I scoffed, casting my eyes downward.

He waited until I looked into his eyes again before speaking. "Well, maybe you're just perfect for me then."

I gazed at him, trying to catch my breath without looking pathetic. I wanted to tell him everything. What I was beginning to feel for him, how he had once again become the only thing that mattered to me, but he shifted and spoke first.

"Listen, I have to go." He reached over to grab his bag. "But I'll see you on Tuesday, ar-right?"

"Yeah," I said sadly, looking up into his gorgeous eyes.

He paused, melting his eyes with mine, conveying so much in just that look. "See you. Save me a dance."

"As if I'd have any other option," I teased.

He crawled out of the tent. A few seconds later, I heard his truck start up. That caused the others to stir in their tents.

I rolled over and sighed, trying to shove my heart back down my throat and into place. I imagined him turning around and coming back for me to stay beside me all day, tangled up in his sleeping bag. That thought created a flutter in my chest. I closed my eyes tightly and squeezed my pillow. Finally, beginning to realize what I needed, everything became clearer. I promised myself that I would put my thoughts into action and change some things for the better.

CHAPTER 42

Visitor

"I don't get it," Lindsay said on the way to dance after hanging up with my dad. "You're driving us crazy. Amy and I have been your personal secretaries, you know?"

I didn't exactly have an answer for her. I had managed to text my dad twice from Amy's phone during my visit with her, reassuring him that I was with her and fine, but didn't go into detail and didn't call him. I also didn't explain why I no longer had my phone.

"Where *is* your phone?"

"I don't have it anymore," I stated simply.

"What does that mean?"

"I sort of threw it against a building by Amy's house."

"So, you destroyed it?"

"Yeah," I smiled, a little ashamed, recalling the utter stupidity of that evening with Amy and way too much to drink.

"Why the heck would you do that?"

"Amy and I were drinking a lot, and then she dialed Jason."

"Ugh, then what?"

"Then I ripped the phone from her hand and threw it at a building."

"You know, you've been very bizarre lately," she said, leveling me with a look that meant she wanted the truth. I shrugged.

"You threw it against a building. You could've at least given it to me. You know my phone stinks."

"Sorry, Linds."

"I should throw mine against a building."

"You should," I said, opening the door to the gym for her.

"Good afternoon, ladies," TJ called out as we approached the crowd.

"Hey," the butterflies in my stomach and I said, greeting the scorching hot guy in front of me. Of course, I've always known TJ was attractive, but now that I'd admitted my feelings for him, attractive didn't even come close.

"Hi, Tommy," Lindsay said.

"How are we?"

"Fine, I guess." Lindsay made a weird face at me.

"Things are looking up," I proclaimed.

"Are they?" he asked mysteriously.

We had a fast day of review. Mrs. Mac had us holed up in groups discussing similarities and differences within the dances we'd learned. I didn't get much time to chat with TJ but held him up after class.

"Let me ask you something." I pulled my bag up on my shoulder and walked beside him. "I'm not going to Coleman today because I'm meeting with my advisor."

"Oh yeah?" He looked puzzled.

"I just wanted to ask if the invitation was still open."

Then he *really* looked confused. "What's that?"

"About this weekend?" I gave him a shy smile. All at once, a huge smile stretched across his face, lighting up his spectacular eyes.

"The wedding? You still want to go?"

"Definitely!" I winked, pulling a "TJ."

"Seriously? You're really coming with me?"

"I am really coming with you."

"Hell yeah, the invitation's still open!" He held my eyes for a moment. "So, you know your boyfriend won't approve of my taking you to Carlyle for the weekend—"

"I don't have a boyfriend." I batted my lashes at him, enjoying his face changing from skepticism to careful joy.

"Really?" He furrowed his brow, trying but failing to keep an even face.

I just smiled brightly at him, knowing in my heart that Mason was right. TJ had been holding out for me all along.

"Well, that changes things, doesn't it?" he whispered breathlessly. The power in his eyes intensified momentarily while his whole body seemed to exhale.

"Hopefully." I blushed, then turned and took off, relishing in the proud moment of my first-ever, purposeful flirting with TJ.

***

On Thursday, TJ was more obnoxious than ever. He threw me all over as we danced. He also deliberately ruined the rotation three times so he wouldn't have to share me with anyone. He kept saying how great this weekend would be, that he couldn't wait, and his mom was ecstatic. Everyone surrounding us gave him dirty looks. Mrs. Mac even scolded him, insisting that he be quiet and rotate correctly.

After dance, TJ headed home to pack up. He said he'd swing over to grab me afterward. On the way to my apartment, I was excited already. I would have the whole weekend to be with TJ, and I planned on telling him everything I had been scared to say before. I'd even decided that taking a permanent vacation from myself wouldn't be a bad idea. Hope was a new and refreshing feeling.

Unfortunately, I had to postpone packing. When I opened my door, I was shocked to see my dad sitting on the couch across from Amy.

She raised her eyebrows quickly, then said, "Well, I'll be in my room. It was nice talking with you, Mr. Winslow."

"Dad? What are you doing here?" I asked.

My dad rose from the couch as I stood in the doorway. He had a tired expression and was clearly unamused. He didn't answer me but only motioned for me to sit.

I slowly made my way over to the chair and sat near him. After a few seconds of silence, he spoke. "I wanted to see if you were okay because we haven't heard from you in a while." His voice was warm and deep. I looked down as he said, "We're worried about you."

When I could finally get up the nerve to look back at him, I felt the pain in his expression and realized at once I had been beyond irresponsible.

"I'm sorry."

"I understand you must be hurt, but you've got to give us a chance. You've got to at least call your mother and me."

With that, he handed me a new phone. I looked up at him uneasily.

"I heard you could use a new one." He stared me down.

"Sorry, Daddy." I managed an awkward smile.

"Now, this nonsense about not talking to us has gone on far too long. We were so worried about you and had no way to get ahold of you."

"You're right. For sure. I shouldn't have given you the runaround with the phone. Sorry, that was totally immature of me."

"Well, thank you for that," he replied.

I took in his hurt expression and let his words sink in. Then, the defiant part of me couldn't hold back the argument building as I processed his next words, "Call your mother."

"But when you say 'call your mother' … what for, Dad? I mean, yeah, I could check in, let you know that I'm fine. Getting good grades and eating well. I just can't go through the motions with her anymore. I'm never going to be who she wants me to be." I shrugged. "I can't give her a chance. You know she's not going to change, so what's the point?"

"Rebecca, your mother is a difficult woman to know. But she does love you and care about you very much. We both do."

"Well, I don't feel it from her. I don't. And if she was so worried about me, she would've come with you, right?"

"It's complicated, honey. Your mom had a really hard time when Rachel died. We both did, but your mother hasn't fully healed."

"Yeah, I know about that. I still see that pain in her. That was over sixteen years ago, Dad, and she still doesn't have any room for me." I clenched my jaw to fight the tears building in my eyes. "She should be more concerned about ruining our relationship than saving the one she barely had with Rachel. Dad, sometimes I just don't even get why you are still with her. She can be so horrible."

He sighed and tried to give his rebuttal. "We've had our moments, but I do love her. I made a commitment to your mother, and I won't break my promise to love her forever."

"I'm struggling to understand that."

"You don't understand what it's like to be completely devoted to one person forever?" My dad made a face at me, stressing something I knew instantly that he'd always known, too. I felt the blood rush to my cheeks, unable to hide the realization of who he was referring to.

And just at that moment, TJ knocked on the door.

"RE-PO man!" TJ called and walked right in. I could tell he felt very ill-at-ease once he saw that I had a visitor. "Oh, I'm sorry." My dad and I looked at each other, able to read each other's thoughts.

TJ turned to back out when he did a double-take and said, "Mr. Winslow?"

My dad got up, and I followed suit. He looked TJ over. "Hiya, Tommy." He grinned and shook his hand.

TJ was amazed, "Wow! It's really great to see you, sir."

"You're a lot taller now," my dad commented politely with the same half-smile.

"I should hope so," TJ replied. After a second or two of silence, he said, "I didn't mean to interrupt...."

"No, that's alright. I've got to be heading home anyway." My dad picked up his jacket and moved to the door. "Give my congratulations to your mother," he said, nodding to TJ.

"Thank you. I will."

"I love you, Daddy," I breathed, hugging him tightly. "I appreciate you coming here," I whispered. As we let go, he gave me a sad but resigned look.

"Think about what I said." I nodded.

"Take care of my daughter, Tommy," he said before shooting TJ a lopsided smile and opening the door.

"Absolutely, sir."

"I know you will." My dad clapped him on the shoulder, then left.

I stood looking at the door for a second in a trance, replaying much of our conversation in my head. Then I inhaled deeply and pushed it aside as I turned toward TJ.

"Is everything okay?" he asked cautiously.

"Yeah," I nodded, then said it again because he didn't believe me, "I'm fine, really." At this, I tilted my head up at him.

"Ar-right." He threw his hands up in defeat.

"I just need to finish packing."

"Take your time."

When I reached my room, I noticed that my overnight bag was already set on my bed next to a small plate of plastic-wrapped chocolate chip cookies. A folded note on top read:

"Snack for the road. Have a great time with my future husband. J/k I like Tommy, but I love him for you.
XO Linds."

I smiled and clenched the note to my chest.

The next thing I knew, Amy came running in with her sleek black dress and forced me to throw it in my bag.

"Whoa, not that one."

"Yes, that one. Your boobs won't explode out of it like mine, but … trust me. *He'll love it.*" She jabbed her elbow into my side.

Knowing Amy too well, I sensed that she'd had her suspicions about TJ and me. "How long have you known?" I whispered so TJ couldn't hear me in the other room.

"Known that he was in love with you? Uh, the first time I met him," she said. I knew I shouldn't dispute Amy. She prided herself on reading people. Besides, my face gave me away.

"Jeez, Miss Rebecca, I'm glad you are finally catching on. Now go have fun and be good. But if you can't be good, be careful. And if you can't be careful, name it after me."

CHAPTER 43

Carlyle

The ride to Carlyle was a breath of fresh air, even with the little bit of rain we passed through. It was as if we were in a different state. There was absolutely nothing around but rolling grass and farmland.

The closer we came to Carlyle, the stronger TJ's southern accent became. It was bizarre. Normally he sounded like every other person from Chicago, yet when he came back from trips home or, in this case, was headed toward home, he picked up a little drawl.

I never mentioned anything to him about it. The drawl made him even more charming to me.

I found myself gazing at him a lot as he drove. Something was building between us. Our stares were longer, our eyes were softer, and our smiles were gentler. By the end of the weekend, I intended on losing my heart and my inhibitions. For the first time in forever, I couldn't wait to let my guard down.

TJ showed me the local points of interest and told me a lot about the history of the land as we approached Carlyle. "The General Dean Suspension Bridge was built in 1859," he pointed out. "Which, by the way, I'm taking you to see tomorrow. It was named after a native to Carlyle, Major General William. F. Dean, who was a war hero," he said, seeming like he wanted to impress me. "Did you know that Carlyle Lake is the largest man-made lake in Illinois?" He didn't shut up the whole ride and got even louder when his favorite country music came on.

"Aww, here we go. This one's a classic, Garth Brooks Ain't Goin' Down," he cheered, getting excited and turning up the radio, thus halting his history of the great Carlyle tour.

In an instant, he was jamming out to a country song. I resigned myself to the thought that this would be one of many I'd hear over the weekend but still rolled my eyes internally.

TJ was so animated, Screeching the song full blast, drumming on the steering wheel, flipping his head around, and I was totally entertained. I also noticed that during our drive, the more he liked a song, the closer he'd get to the steering wheel. It seemed he'd break through the windshield.

"Hey!" he shouted in his cracking, singing voice. I was so amused. I could watch him pretend to sing well all day.

For a minute there, he looked like his ten-year-old self riding on his beat-up bicycle singing, "Walking on Sunshine," as we pedaled down the street.

We were getting close to his house, and a nervous excitement built up inside me. TJ was unbelievably thrilled to be going home, a feeling that was completely foreign to me. The clouded skies showed a touch of pink as dusk approached at the end of our road trip.

"I'll show you around tomorrow," he said, turning down a gravel road. Then: "You realize my mom's gonna attack you, don't you?"

I snorted.

"No, seriously. And I'm sure she'll start crying, so be prepared." It didn't seem real to me that I could mean so much to someone.

"This is it."

He turned the corner again and pulled into the cutest little cul-de-sac. There were only four houses, all surrounded by huge grassy fields. Corn and soybean fields lie beyond that. His house was a charming country ranch. Everything was perfect, from the shutters to the flowerbeds to the swing angled in the front yard at sunset. I was amazed when I saw how many trucks and vehicles were crammed into the driveway and along the two-story next door. TJ squeezed his truck into the driveway, as well.

"Here she comes," TJ said, opening his door and stepping out of the truck.

I pushed open my door and looked up to see a crowd of relatives shuffling out of the house. His mom approached the truck with her hands clasped together. He was right. She was crying.

TJ stood by the front of the truck near me, smiling proudly. His mom looked the same but with some wrinkles and a few extra pounds. She had the same flyaway, strawberry-blonde hair. Her eyes were bleary with tears.

"Oh, my sweet Becky!" Mrs. Lawson cried. She threw her arms out and squeezed me tightly. She didn't let go for a while. I was nearly brought to tears, too. It felt surreal to be hugged so tightly by a mother figure. "Look at you." She backed off and held my right hand as she wiped her face with her left. Then she looked me up and down and hugged me again. "You're an angel," she said, wiping her eyes again. "Isn't she just beautiful?" she asked, glancing at TJ.

"Absolutely," he grinned at me. "Hi, *Ma*," he said, faking that he was mad because she hadn't given him any attention yet.

"Hi, sunshine." She kissed him, then furrowed her brow. "Why in God's name did it take you so long to bring her to me?" Mrs. Lawson asked as she lightly smacked TJ's shoulder.

"Becky darlin', how are you?" came the deep, raspy voice of Grandma Noreen Lawson. She, too, looked very much the same, although she seemed weaker somehow. She still managed to squish me in her big, beefy arms.

"I'm good. Thank you," I breathed.

"It's just wonderful to see you again," Grandma said.

Katie said hello and hugged me, too. Then TJ introduced me to his mom's fiancé. "And Beck, this is Howard." He smiled, motioning toward him.

"Well, well, it's my honor to finally meet you, Beck," he said, shaking my hand.

"Thank you. It's nice to finally meet you, too."

His eyes were small yet endearing. When he looked at you, it somehow felt that he could see within. I got the impression right away that he was a typical, good ol' southern gentleman. I almost laughed, remembering a comment TJ had made before about Howard's ears. They stuck out quite a bit, making them look even larger than they actually were.

Beyond Howard were a slew of others: handfuls of aunts, uncles, and cousins, then Mason, Jenna, Tana, and Mason's grandparents, Edna and Joe. Whew! Talk about a crowd.

TJ gave me an encouraging smile before taking me inside with the rest of the guests. We all sat down at a huge dining room table just outside a cozy kitchen. Katie sat on the barstools at the kitchen island next to her cousins. Tana ran wild. The house smelled of mouth-watering country-fried chicken. Grandma and Mrs. Lawson had teamed up to make a delicious meal topped with mashed potatoes, biscuits, and green bean casserole.

Mrs. Lawson explained to the crowd how TJ and I would camp out in the backyard together and swim and ride bikes all day long. She said how precious we were, then started tearing up again because there we were "sitting together after all this time."

I could tell that TJ didn't want me to feel uncomfortable, so he started telling the story of how Howard and his mom had met. Everyone was amused by his retelling. He explained how his mom had cried during the whole movie on their first date, and Howard had thought he blew it. TJ could light up an entire room with just his energy and wit. The mood mellowed a bit, which I was thankful for.

Everyone stayed at the table long after the plates were cleared. Katie helped Tana play dress-up. She would come out and model for our crowd. Tana was adorable, especially when the dresses and boas hung off her shoulders. She still thought she was beautiful.

Katie showed me her room and said I could stay there with her. It was massive and had an adorable reading nook with all kinds of plush throw pillows. She had a super-comfy queen-sized bed draped in a hot pink fleece comforter. Her room was covered from floor to ceiling in pink decorations and cheerleading memorabilia. It was cute but a little much for me.

After showing me a million photos of boyfriends, new and old, making gagging noises and whistling as she explained each, TJ came to get me to play Gin Rummy. Mason and his Grandpa Joe were huge card sharks. Howard laughed quite a bit during the game, which got everyone else laughing because he had a whistling cackle. Grandma Lawson won the first hand, which took a long time. They were just getting ready for another hand when Katie excused herself to go to bed, and I decided to follow her.

Once TJ heard me thank everyone for a great dinner and say my good nights, he shot up and came over to me.

"Hey, you're going to bed? You ar-right?"

"Yeah, I'm fine. Just a little tired."

"Ar-right, just gimme one sec, and I'll...." He moved to tell the others goodnight, but I stopped him.

"No, no. Go play with them. I'm okay, really," I insisted.

"But you're my guest. Come on."

"TJ, I don't need you to babysit me. I'm fine. Please, hang out with your family for a while," I said, assuring him. He looked deep into my eyes, then said, "Ar-right, just ask Katie if you need anything. You know you're getting up early tomorrow."

"Oh, great."

I made my way down the hall and into Katie's room. She had just come in with pajamas on. "Hey, Becky, how are things with that boyfriend of yours?" she asked. I noticed her smirking a little as she began crawling into her bed. I stared at her watchfully.

"Well, actually, we're not together anymore."

"You don't say?" She was smiling big now. I couldn't help but smile back. "Well, it's all for the best. He was just all wrong for you. Not your type. Good night." Then she pulled the covers over her head. I grinned, thinking that I couldn't agree more.

CHAPTER 44

Second Kiss

After Grandma Lawson's signature filling breakfast, TJ told me to prepare for the royal treatment. He was going to show me every corner of Carlyle. We were out front when TJ suggested I put my hair up. I just looked at him quizzically for a moment as he continued walking across his yard over to Mason's driveway. TJ then motioned toward Mason's motorcycle. My eyes grew wide in surprised delight.

"No way," I said, moving closer to examine the bike.

"You up for it?" he asked, his head tilted at me. Without waiting for my response, TJ bent over and grabbed one of two helmets on the ground by the bike. He gave me one and tucked the other one under his arm.

"Yeah, I've never been on one."

"Seriously?" he asked

"No, but this is so cool!"

"You seem downright chipper, Beck."

I wrinkled my forehead at him.

"I thought you'd give me grief for getting you out here so early."

"No," I said.

I looked him over and thought about how relaxed I was becoming. His family was so cute and welcoming. It was a great feeling. I was completely at ease having him with me.

"I don't know what it is. I feel this peace here. Is that weird?"

He shook his head.

"I feel like I'm home. I already love being here," I whispered, looking into his eyes.

TJ held my gaze and searched even more deeply into mine. "I love you ... being here," he said finally with the slightest smile and bright, yearning eyes.

I gave an internal gasp as we stared at each other for a moment, then sensed him moving closer to me.

Mason's screen door suddenly squeaked, and his grandparents came walking out onto their porch. TJ bit his lip, looking down at me.

"Oh, are you taking the bike, Tommy?" Mason's grandma, who was TJ's great Aunt Edna, called out. She started over in our direction.

"Yup. Unless you and Joe need it," he teased.

"Lord have mercy," she swatted at him. "Just be careful now."

"You bet."

Edna and Joe opened the doors to their car and got inside.

"Huh," TJ grinned, his nostrils flaring.

"Yeah," I mimicked his amused but disappointed look. "That would've been a nice first kiss moment."

"Second kiss," TJ shook his head, correcting me.

"Right," I playfully apologized.

We looked at each other for a beat, then the sound of the car starting up on the far side of the driveway gave us the push to get going.

"Come on, Beck. Carlyle is waiting for you."

TJ pulled on his helmet, slid over the front of the bike, and I hopped on behind him, following suit. Although he said since it was my first time, he'd be gentle; he took off like a maniac. It was an amazing feeling. My stomach dropped, and I flung my arms tightly around his trim body. We zoomed down one-lane avenues, my eyes tearing up from the gust of air we cut through. I had a feeling TJ was showing off by turning low at every chance. The bike glided along, cornering perfectly. After a few moments, I found balance on my seat and let my arms fly out to the sides. The cool wind rushed past me in a thrilling jolt. I arched my neck skyward, and my vacation from myself transformed into a permanent leave of absence. I was free.

SECOND KISS

What a perfect setting: my first day at TJ's house, we were, as usual, out riding bikes. I smiled, remembering the time when that was all it took to make me happy—spending entire days riding our bikes around.

True to his word, TJ showed me every part of Carlyle. We visited his high school, Howard's fishing shop, the park district where his mom worked and spent the better part of the afternoon at Carlyle Lake. We even walked across the General Dean Suspension Bridge. It was exhilarating and terrifying when TJ started bouncing on it in an attempt to unhinge me.

Later, we went to Wonderburger, a hole-in-the-wall restaurant which TJ told me was *the best* place to get a hamburger and shake. It was a tiny 1950s mom-and-pop diner with one long u-shaped bar to sit at and eat.

Given how small it was, the food was surprisingly delicious. I had to give him props for one of the best burgers I had ever tasted. The owners were so friendly and talked with us the whole time. TJ rambled on and on to them about me and our history. They said our meal was on the house on account of Janet and Howard getting hitched.

Our last stop before heading back home was to check out a *special attraction* just five minutes away from everything else.

The main highway soon led to a gravel road, which wormed around until suddenly opening up to a stunning landscape of willows and massive oaks. Set back like something out of a fairy tale stood the sweetest little country house I could ever imagine. It had a big, peaked front roof and was half brick, and half siding, with a white front porch hugging the home. Bushes and shrubs decorated the front and sides of the lawn. Beds of tulips and daffodils flanked the pathway from the drive to the porch. My eyes danced, taking it all in. The house was magical.

"This is Howard's house," TJ explained, catching my expression while getting off the bike and helping me down. He took a key out of his pocket and showed me inside. The house was so warm and inviting. The scent of cinnamon filled the entranceway like a Cracker Barrel restaurant. Everything was neatly in its place. A huge stone hearth surrounded the fireplace in the center of the living room. An antique cherry china cabinet displayed relics, no doubt of Howard's family. The smooth, dark, hardwood floors completed the classic elegance and wrapped us in its country charm.

I investigated the family room while TJ headed for the kitchen. A handful of photos of Howard and his family graced the mantel, and there was even one of TJ and Katie from a few years back. Also included in the display were landscapes of lakes and images of piers and boats that all revealed Howard's love of fishing. My favorite was a close-up of Howard and TJ standing shoulder to shoulder, a huge fish held between them. TJ smiled ear to ear.

"Howard doesn't drink," he said, handing me a bottle of ice-cold root beer. "Let's go swinging." He winked and offered his hand to lead me to the front porch swing.

"Do you like it?" he asked, taking a swig and gesturing to the house.

"Of course. It's perfect."

"After tomorrow, it'll be mine," he explained. I turned to him, unsure I'd heard him right.

"*This*? This will be your house?" I asked, eyes wide.

"Yeah. Houses here pretty much just get passed down in the family. This is where Howard grew up, and he doesn't have any kids so, I'm kind of his kid tomorrow."

"They'll just live at your mom's?" I stared at him then looked around again.

"Yeah. She doesn't want to leave my grandma there on her own. And it just makes sense. Katie's still there. It's bigger, a bit closer to town."

"Wow." I got really quiet after that. A few moments passed with my emotions building inside me. What an awesome situation for TJ. How ironic that earlier in our history, my family was the one that supposedly had it all: the upscale house, a picture-perfect family of two kids, a dog, a BMW, and a pool. It was all for show. We had nothing where it counted. A pain seeped into my chest. "You're so lucky."

"I know," he said, looking down.

"No, not just this," I said, and he looked at me. "Your family." Repressed tears welled up in my eyes. "They support you with no questions asked." Now, I clenched my jaw and looked away, yet still felt his stare.

I reasoned with myself to speak up. How long would he continue to be patient with me if I kept everything to myself? How long would he be willing to figure out all my emotions based on his hunches? He had shown his whole life to me in a matter of hours, and I had given him nothing.

It was time for me to finally open up.

"I wasn't home for spring break. I went there but didn't stay the week."

He looked confused, so I continued. "Taylor drove Lindsay and me home Friday night, and I left my house on Sunday. I had this ... awful blow-up with my mother. It was about Jason, and yet it wasn't about *him* at all."

I huffed out a big breath.

"You see, I hadn't talked to Jason since that night at the bar. He left us there, in the parking lot. Linds and I ended up walking home."

TJ narrowed his eyes at me. "He left you? Beck, why didn't you—"

"I couldn't go back in the bar. It's not a big deal anymore. That was the last straw. It's over. It's been over. I think I just started dating him to attempt some connection with my mother. She was nuts about him. She's the reason we met since his mom, and my mom are friends. I hadn't dated a whole lot, and after the relationship with the nonconformist, I guess she decided it was time to step in. Like she always does." I inhaled and continued.

"Conveniently, I was attracted to Jason, and he was very determined to win me over, so it worked for a while. When I was with him, it was the easiest time I'd ever had with her. We'd never been closer, at least in my opinion. I actually laughed with her a little and had a few real conversations. It was like I wasn't me. I was the daughter she really wanted."

At last, the tears gushed through effortlessly. I'd pent up so much from a lifetime of feeling inadequate.

TJ drew nearer and smoothed his hand up and down my back without a word, waiting for me to finish. "So, this semester, things became … different."

I glanced at him and saw he was trying to hide a grin. "You came back to me, and I finally felt like I hadn't been myself in ages. I started becoming who I wanted to be, and of course, my mother was not on board with that. When Jason and I had that appalling fight, my mother found out that we weren't speaking. She wouldn't shut up about him. Said we should work things out. I told her it was over, and she should let it go, but she couldn't," I shook my head and paused. "My mother invited him over."

I stopped again and took a breath as a new set of tears ran down my cheeks. "As much as I should've expected it, I still couldn't believe that she gave no regard to what I wanted. She didn't care one bit about how I felt or what was bothering me. I finally realized that she never would. No matter what I did. It was just like Melanie Abrams all over again. Her molding of me and trying to fit me into the neatest presentation box she could approve of."

TJ's hand continued to make a path up and down my back.

"Anyway, I couldn't take it anymore, and I started yelling at her. 'What is wrong with you?' I literally screamed that I was not doing it again, her meddling with the people I chose to have in my life. So, I left and took a bus to Amy's and stayed there for the week."

It was all coming out and becoming easier to breathe. I felt TJ's warm body as he sat with me, silently encouraging me to let everything out.

"I don't want to go back. I can't. It's not home to me. It has never been with my mother's constant disapproval," I said, dabbing my face with my sleeves. "My dad came to see me because I hadn't talked to them since I'd left. That's when you saw him on the couch. He was trying to change my mind about my mother. He said to give her another chance. And now, I don't know what to do. She didn't come to see me. She hasn't attempted to call me."

SECOND KISS

TJ allowed me to melt in front of him without any interruption. He just sat calmly listening and let me finish my confession. After a period of silence, he spoke. "I'm so sorry that you've had to go through all of that, Beck. It kills me to hear how unhappy she's made you. If you don't want to go home, you don't have to." He tilted his head toward the house and smiled. "Stay with me."

I smiled back through watery eyes.

"I'm proud of you, Beck," his voice got a little louder. "It took a lot of guts to make a move like that. I really think your mom needed to hear that from you. Hear all of it. Now maybe she'll come around."

I had confessed so much to TJ, but his remark about my mother hearing "all of it" made me tense up for a minute. She hadn't heard all of it. I'd only yelled at her on the surface and ran away like she did all the time. Like I did all the time. I hadn't expressed everything after all. I didn't say the one piece that hurt the most: the one person who haunted me.

I looked at TJ, wondering if he noticed my concern. But he seemed so relieved to hear me vent my emotions that I knew he hadn't caught onto the new anxiousness I was feeling. For now, I kept one last secret tucked away.

It was a start.

He grabbed my hand. "I'm proud of you for sharing that. Really. Thank you." His lips touched my hand.

We shared a moment looking into each other's eyes, and I breathed in deeply, feeling the fresh air move throughout my body.

"See? That wasn't so bad, was it?" He smiled, wiping the last of my tears away.

"No."

"Kind of feel like the weight came off your shoulders a bit?"

"You mean the air out of my tires?" I smiled at him.

"Yeah, I guess that one really didn't make sense," TJ chuckled.

Breathing in slowly, I felt myself calming down further and further. I couldn't pull myself away from gazing into TJ's spectacular blue eyes, a little in disbelief that someone could possess such brilliant features.

"You have the most amazing eyes," I whispered. "Have I ever told you that?"

He shook his head lightly. "You have the most amazing lips I've ever seen," he breathed, staring at my lips.

I made a slight gasp at his comment as a heady feeling swelled inside me. "My lips?" I asked.

"Yes. Those lips have been driving me crazy for a while now."

My breaths suddenly became shallow, and I found myself staring at his mouth as well. "You know," he began. "This could be a great second kiss moment."

But it couldn't be, we realized, seeing Howard and Uncle Chuck drive up the path. "Or maybe some other time," TJ said, shaking his head and laughing.

***

After a quaint wedding rehearsal at St. Margaret's that night, we were off to the local hangout and karaoke spot. TJ warned me that I would be a bit out of my element, but I was actually looking forward to it. This tiny little town was growing on me in a way I had never imagined possible.

We had pizza and beer by the pitcher. Howard kept to his root beer, which he was famous for. Mrs. Lawson gave Katie the eye when she tried to get a beer for herself and her friend Sarah. But minutes later, Grandma slipped the girls two glasses.

Howard gave a touching speech thanking everybody for being there. "Well, after all these years of searching, I've found my true companion. Janet, you are a gem to me. You light up my soul," he said to a quiet crowd.

TJ looked at me instead of at Howard. He grinned sweetly. I returned his smile and turned back to Howard's speech.

"I guess you could say I'm a happy man. But come this time tomorrow, I'll be the happiest man who ever lived."

Janet dabbed her eyes as he leaned in and kissed her softly. The crowded house awwed and applauded. Then it was karaoke time.

"We have a special song for my mom and Howard," Katie cheered enthusiastically after she'd taken the microphone. "It's my mom's favorite!"

She grabbed Sarah's hand and pulled her forward to the mic. Sarah giggled, red-faced as Katie set up the song with the DJ. The two girls argued in whispers with each other for a moment, and then the music began. As soon as they started singing, everything stopped, and each person in the bar was glued to their angelic sounds. Their harmonies were perfect at each chord as they sang "When You Say Nothing at All." It was truly magical.

Mrs. Lawson bawled through the whole song. Howard sat smiling at Katie and Sarah with his arm around his soon-to-be bride. When the girls finished singing, the whole crowd erupted in applause. It was beautiful. TJ glowed with pride.

After that, the party really got jumping. Janet and Howard danced to a German folk song sung by Uncle Chuck. TJ graced everyone by singing some other country song that I, of course, didn't know. He was very entertaining as always. Despite his awful singing, he received several hoots and hollers when he finished. I could only smile widely as he sat back down beside me.

"Now, why is it that you can't sing like your sister?" I teased. TJ's mouth dropped open in mock shock.

Mason leaned in and answered, "Cuz he hasn't been kicked in the balls enough yet." We all shared a good laugh and the evening died down soon after.

***

Back at the Lawson house late that evening, TJ, Katie, and I talked over a batch of caramel brownies that Sarah's mom had dropped off for the family. We all stood around the kitchen island, savoring each bite. Katie seemed jittery while TJ looked tired and serious for once.

"Are you heading to bed?" I asked.

He kept looking down. "I should…. I have to get up early and fish with Howard. But no, I gotta write my speech."

"Tommy, you slacker!" Katie chided as she put a gallon of milk away.

"That's right," I said, forgetting that he was the best man. "You didn't do that yet?"

"Naw, but I know what I'm gonna say." He gazed at me with a tender smile.

"Hey, where's your shirt that you need ironed? I'll just do it now since I won't be able to sleep," Katie offered.

"Aww, thanks, Kate. It's hanging behind my door."

"You're welcome," she called, walking away. "Good night, Becky!"

"Night."

TJ and I sat on stools beside each other. He was unusually quiet.

"You okay?" I asked.

"Yeah," he said softly, peering up at me. "Just taking it all in."

A few silent seconds passed as we matched each other's gaze.

"I had the best day with you," I whispered. "Thank you."

He flashed his adorable smile at me then burrowed his eyes intently into mine. As I gazed back into his crystal eyes, my stomach fluttered once more. I couldn't wait another minute to finally kiss him.

"TJ, I need this second kiss moment."

He cradled my chin in his hand then gradually leaned in, not taking his eyes off my lips. I leaned in, too. He moved his eyes back to mine right before we touched, and I closed my eyes as we pressed our lips together. My heart raced, and I tried to control my breathing. His mouth was so soft and inviting. The gentle push and pull of his lips on mine made my blood tingle like I was meant for his lips only. After nearly a dozen long kisses and trying to take in as much emotion as we could, TJ pulled away.

"Whew," he breathed out slowly, without taking his eyes off my mouth. "I gotta write my speech," he said as if trying to convince himself while still entranced by my lips.

SECOND KISS

We kissed again despite his confession. He reached his hand up, cupping my neck in soft yet aggressive persistence. My lips moved over his, passionately drawing him in.

After a few moments, he pulled back abruptly, looked into my eyes, grabbed my shoulders, and kissed my forehead quickly. The next thing I knew, he had shot up and jogged away.

"Damn. I gotta write my speech."

TJ dashed over to the kitchen sink, turned the water on full blast, dropped his head under the stream, then shut it off and scampered out of the kitchen, dripping everywhere.

"Good night, Beck," he called, racing into the office, and closing the door behind him.

I laughed myself silly at how crazy he was. After wiping tears from my eyes, I sat there in the kitchen for a while, reminiscing about this most perfect day. For the first time in forever, I was exactly where I wanted to be. I thought of TJ all night long.

My heart no longer belonged to me. It was his, as it always should've been.

CHAPTER 45

Vows

"Becky, it's so good to have you here." Mrs. Lawson squeezed me the next morning.

"I'm thrilled to be here, really."

"Forgive me for getting crazy. I've got a million things to do, and the family will be here any minute." She straightened some newspapers on the counter and placed dishes in the sink.

"I can get that for you," I offered, stepping to the sink.

"Oh, you're a doll. I'm gonna jump in the shower, so just tell Aunt Kathy, Aunt Peggy, Uncle Roger, and the cousins to fix themselves something to eat, or go ahead downstairs."

"Sure."

"It truly is so wonderful to have you back," she gushed. Her eyes welled up, and she grabbed my hands in hers. "Tommy adores you."

I smiled shyly.

"He always has. You mean the world to him. Ah, look at me, blubbering away," she said, grabbing a tissue and blowing her nose. "It's gonna be a long, emotional day, huh? I hope Jenna's got some strong mascara for me. Well, I'm off." She left the kitchen and headed to her shower.

After straightening the kitchen for Mrs. Lawson, I moved about the office and living room of the house, looking at family photos. They had a ton of pictures hung up: country houses, the old farm, extended family, a young Noreen Lawson with Grandpa, TJ, and Katie from years ago, his mom and dad on their wedding day. I also saw a sweet photo of Janet and Howard. I snatched it temporarily and headed back to Katie's room to sketch it out and try to make a wedding gift.

Meanwhile, a dozen aunts, uncles, cousins, Katie, and Grandma returned and chatted wildly as they prepared another Lawson breakfast. I put the finishing touches on the picture then set it on a table in the foyer.

The family gathered around the table, chitchatting. Katie was at the stove with wet hair, still in her robe, frying bacon and assisting Grandma. We heard the back door slam, and a few seconds later, the shower down the hall turned on. TJ must've come back from fishing with Howard and headed straight to wash up.

I felt a nervous tingle creep up my back in anticipation of seeing TJ. Now that we had kissed, our friendship was becoming something much more. I kept glancing down the hall near the bathroom, hoping to catch a glimpse of him, wanting to capture every view of him if possible.

TJ's extended family headed downstairs to the finished basement to hang out until breakfast was served. I helped Mrs. Lawson with a few final wedding favors, tying ribbon, and attaching cards. She was so emotional. The morning was perfect chaos.

Aunt Peggy busily set the island with stacks of plates, forks, and knives. Then a familiar rendition of "Walking on Sunshine" resounded in the hallway. My head whipped around to see a freshly showered TJ with glistening golden hair approach the kitchen wrapped only in his towel. My mouth dropped the second I saw him. His six-pack and sculpted shoulders glowed in the morning light. I forced my mouth shut and swallowed hard to avoid panting at his gorgeous physique. He purposely evaded my eyes, probably enjoying himself.

"Good morning!" He kissed Katie on the cheek and stole a piece of bacon as she flipped it.

"Get out of there! It's too hot, anyway," she snapped.

"Good morning, ladies." He kissed both Grandma and Aunt Peggy, who giggled.

"Morning, sugar. Ain't you something today." Grandma smiled at him.

"Good morning, beautiful," he said charmingly to his mom and leaned in to kiss her.

"Hello, my sunshine." She patted his face. "You should put some clothes on."

He then sauntered over to me, and I bit my lip to stop smiling. He leaned close, and our eyes held each other's. "Morning, Beck," he whispered. I lost myself in his gaze for a moment. Then he kissed me sweetly on the lips, pulled away, and sat beside me.

"Morning." I smiled gingerly at him.

"So, what have we got here?" he asked, looking at the favors.

"This darling girl has been helping me all morning," Mrs. Lawson said.

"Oh, yeah?"

"Did you catch anything?" Grandma asked.

"Naw, just two small bluegills. Howard caught a pretty nice-sized bass, but not much. Beautiful outside, though."

"Yep, Janet. The Lord's given you a good one," Aunt Peggy declared.

***

By late afternoon, Mrs. Lawson and Katie were dressed and dolled up. Their family was taking photos outside when Jenna offered to fix my hair and make-up, too. It was actually nice having a little help looking pretty. I thought of my mother and how thrilled she'd be to see me decked out in a dress adorned with make-up and jewelry. Amy's dress certainly did the trick. I felt like I was on cloud nine and now looked the part. Thick mascara defined my lashes, and lustrous chestnut curls graced my shoulders. We had just finished getting ready when I heard TJ's voice coming near Katie's room.

"Hey, Beck! This is so awesome that you...." He came in holding the sketch I made but was frozen in the doorway, mouth on the floor. It took me a second to realize why he'd stopped speaking. Then Jenna and I looked at each other and giggled.

"Yeah, she's a fox," Jenna said, inching past TJ in the doorway. "I'll take this for you." She grabbed the picture from his hands and left the room.

"You look amazing," I said, scanning him from head to toe. TJ did look incredible in a dashing black tuxedo. His face was smooth and flawless. His gleaming, golden hair was arranged in a purposeful, disheveled manner. He was beyond stunning.

TJ was still gaping at me with wide eyes, his mouth curling into a smile. I just laughed at him. He blinked again and again as if trying to awaken himself from a trance. "Wow," was all he managed to say.

"There's something wrong with you," I laughed.

"Absolutely," he said, looking me up and down. "Come here," he whispered in the most seductive way ever. I licked my lips and felt warm and calm as my body instantly smoldered. Then I moved as close to him as I could, obeying his request. Our eyes blazed into a deep stare. "Drop. Dead. Gorgeous," he enunciated each word in a sultry voice. I couldn't help myself or wait one more second to take him in. I leaned up and kissed his open mouth.

The whole room felt like it was spinning. He kissed me so intensely that my knees were about to buckle. I wrapped my arms around him, pulling his body closer, and delved into his warm, moist mouth. He pressed his hands on the small of my back, moving up to cradle my face, then pull at the back of my neck. His whole body wanting me.

"It's just beautiful!" I heard Mrs. Lawson cry, coming down the hallway. We froze and wiped our mouths and the guilty expressions from our faces. She met us in the hallway with a tissue in her hand, having just seen my picture.

"Becky, sweetheart, I can't believe you did this."

"Do you really like it?"

"I love it. You made this today? It looks so professional. Howard is going to love it. Thank you. It's incredibly special."

"You're so welcome," I said as she hugged me.

"Did you see this, Tommy?"

"I did. It's awesome." TJ beamed at me.

"You are so talented! Oh, my goodness, and you look so beautiful." she examined me at arm's length.

"So do you," I said happily.

Mrs. Lawson looked so lovely in a pearl-white gown with lace-capped sleeves. Her hair was curled up and set to the side with a delicate white lily pinning it back.

"Is everybody ready?" she called as she walked out of the room. TJ and I followed the herd of people marching down the hall and out the door. Then we were off to the church in a convoy of vehicles.

The wedding ceremony was enchanting. It seemed the entire town showed up to fill every pew and line the walls of the cozy church. The sun poured through the textured stained-glass windows. Father Jim bestowed his blessings on Howard and a teary-eyed Janet in a brief, emotional ceremony. After many photo opportunities, we headed to the reception just a short ride away.

Father Jim once again blessed the union of Howard and Janet and said grace before the meal was served. At last, it was time for TJ's speech. I felt anxious for him as the priest handed him the microphone. Of course, I was sure he didn't feel nervous at all about his presentation to a crowd. He lived for these moments, a trait I would never share with him. He stood up and graciously accepted the microphone, looking perfect. I blushed as I scanned his body again, still feeling his lips on mine. It was surreal to think that he was now more than just a friend. I was completely lost in TJ, head over heels.

"Hello everybody!" he called. Several greetings echoed back. "I'm Tom. I'll be your speaker tonight. Uh, as most of you know, I'm a pretty shy guy, so...." There were a few breakouts of laughter. "This might be a little tough for me." More laughter followed, and TJ smiled.

"Initially, I was going to sing this whole speech. I know a large group of you guys were out with us last night for my repeat killer karaoke performance, so you know what a brilliant singer I am." Cries of laughter erupted. "I had it all mapped out with the chorus and whatnot, but I didn't want to go viral online. We'll save that for later when Mason's grandpa Joe leads everyone in the Macarena."

Howard gave a belly laugh, and everybody burst into laughter again, glancing at a pink-faced Joe sitting beside Mason.

"But really, it's a very special night," TJ continued. For my beautiful mom, Howard, for Katie and me, and my whole extended family."

He paced back and forth a bit. "My mom is … amazing, as you probably all know. She really gives so much to everybody but herself. So, I'm glad she's finally giving herself this awesome gift. The gift of Howard." TJ winked at him. "I have *never* in the eleven years that we've been in this town heard one mention of ill will about Howard. He is literally the best guy I've ever known. To use his words from last night, my mom is his true companion. How fitting to be a true companion to the person you are closest to, the one you spend your life with. That's marriage right there. Howard is an ideal companion for my mom. And now, he's family, too. Family means everything." He paused.

"I was six years old when my dad died." The room quieted, and everyone fixated on TJ. My heart fell upon hearing the mention of his dad. "That was really hard for me. And I realized more recently how hard that must've been for my mom." He grew somber, and I heard a few sniffles around me. Then he looked right at me. "To lose that person you love so much." Our eyes held each other, and my heart melted again as I focused on his words. "But then it happens again, and you find that true companion of yours once more. All hope was not lost." As he choked up, he returned his focus to the speaking, pacing a little more as he finished.

"My family is complete again, and my father has come back to me." TJ swallowed and looked at Howard. By now, the whole room was in tears. "In all of the qualities in Howard. His patience, gentleness, work ethic, and the love of the most fantastic lady. Howard has all of that. That and the biggest damn set of ears this side of the Mississippi." Then, at last, there was an eruption of laughter to break the serious moment.

Howard heaved back and forth in his chair with big belly laughs that got everyone roaring.

"Oh God," TJ laughed and rubbed his eyes. "So, this toast is to Janet and Howard, Mom and Dad, to family, to that true companion," he raised his glass slightly higher and looked my way. "God Bless!"

Then there were shouts of Amen and agreements as we all raised our glasses and toasted with TJ. "Now, let the good times roll!" TJ announced, and everyone cheered along as TJ headed off the stage. Howard gave TJ a huge hug with several pats on the back, and Janet hugged and kissed him in between sobs.

I stared at TJ for a while after that, smiling at him with pride, positively bursting, but mostly lost in the nostalgia of it all. In between talking to Howard or interruptions from his family, he glanced at me and winked. Although it was a small town, the reception was unbelievably crowded. TJ was very hard to spot after dinner. The first few dances passed, and I didn't let it bother me that I hadn't seen him. I longed to be near him but knew he had to be there for his family first. Besides, he was magnetic, attracting everyone to him effortlessly.

***

I danced for a while with Katie, Sarah, Katie's cousins, and Jenna and Tana, but I was constantly on the lookout for TJ. Katie's cousins slipped her drinks by the fistfuls. She was getting louder and louder.

Finally, the music slowed, and several people cleared the floor, me included. Mason, Jenna, and Tana danced together. It was so sweet to see them sway wistfully with their daughter clenched between them. After a minute, I felt a hand grab mine.

"Come on."

TJ had determinedly pulled me up and shuffled me onto the dance floor.

"Hey," I whispered as we began dancing slowly.

"Beck, I'm so sorry. Are you having an okay time? I feel like I haven't seen you all night. I swear I haven't been avoiding you—"

"That's okay. You've been busy with everyone. I understand."

"Yeah."

We moved lightly to the music and let our pace slow.

"I liked your speech," I said, folding my arms around his neck.

His eyes sparkled. "Oh yeah?" He wrapped his arms around my waist. "Which part was your favorite, though? The singing?" he teased.

"Um, yeah, no. That wasn't my *favorite* part," I played along.

"No? What about the ears thing? That was funny, right?" I rolled my eyes. Then he smiled. "Well, I'm glad you liked it. I was really hoping you would. I put some subtle hints in there for ya. I don't know if you picked up on any of that at all?" He raised his shoulders in a teasing way.

"I got most of it."

"Good, cuz you know, I'm not a very good writer, so…" He stopped and softened his eyes a bit. "I don't mind just coming out and telling you." He paused for a while and brushed my hair off my shoulder. I breathed deeper as TJ searched my eyes. "Beck, I am completely … in love … with … Joe.…" He threw his arms up. "Yes, you made me say it." I tried to hold back my smile by biting my lip and looking off to the side. "I mean, he's a catch. A catch and a half. Ya know? Look."

I gave him a scornful smile but glanced to the nearest table where Joe, Mason's Grandpa, sat slumped in his chair, knuckle-deep, picking his nose. TJ was rolling at my expression. So much for the serious conversation. That was TJ, though.

"Ar-right, sorry, sorry." He calmed down. "Seriously, Beck."

I smiled to myself, thinking he could never be serious.

"You do know that you are my everything, right? I mean, if you've been paying any attention at all for the past sixteen years or so, you'd know this," he teased again. I couldn't help but smile, too.

Then the music stopped, interrupting TJ's confession. We heard his favorite swing song, and he stepped back and regarded me in the most delighted way. I gave him an "Oh, God" look.

"Yeah! Come on, Beck!" He was loving this.

I twisted one corner of my mouth up in a half-smile, knowing I had no choice at all. Humoring TJ, I took his outstretched hands and all at once became wrapped up with him in his favorite dance. We were brilliant. Mrs. Mac would've been so proud. He danced in the most charming way: smiling, throwing me around, and leading me in and out of twists and turns like the true showman he was. After only a few moments, a large circle of people had formed around us, cheering. We bounced and kicked in perfect rhythm and even nailed his favorite Bow Tie move. It was a blast. Riotous applause broke out when we finished, all out of breath.

***

The rest of the night went by in a blur. TJ danced and played with the adorable Tana. He spun her around like a top until she giggled loudly and fell on her bottom. Later, I joined in their game of hide and seek behind the tables and chairs.

Several polkas in a row allowed Howard's family to have some time on the dance floor. They were all very good and entertaining, as if they'd been part of a traveling act. Katie and Sarah attempted to join in, but they really just threw themselves all over the dance floor in a drunken mess, laughing wildly. TJ took it upon himself as the big brother to cut them off and gave Katie a quiet but stern warning to slow down and pull it together. Shortly after their polka, Sarah's family took her home.

Mason and Jenna were having one of their typical disagreements over by the bar. That led to loud cursing and Jenna attempting to storm out. The night ended for us after I found Katie on the bathroom floor. I picked her up and tried to move her closer to the doorway when Grandma Lawson stepped inside the ladies' room.

"Well, she's had enough, I'm guessin'." Grandma shook her head and helped me lead Katie to a bench in the lobby. "I'm gonna fetch Tommy and tell him it's time to hit the road."

Katie swayed this way and that on the bench, mumbling and crying about Zack, her ex-boyfriend. I couldn't really understand her, so I uttered a lot of uh-huh's. A few seconds later, TJ entered the lobby, shaking his head at Katie.

"What did I tell you, Beck? Worst drunk ever."

The four of us headed toward Grandma's Chevy pickup in the parking lot. TJ was pulling Katie along with her arm over his shoulder when they stopped abruptly, and we heard a sickening splash. I turned to see Katie leaning over while poor TJ held her far away from himself.

"Can we throw her in the truck bed?" he asked.

"No, we'll just get home quick," Grandma answered.

After a few more minutes of stabilizing Katie, we headed back to the house at great speed, thanks to Grandma. At one point, Katie started to mumble about not feeling well, so Grandma rolled the windows down to cool her off. It was quite a ride. The cold night wind was deafening and silenced us all. And with the window down, it was soon freezing. I crossed my bare arms, trying to stay warm as I recalled the evening, moments with TJ, and knowing that our night wasn't over yet.

My fluttery stomach made my chilled skin prickle even more. I could almost feel TJ's eyes watching me in the rearview mirror as if he was having the same thoughts. I forced myself to stare out the window rather than turn around to meet his eyes.

Finally, we were home. TJ carried Katie to her bed. Grandma said her goodnights and headed back to her wing of the house. As TJ was getting Katie wiped up and tucked in, I snuck over to his room. I sat on his bed reminiscing about the night, the whole weekend, being with his family, with him. I felt completely at peace and so alive, so at ease, and so loved. Although he didn't come right out and say it, I knew how much he loved me.

The semester that we'd shared, plus all our childhood days, was proof enough. He had shown me his love in every smile, wink, and in every compliment all my life.

I got up, put the radio on low, and turned the old-fashioned knob until I found a sweet melody. I kicked off my shoes, pulled the few pins out of my hair, and set them on his dresser. Then I shook my hair out and ran my fingers through it. When I glanced at the doorway, I saw TJ leaning against the door jamb staring comfortably at me with his tie off and collar unbuttoned.

"How is she?"

"She'll be fine." He tossed his hand in a casual manner.

TJ took a step in and threw his jacket over the back of his desk chair. The soft ballad humming in the air caused him to glance to the radio and then back at me with a smile.

I turned and sauntered up to him, my eyes finding his. "You owe me a slow dance."

The sweetest, shyest smile spread over his face. I grabbed his hand and pulled him closer. He draped his arms behind me, and we rocked slowly to a low country song. I closed my eyes as I pressed my face into the crook of his shoulder and neck. His warm scent filled my senses, and I moved my arms tighter around his neck. I had no idea I could feel that way. The overwhelming love I felt for him was like a wave crashing over at high tide. There was nothing in the world I could ever want as badly as to be with this man for eternity. I squeezed my eyelids tighter and said a silent prayer of thanks that TJ had come back to me.

He smoothed my dress up and down while pressing himself to me. I breathed in deeply, caressing the back of his neck. We continued to sway with our chests heaving up and down until I pulled back. His mouth was opened the slightest as his eyes penetrated me. I knew I had to confess how much I loved him.

"Do you have any idea how crazy I am about you?" I breathed, looking from his eyes to his lips.

He smiled with his eyes, and I could see the flighty TJ awaken. "How crazy? Are we talking midnight robbery crazy or drunken, naked, skydiving crazy?"

I pinched my lips together, trying to fight a smile. "The latter."

"Wow! That's really crazy, Beck. You must like me a whole bunch." He touched my cheek with his fingertips, then traced them over my lips slightly.

"I've loved you my whole life." I heard the catch in my throat.

"I know." He kissed me softly. "So, you like it here, right?" he whispered, his lips grazing my neck.

"Yes," I said, trembling.

He moved his head up and looked down at me again, "I hope so because this is where we're gonna live."

The air vanished from the room as I gave an internal gasp. I stared at him.

"You are mine now. Forever. You know I'm never gonna let you go, right?" He was suddenly adorably defenseless. "Are you gonna be okay with that?"

I was awed at how vulnerable he'd instantly become. My heart leaped at his need for me, and I smiled sweetly, knowing how perfect it was.

"Absolutely."

His whole body relaxed. Then with scorching eyes, he urged his lips to mine. My face and body became weak and aroused at the same time. He cradled my face and kissed me avidly. We were wrapped up in each other's embrace, kissing passionately. It felt like ages of pulling, teasing, and taunting each other's mouths and necks. I reached behind my back and unzipped my dress, so it fell to the floor. He stood with his lips parted, his eyes raking me up and down. He unbuttoned his shirt, cast it down, and grabbed the back of his t-shirt, pulling it over his head to unveil his chiseled body. His willing arms grabbed me, and he kissed me hard as he led me onto his bed.

I felt the softness of the comforter curl around my body, the silkiness of the sheets graze my bare legs. Exquisitely, TJ's warm body draped over me and covered me with his desire. His lips slowly savored a path of wet kisses from my mouth to my navel. He looked up at me with a new and unrivaled intensity. Those gorgeous eyes aching for me. My breath quickened, and my body flushed in anticipation, waiting for him to overtake me.

We kissed, caressed, and held each other all night. I could never imagine a more intimate display of affection. It was an entirely different kind of passion. He was my world, and amazingly enough, I was his as well. After experiencing the sweetest bliss, TJ fell asleep with his arms wrapped around me. The next morning, I awoke to a sun-filled room and was overjoyed to see TJ still sleeping peacefully beside me. I kissed his head and closed my eyes again, willing the dawn to hide back under the blanket of our perfect night.

CHAPTER 46

Revelation

Three weeks had passed since the wedding, and the spring semester was nearly finished.

So much had changed, and I was truly elated.

I had the most adoring boyfriend in the world; I'd switched my major and discovered the beauty in country music. Also, as it turned out, TJ *could* actually sleep past the first light of morning.

Everything was perfect. Except. Two problems remained. First, I still hadn't spoken to my mother. Guilt over not reaching out was piling up on my shoulders. But then she hadn't reached out either. Second, nightmares of Rachel still filled my dreams.

And then one night, I had the nightmare and woke up calling out. TJ was beside me and sat up, alarmed. He consoled and reassured me that everything was okay. I laid back down and tried to rest, but it was no use. I couldn't sleep, so I waited a little longer until TJ had dozed off again. Then I climbed into my yoga pants, pulled on my socks, grabbed a hoodie, and tiptoed out of my bedroom.

Lacing up my shoes, I spoke silent messages to myself as usual: *breathe. You're okay. It'll pass. Just keeping moving.*

I wouldn't let it ruin my day. I would shove this nightmare down again and plead with Rachel to let me be. All these thoughts pinged around in my mind as I jogged down the steps, across the courtyard, and onto the nearby trail. I was picking up speed, but it didn't extinguish the panic of the dream. I'd have to lap my route until I was too exhausted to run anymore, and sleep could come peacefully. But that frustrating knot of worry lingered, pushing against me like a gust of wind.

And suddenly, as I looked up the trail, there was TJ standing in the middle of the path ahead of me, hands in the pouch of his hoodie, scrutiny marking his face. He was waiting for me.

I slowed to a walk and moved forward a few steps despite a new bubble of anxiety in my chest. He didn't say anything but just remained there, watching me.

"Hey," I said stupidly, delaying the inevitable. He was there to talk.

"What's going on, Beck?"

"I just needed some air and wanted to go for a jog. I didn't want to bother you." I fiddled with the string on my hood. TJ watched me calmly. *Ugh.* His behavior was so different from his typical vibe that my pulse quickened even though I was standing still.

"Are you sure that's it?"

I could only stare at him. TJ didn't waver. He wasn't going to say anymore. He knew I was holding back. Like always.

"No," I admitted, swallowing the lump in my throat.

"What are you running from?"

"I'm not running from anything. I just had a bad dream, and…." I stopped and kicked at the path under my feet, then peered up at him warily.

"Have you been having the same dream more than once or twice?"

"Yes."

"A lot more than twice?" he asked with growing disbelief.

"Yes." I gave him a heavy look.

He looked me over, waiting for me to explain. So, I told him. All of it. My dead sister haunting my dreams. The repetitiveness. Rachel's eerie path that went on forever. Seeing my face instead of hers. When I was done, I let out a slow breath.

I could sense how hard it was for him not to rush over and hold me as I spilled out every horrible detail of this nightmare. I saw the pain on his face. But whatever he was trying to get across to me must've been even more urgent because he stayed put, making me fight through it.

REVELATION

"We've never really talked about Rachel," I croaked.

"No, but I saw her picture at your house, and my mom talked about it, too, a long time ago. That is pretty much how we met in the first place, right?" TJ looked down and swatted a piece of gravel with his shoe. Awkward silence buzzed in my ears. "So, why are you still running, Beck?"

"What do you mean? I just told you...."

He cut me off. "If you're still having this nightmare, maybe it's not Rachel. Don't you think? What are you running from?"

"I'm not...."

"You've been running from your problems since the day I first met you." His words seemed harsh, but he moved closer now and spoke more softly.

I looked into his eyes and could almost see my younger self reflected in the warm specks of blue.

And then I was instantly transported to that day....

I saw my pudgy bare feet slapping the sidewalk after escaping the house when my mother collapsed in the dining room. I saw the whirl of my pedals chasing away her playdate with Melanie Abrams. I felt my bags swinging behind me as I tore down the street headed for Lindsay's and the train to Chicago. I saw a glimpse of the nightmare. The trail. The eerie sunset. The girl with the dark, bouncy hair walking ahead. She turned around. I reached for her, but she backed away, no expression on her face.

My mother's face.

Tears welled up in my eyes with the truth that I had always been chasing my mother. Wanting her attention, her love, her to be my *mom* again. I stumbled forward, and TJ lunged and grabbed me. He rubbed my back and let me catch my breath. I sobbed into his soft sweatshirt for a long time.

"Just to be clear," TJ whispered. "There is *nowhere* you can run that I wouldn't find you." I clung to his waist, and he rested his head on mine.

Then TJ tilted my chin to meet his eyes. "Beck, my love. Too much air in those tires." He grinned sadly at me.

It wasn't a comical moment, but it was just what I needed to break my sorrow. I nodded, a slight smile mixing with my tears.

"We're gonna work on this," he promised.

CHAPTER 47

Truth

TJ, my great ally, and protector took it upon himself to get to the root of the problem: my mother. Within a week, he had devised a plan.

I tried to hold on to his positive influence as I sat gripping the seat of his truck while we turned onto my parents' street. TJ, as always, sensed my nerves and reached over to grasp my hand, allowing me to forgo gripping the sides of his passenger seat. His hand was warm, smooth, and comforting as always. He gave my palm a gentle squeeze as if reassuring me for the hundredth time that this would turn out well.

"Which one?" He scanned the neighborhood of towering brick homes and perfectly landscaped lawns.

"Fourth one on the left."

He nodded and veered to the left, then slowly rolled up the drive. The unease in my stomach increased as TJ shifted to park. I hadn't seen nor spoken to my mother since the spring break incident. Time certainly wasn't healing all wounds. In my case, it had only made my anxiety about being with her worse.

"Beck, it'll be okay," he reassured me yet again. All I could do was exhale.

"What's the worst that can happen? She won't talk to you? Well, she's already doing that. So, nothing to worry about."

TJ opened his door and rounded to my side. He pulled open the passenger-side door and held out his hand. I momentarily looked up at him and wished I hadn't. He was so beyond gorgeous, smiling at me with a hint of a grin that I sighed, breaking my anxious stare. I took his hand to get out of the car. TJ kissed the top of my head, evidently praising me for being brave.

My lead-filled legs cooperated for the most part and solidly climbed the steps. I stood at the door and rapped on it twice. Then I slowly pulled my hand back down and into the cradle of TJ's palm. As a shadow moved steadily closer to the textured glass panel of the door, I sucked in a breath.

There was a momentary fumbling at the handle; then, the door swung open. My mother stood before me. Her lips parted. She was speechless. We locked eyes.

"Hi, Mrs. Winslow," TJ stated in an even tone. "May we come in, please?"

Her eyes shifted to TJ's then fell to our locked hands. She nodded slightly and backed out of the way to let us enter. We walked in, and I took a moment to close my eyes and steady my breathing. TJ had promised me that he would do the initial talking so that I could get a few minutes to gather myself.

"Suzanne? Who is it?" My dad appeared at the end of the hall. Catching sight of me, he grinned. He didn't say anything as he sauntered up to me with his arms open and hugged me like the prodigal daughter returning home.

"Dad," was all I could muster, hugging him back.

He released me and cuffed TJ on the shoulder, then hugged him as well.

"Hey, Mr. Winslow." TJ smiled, returning the hug. "If it's ar-right with you, we'd like to talk for a little bit." He glanced between my parents.

"Yes, that's a good idea." My dad smiled, gently eying my mother.

"Why don't we sit over here?" my mother put on her best hostess voice, but her eyes betrayed her. She was not at ease with this situation. Regardless, she led us into the front room and sat stiffly on one of her suede chairs. She was even thinner than the last time I had seen her. Her eyes were glassy and dark circles peeked out from under layers of makeup. In a way, I did hope that she'd been making herself sick with worry for me. But my head argued with that. *I can't be the reason.*

We sat down on the loveseat, and TJ held my hand. I'd formulated what I wanted to say. But as we'd agreed, TJ would start for me.

"We wanted to come today to hash things out a little bit. There's been some tension and hurt feelings, and we think it might be a good idea to see if some mending can happen," he said.

As I kept my eyes glued to the hardwood flooring, I listened to him work his careful argument and sensed my dad nodding along.

"Here's the thing...." I glanced at TJ noticing a slight change in his voice. He directly addressed my mother. I eyed her quickly and noted the discomfort in her whole body as he spoke. She fidgeted with her hands and shifted in her seat. "I love your daughter, and there's *nothing* I wouldn't do for her." My heart lunged in my chest, and I leaned into his shoulder, feeling once again that I didn't deserve the love he gave me but swimming in gratitude over it. "I know she's unhappy with how things are right now between the two of you. So, Mrs. Winslow, I was hoping you could help me out here and take some of this uneasiness from my girl." He grinned at my mother, and she attempted a grin back. I figured that was my cue to start talking, but with her being so guarded, it felt like we needed a change of scenery to start the discussion.

"Mom, would you walk with me?" I asked, my throat dry.

She took a moment to respond, "Fine." Then she rose from her seat and headed slowly to the door. I glanced at TJ, who gave me an encouraging wink. I followed beside her.

We were quiet for a few minutes matching our pace along the sidewalk, leading to the secluded bike path around the neighborhood lake. Like always, my mother wasn't about to apologize first.

"I'm sorry that I fought with you and avoided you," I started. "Sometimes, though, I don't know how to talk with you. I feel like half the time, you just talk at me, not with me. I don't feel like you notice me ... the real me." I studied the path below me, watching my feet move in unison with hers, hearing her intake of breath.

"I've always wanted what's best for you," My mother finally spoke. Out of the corner of my eye, I saw her fidgeting with her hands.

"What's best for me? Or what's best for you?" I had to push it.

I raised my eyes from the path and caught her glance for a second; then, her gaze moved to the road ahead. She pursed her lips, seeming to consider her next comment carefully. Then her voice filled the air: "We're different people, Rebecca. We see things differently."

"I know that, but how do we get past it?"

A few moments went by as we strolled along the path, winding around the lake. She was searching for the answer to my question, and I had almost given up hope that she would respond. I was sure she would close up again and be finished with our awkward conversation.

"I feel that we can't come together if I am excluded from your life." She didn't look at me as she talked, and I tried to see into her mind.

True, I was tight-lipped about a lot of things. *Had that affected her all this time?* I thought quickly of all the fun I'd had with my dad, with TJ, and the girls. Everyone but her. We never had our *thing* to bond over. Until Jason. *Was that why her defenses had been up for so long? She felt left out? Was there a chance that it wasn't really about Jason for her either? Had she finally made a connection with me through him?*

I thought about it honestly and conceded it might be part of the big picture. She had admitted some insecurity to me for the first time. I had another insecurity of my own to add.

"I get that. And I can work on that," I offered.

She swallowed hard but kept her eyes and chin forward.

"I feel that we can't come together if I'm not accepted for my own abilities and choices," I confessed.

She nodded but still didn't make eye contact with me.

I wanted her to yell or plead with me.

I wanted her to beg for forgiveness. To tell me I was important. More important than Rachel. Me, Rebecca. But I knew she wouldn't confess anything like that.

It was up to me to say it. The last part. The fear that had been hanging over me forever that I'd never spoken of to her. The whole cause of every nightmare.

I steadied my quivering chin, "I'm never going to be Rachel, Mom."

Her mouth flew open in surprised pain. She whirled her gaze to me, and I could tell she was trying not to cry. But I was brave enough to keep my tear-filled eyes on hers, to let her know that I meant it.

"Of course," she said sadly.

Then I had to look away and gather myself for a minute longer. It was out, and I wanted my mom back.

Although I didn't look directly at her for the next few moments, I gathered the change in her demeanor. She seemed to bear the weight of my confession in her whole body. When the silence lingered longer, I finally stole a glance at her face and saw the anguish behind her eyes.

My mother turned her sorrowful eyes to mine, grabbed ahold of my hand, and kept it cradled in her own.

I felt the coolness of her narrow fingers, of her perfectly shaped and silky fingernails, but somehow that simple touch warmed my hand instantly. I fought back a wealth of tears and radiated warmth back into that hold I had been longing for.

For so very long.

We walked for a while longer in silence, just listening to the wind rustle the leaves in the trees surrounding the path. She didn't throw her arms around me, embrace me, or cry a bundle of repressed tears, but the anxiety had melted off my shoulders. I could breathe a little easier since I had finally confessed everything on my heart.

We would have to work at our relationship again and again. It wouldn't be better suddenly like a bonfire blazing, but at least a spark of kindling existed between us now. Each continued step we took that distanced us from home brought us closer to each other.

Epilogue

Just a week remained of the spring semester. The whole gang was out at the intramural fields, ready for a game of football. TJ and I sat side-by-side in the grass, chatting with Lindsay and Amy, who was having a smoke.

"So, what did your advisor say?" Lindsay asked.

"I'm in for intersession," I said matter-of-factly. "I should hopefully graduate just a half-year behind schedule."

"Well, that's good," she said positively.

"Mom and pops know your plan?" Amy asked, eyes wide.

I looked at TJ quickly. "Yes, they do."

"Art major, huh?" Mason asked. He grabbed Amy's cigarette, took a puff, and handed it back. "So, do you need any nude models for your class or what?"

"We're good, but thanks," I laughed.

"That's a handsome offer, man," TJ commented, looking up at Mason.

"Handsome indeed." Mason nodded.

"Huh, well, Miss Rebecca, what a coincidence, Tommy boy is staying for intersession, and now you are too! And with our apartment set for renovations this summer, where on Earth do you think you can crash?" Amy asked, sarcastically eyeing TJ, who grinned broadly.

"I'm not sure," I teased.

"Tommy boy, is there any way Miss Rebecca can stay with you?"

"I don't know...." He shook his head, squinting up at the sky. "It's pretty crowded at my house," he mused.

"Oh, come on. I could share the couch with Al," I flirted, leaning close to him. He grinned, staring at my lips. "Naw, you can have my bed." He kissed me softly. "I'll share with Al."

I giggled at his silliness then kissed him back harder.

EPILOGUE

"Ok, you guys are too disgustingly cute." I heard Lindsay announce.

"Hey! Either get a room...." Brandon shouted, shuffling the football from hand to hand.

"Record it, send me the link...." Mason added.

"Or get moving. Are we playing or what?" Brandon griped.

"Yeah, Beck's on my team," TJ added.

With that, we were up and in battle. TJ guarded Trevor with a devilish glint in his eyes. I was right on top of Mason, who was trying to distract me with goofy raised eyebrows and puckered lips. Brandon hiked the ball and palmed it, searching the field for an opening. I shadowed Mason's every step. Seeing a gap between TJ and Trevor, Brandon launched the ball toward Trevor. TJ caught sight of the ball, lurched to Trevor's side, and tapped and secured it to his chest. He steadied it and dashed to the opposite side of the field.

Watching him, it was as if I could see TJ years later in our life, running with the football across the front yard of our perfect country home. I could picture a six-year-old boy chasing TJ alongside a chestnut-haired toddler, her eyes like the bluest sea. I could imagine TJ exaggeratedly toppling over with the ball and tickling them into a fit of laughter. I envisioned him winking at me for shaking my head at him from the porch swing.

But there was a lot of living I had to do before then. I didn't know how my mother and I would manage our relationship. I wasn't sure exactly what opportunities my new major could create for me. Yet, with TJ by my side, I knew everything would be ar-right.

Acknowledgments

First and foremost, I need to thank my family and friends for their unyielding love and support.

To my fun, obnoxious, hilarious, feisty, and loyal husband for believing in me and making life interesting. Love you, Ships. ;0)

To my children for helping me truly understand that love knows no bounds.

To my adorable and wonderful dad, who is the sweetest man on Earth.

To my beloved and remarkable mom in Heaven, I miss you every day.

To my amazing and compassionate sister Sue, my best cheerleader. For your selflessness and hours and hours of help. You are awesome. I owe you. Big. Huge.

To my brother Mike, for his advice and reviews. Thanks, bro.

To my brother Mark, for being my best playmate and companion growing up.

To my BFFs Michele and Maris, for being my extraordinary *forever* friends.

To my EIU girls for all those fantastic years then and now. This story would NOT exist without you. Especially you, Karen. ;0)

To Mike, Stephanie, and Liz for suggestions.

To my book club girls for their early praise.

To my teacher friends for humoring me with my weird entertainment for twenty years. Best Team!

ACKNOWLEDGMENTS

To Hilary and her phenomenal team: Ashley, Mats, Jen, and Heather—thank you! Hilary, most of all. My extractor-extraordinaire and Book Goddess. You have done so much for me and have become a dear friend. Thank you for your time, for your brilliance and guidance.

To Jean Lachat photography, Allison, Tommy and Gigi, and Leslie Campins Photography for your beautiful photos.

To the staff at St. Victor's, Marian, and Eastern for your tireless efforts to get through to your students.

To my own students: past, present, and future. When you believe in yourself, anything is possible. I believe in you.

Lastly, to my 13-year-old self, I see you. Thank you for your creativity and imagination.

About the Author

Margie Janes grew up in the suburbs of Chicago. She graduated from Eastern Illinois University, where she met her husband, Bill.

Now, an elementary school teacher, she is fortunate to spend her days teaching, connecting with, learning from, and entertaining a room full of 9-year-olds. Margie began writing *True Companion* at the age of thirteen after being inspired by Phil Colin's 1990 music video "Do you Remember?" The video features a girl and boy who instantly connect and create a friendship until they are separated by an event.

She loves reading, writing, watching movies, spending time with family and friends, cheering at her kids' sporting activities, and playing with her rescue pup. *True Companion* is not your ordinary girl-meets-boy novel. Margie crafted this novel over thirty years, writing from a child's perspective when Beck was a little girl, a college student's perspective when Beck was in college, and a mother's perspective when she wrote the part of Janet.

True Companion is her first novel.

Made in the USA
Middletown, DE
23 July 2022

69805313R00168